Bethan Roberts was born in Oxford and brought up in nearby Abingdon. She teaches creative writing at the University of Chichester and for the Open University. Bethan Roberts was awarded a Jerwood/Arvon Young Writers' Prize for *The Pools*. Serpent's Tail also publishes her second novel, *The Good Plain Cook*. She lives in Brighton.

Praise for *The Pools*

'A complex anatomy of a murder, *The Pools* brilliantly evokes the sickening recognition of a wasteful death. Bethan Roberts is a fearless writer whose first novel raises questions about fate and responsibility that remain with the reader long after the last page has been turned. A compelling debut' Louise Welsh

'A wonderfully self-assured debut... There is a forbidding feeling throughout the novel – an almost audible hum of misgiving coming off the pages. Superb' Ruth Atkins, Booksellers' Choice, *The Bookseller*

'An unsettling and disturbing tale of awakening sexuality and predatory parents' Patricia Duncker

'A tense thriller that reminded me of Julie Myerson's *Something Might Happen*' Viv Groskop, *Eve*

'Brilliantly illuminating… A beautifully understated debut'
Easy Living

'A cool and relevant novel… like an urban *Cold Comfort Farm*… An expertly crafted book' *Sunday Express*

'The kind of first novel that takes your breath away… a beautiful, unsettling book' *Sainsbury's Magazine*

'Carefully dissects the bubbling tensions of ordinary lives… heartbreaking' *FT*

'A sense of controlled menace broods over every scene, as if the book's tragic outcome were inevitable' *Guardian*

'Tightly drawn, sharply focused and the writing has the clarity of a good short story' *Mslexia*

'A haunting glimpse of emerging adolescent sexuality and of adult lives wasted by grief. This is a convincing and haunting debut that evokes an uneasy and menacing Middle England' *Time Out*

Bonus material

Turn to page 282 for Bethan Roberts' account of writing *The Pools* and 'Snooping in Other People's Houses: some thoughts on writing *The Good Plain Cook*', followed by the first chapter of her second novel.

the pools

Bethan Roberts

A complete catalogue record for this book can be obtained from
the British Library on request

The right of Bethan Roberts to be identified as the author of this
work has been asserted by her in accordance with the Copyright,
Designs and Patents Act 1988.

First published in this edition in 2008 by Serpent's Tail
First published in 2007 by Serpent's Tail,
an imprint of Profile Books Ltd
3A Exmouth House
Pine Street
Exmouth Market
London EC1R 0JH
www.serpentstail.com

Designed and typeset by Sue Lamble

ISBN 978 1 84668 651 1

Printed in the UK by CPI Bookmarque,
Croydon CR0 4TD

This book is printed on FSC certified paper

Mixed Sources
Product group from well-managed
forests and other controlled sources
www.fsc.org Cert no. TT-COC-002227
© 1996 Forest Stewardship Council
FSC

For Mum and Dad, with love

For Mum and Dad, with love

prologue

Howard
Christmas, 1985

Since the night he disappeared, she's kept her hands to herself. No fingers stray towards me as we lie together, not sleeping. At seven o'clock I shake her shoulder. The brushed cotton of her nightie is soft against the rough skin of my fingertips. I know it's rough because she used to tell me, in bed. If I stroked her back she would say, 'Howard. Skin's catching.'

I shake her shoulder and she ignores me. So I speak. 'Time to get up, Kathryn. Come on now, time to get up.'

Her arm twitches, but there's no sound. So I try again, a bit sterner. 'Come on, now. You have to get up. This morning you have to get up.'

Neither of us has slept, of course. For the last hour I've been watching the blue-grey light push through the curtains, listening to her breathe. From her shallow, quiet breaths, I knew she was awake, too; probably her mind was stuck, like mine, on that moment when we saw the police-woman opening the front gate, carefully closing it again, and taking off her hat as she walked down our path. Then we knew they'd found his body.

I rise and leave her, knowing it'll be ten minutes before she'll move. But when I come back from the bathroom she's standing there in her winter nightie. Her hair is still in waves, but they're all in the wrong place, as if she's wearing a wig and it's slipped. There's a big patch of mottled red on her chest where the cotton has made its imprint.

On our wedding night she wore a very different nightie. It was all layers of stuff, a bit see-through, short, well above her knees. But it hung there as if it wasn't on her body at all, as if she'd just stepped into a tepee made of nylon. 'What's that you're wearing,' I said, smiling, wishing I could see more of her lovely curves. At the power station Christmas parties I knew the other men were watching her, their eyes following her movements; some of them even looked slightly scared if she spoke to them, I noticed that. They would lean towards her to catch her voice. They patted other women on the hips, shouted things out as they passed, but with Kathryn it wasn't like that. Even her hair seemed curvy to me, and her eyelashes, the way they swept up off her cheeks just as women's eyelashes are supposed to. I never saw any other girl with eyelashes like Kathryn's, except at the pictures. On our wedding night she touched a layer of nylon and gave me a twirl. 'It's a powder blue negligee,' she said. 'Can't you tell?' And she lifted up the hem and laughed.

I reach out and hold her elbow for a moment, but she doesn't make a sound; she just stands there, waiting for me to let go. I release her and she walks past me, out of the door. Then I hear water running in the bathroom.

When she comes back her face looks a little pinker so I ask her, 'What'll you wear?'

She looks up at me with clouded eyes. I lean forward and press my forehead to hers. The tip of her nose is cold against my cheek.

'What'll you wear, Kathryn?'

'Anything. Anything.' She lets her weight fall against me.

I sit her down on the bed. 'Right then, let's have a look.' I go through her whole rail, my fingers trailing over dresses, skirts, blouses, and there's nothing black. I pull out every drawer and pick through the folded corners of her knitwear, and there's nothing black. Plenty of brown, and quite a bit of blue, but no black. I think it best not to say anything. Instead I select a dark brown pleated skirt and a navy blue jumper.

'This is nice,' I say, laying it all out on the bed beside her. She stares at the skirt but doesn't move.

'Come on, Kathryn. Let's get that nightie off.'

I wait a few moments, in case she stirs.

She lets me hook the hem of the nightie round my fingers and lift it up to her thighs, and when I say, 'Lift your bottom up for me,' she does so. She sits there naked on the bed, her arms clutched round her waist. The skin on her forearms hangs. In the half-light of the bedroom I can see the curves are still there; a little wilted, but still there.

'Here's your knickers,' I say. 'Are you going to stand up for me?' I hold the knickers out so she can step into them. 'No? All right then.'

I lift her left foot, guiding it into the elastic hole. And as I lift her right foot I smell her there above me, all sleepy brushed cotton and something faintly vinegary, and I find myself stopping and dropping her foot back down again, so she's sitting there with her knickers round one ankle, and I'm resting my cheek against her shin and mouthing *Robert* without making a sound and knowing our son is dead.

She must feel my breathing go heavy, because she puts her hand on my head and we sit like that for a few minutes, my knees digging into our thin purple carpet, my cheek feeling the dry tissue of her shin and the knobbles of bone in there, all rounded, like a row of marbles.

'I should have bought a black dress,' she says.

I lift her right foot again. 'No, no. It's all right. People don't wear all black at funerals these days.'

I guide the knickers beyond her knees. 'Lift your bottom up for me.'

I keep thinking of the time I took Robert to the Tank Museum. Kathryn refused to come in, waited in a café down the road, wearing her red raincoat (she used to wear a lot of red), sipping a milky coffee, reading a novel. At least, that's how I imagined her as I walked around that place, yards of camouflage and unspeakable weapons everywhere.

In that museum there were lots of fathers and sons. All the fathers seemed to have big hands with which to guide their sons around the *Whippet*, the *Sherman Crab* and the *Somua* tanks. They would stoop and point, ruffle hair, share interesting facts. I didn't know anything about those grey and brown hunks of metal. I knew about turbine halls, not armoured vehicles.

I walked behind Robert as he ran ahead. I'd never seen him so excited. I let him weave between the tanks with his anorak wrapped around his waist in the way he liked. I smiled as he sat in the cockpit of the armoured Rolls-Royce, his hair sticking up on the crown of his head, his straight teeth shining.

When we got back to the café she embraced him as if he'd been gone for weeks, and he told her all about the tanks in one long breath, and her eyes lit up at the very mention of the word *missile*, even though she'd refused to set foot in that place. 'Did you enjoy it, Howard?' she asked me. I hesitated. Robert said, 'Dad *hated* it.' And they laughed.

The iciness of the kitchen floor seeps through the thin soles of my slippers. I warm my hands in the steam of the kettle. The blind with the fruit and veg print is moving slowly in the draught from the window. Sucked in, blown out. I drop the cold tea bag from the pot into the bin. I can't cook like Kathryn so the bin is full of empty tins. She used to feed Robert plenty of meat; chops grilled with a little salt, boiled potatoes and tinned peas on the side. I never understood it. She doesn't like meat much, but for her son she let the fat ooze over the bars of the grill and fill the kitchen with a sweet stink.

For the last fortnight she's said nothing as I've handed her beans on toast, spaghetti on toast, cheese on toast, night after night. She says nothing, chews on a corner, leaves the rest. Since the night he went, we've eaten our tea on our laps, in front of the television. And we do not watch the news.

I almost pour the tea into the mug he bought for her, years ago – the one with 'World's Best Mum' on the side. When I say he bought it, I mean of course that I got it, and said it was a gift from him on Mother's Day. He must have been about six. She looked pleased, but she never used it. Kathryn doesn't go in for that sort of thing, slogans.

I jerk the spout away so quickly the tea burns my hand. Then she's there, standing beside me in the kitchen, wearing the brown skirt and the blue jumper. She's put some earrings in.

'You've got earrings in,' I say, pushing the mug behind the teapot.

'I'll take them out,' she says, quickly, before I can tell her that I like them. 'It was a mistake. What was I thinking? Earrings.'

'Right,' I say. 'Tea.'

Eleven o'clock. The car arrives in plenty of time for the service. We stand in the hallway. I am wearing my only black suit; it's a bit tight round the waist. It's all right, though, because I've put a belt round and left the top button undone. I hold out Kathryn's wool coat. She slips her arms into it, and I heave it onto her shoulders. I button it right to the top; the collar is so high it's like I'm tucking her neck into it. I comb her hair, which sticks out above her right ear. The ends of it look frazzled, as if they've been burnt.

'Have you got any spray?' I ask.

She looks at me. 'Spray?'

'For your hair.'

'No,' she says.

'A hat then.'

'I've never had a hat.'

'Oh. Right then.' I smooth the shoulders of her coat. 'You'll do,' I say.

She reaches past me and opens the door. Outside, a blast of wind brings water to my eyes as I hurry to keep up with her, to keep hold of her herringboned elbow.

Joanna
Christmas, 1985

I know Shane's not coming. I sit on the seat of the twitchers. I know he's not coming. But I wait. I grip the seat until my fingers go dead, and I wait for him.

Pink hoop earrings, pink pencil skirt. I'm ready, should he stride past, Walkman blasting. I'm ready, but I know he won't come. No one's seen him since that night. Not even me.

Rooks scream in the spiky trees. Everything's frozen, even the air. It bursts in my lungs when I inhale.

The only thing moving is the steam in the sky. It coughs out of the power station cooling towers. It never stops.

I stretch my fingers out and let the blood flow back. Then I grip the seat again.

They found Rob's body down here a week ago. I saw it on the news, like everyone else. There were nets and dogs and more police than you've ever seen in Calcot. They came to my house and asked me, when was the last time I saw Robert Hall? How did I know him? Who were his other friends? How did he seem when I left him? I didn't leave him, I said. I went to look for him. But he'd gone. They'd both gone. The policewoman had lines scored around her mouth, and shimmery purple eyeshadow. I kept looking at it because she'd done one eye darker than the other, and it made her lopsided. I know it's hard, she said, but try to remember. She put her hand on my shoulder. Robert's friend Luke said there was someone else there. Was there anyone else with you? Was there anyone else there that night? No one, I said. No one else was there.

It's all quiet now, though. The police have gone. They found Rob's body, and they stopped looking for Shane.

Rob came into the shop where I work weekends not long ago and bought some Dairy Box for his mum, for Christmas. I told him that she'd want Ferrero Rocher, pointing to the gold pyramid I'd just stacked. We laughed. His flawless cheeks glowed.

They'll be grey now, though. Bloated from the water.

No one's found Shane. But he's probably looking for me. If I sit here long enough, he might come. I might hear his beat. He might put his hands on my head.

If he does, I'm not sure what I'll do. I might scream. I might run off. But I'll let him touch me, just once.

Shane's hand would have covered Rob's whole head.

Instead, Simon comes.

I know it's him before he sits down next to me. I recognise his sigh, the expensive-sounding crunch of his leather boots on the frozen mud.

We sit for a long time, looking at the pool. There's still police tape round the other side, where they found the body.

Mum didn't come to the funeral, but Simon did. He

didn't come with me, he just appeared at the last minute, sat behind me and breathed his damp air on the back of my neck. I didn't ask him to do that. After the service, I slipped out before he could clutch my elbow and say my name.

He must have followed me down the lane to the pools, telling Mum he was going to do some birdwatching. Promising he'd bring her something back. Kissing her pout before he left.

He inches along the bench, closer. I let him sit there, in silence. I know he doesn't know what to say to me. He steals the odd sideways glance at my face. I keep looking at the pool, though. I don't want to see his eyes.

Then he reaches into his coat pocket. Brings out a bar of Bourneville. Slides a finger beneath the red paper wrapper. Pops it open. Rips back a piece of foil. Offers it to me.

I snap off a block and put it in my mouth. Let it melt.

part one

Howard

one

Summer, 1965

Kathryn worked in the library. She looked like she belonged behind that counter, smiling at the borrowers, stamping the books, answering the phone in one breathless phrase, without even thinking. She looked so capable there.

I wasn't a library person, but that was the time of my first rose. It turned out to be a beautiful one, too, *Rosa gallica*, one of the oldest known varieties, deep red with generous petals. I hadn't a clue what to do with it. It was an impulse buy on a visit to a nursery with Mum. I was seduced by the photograph tacked to the frame – all that promise. All that redness. I left it by the back door of the kitchen for a while, studying it every morning for signs of growth, afraid to leave it to its own devices in the garden. Mum suggested I consult a book. 'Roses are for outdoors, Howard,' she said. 'It'll perish inside.'

The library was new then. It was built to match the multi-storey next door. It was a sunny July day when I went down there; from the window of the bus I watched the cow parsley swaying in the verges.

When I opened the heavy library door it took my eyes a few moments to adjust to the gloom. Kathryn was behind the counter. She was wearing a red blouse; the white of her neck was startling against her scarlet collar. And I noticed her hair of course, all dark and wavy and resting there on her small shoulders.

I didn't go to the counter straight away. I spent about fifteen minutes weaving in and out of the shelves, trying to decipher the shelving system on my own. (Kathryn later explained about the Dewey Decimal. Roses are 635.933.)

I could see that Kathryn was on the phone, so I hung about, looking at the noticeboard, until I heard her say goodbye.

I brushed my hands across my shoulders – in case of dandruff – and then I approached.

She looked up. Her nose was just that little bit too large for her face. But it matched her lips somehow, the size of it, because they were full and curvy, like the rest of her.

'Can I help you?'

'Roses,' I said. 'I'm looking for books on roses.'

We pretended not to recognise each other, although I knew who she was, and she told me later that she knew my face on that first day. 'I knew who you were all right,' she said.

She'd been married to Jack Welch. He was killed in a motorbike accident not six months after they were wed. They were quite the couple in their courting days, Jack with his winkle-pickers, and Kathryn with her shiny hair. You'd see them racing through the village, her hands tight round his waist, her skirt dangerously close to the back wheel.

After Jack died, no one saw Kathryn for a year.

And there she was in the library, a widow at twenty-six, showing me a whole shelf of gardening books, with several solely dedicated to roses.

'Are you a member?'

I didn't know what she meant. I thought I could just stroll in and borrow a book.

'No. But I'd like to be.'

She showed me the forms. I filled in each section, taking care not to let my letters spill over the printed lines. She watched me as I signed my name with what I hoped was a flourish. I pushed the forms over to her for examination, and she ran a finger along the lines, checking each one. 'Howard Hall,' she read out. 'Totleigh Way, Calcot.' She looked up. 'That's near me.'

I went there as often as I could after that, sometimes taking the bus on a Thursday after work, as they stayed open until seven that night.

She did something special when she answered the phone. She said, 'Good evening,' before she'd even started. Not just 'Hello', or plain 'Darvington Library', as I'd heard the others do. With Kathryn it was a three-part structure. 'Good Evening. Darvington Library. How may I help?' Her voice sliding up and down. And she always reached for a pad and pencil as soon as she picked up the receiver. She knew she might have to make a note, and she didn't want to keep anyone waiting while she searched for the appropriate equipment.

I noticed the way she'd dampen her forefinger with her tongue before she flipped through the membership files. And the way she closed the filing cabinet drawer with her hip, twisting her body and slamming it into place.

On my fourth Thursday evening I promised myself I would speak, phone or no phone, filing or no filing. I'd go right up to the desk and ask her something. Interrupt, if necessary. I'd say anything I could think of. All I had to do was open my mouth and let the words come out.

I spent the journey there looking at my reflection in the bus window. The fields smeared past. My nose looked big and red, pockmarked at the sides, the nostrils flaring slightly as I breathed. I licked a finger and smoothed it over an eyebrow, as I'd seen someone do in a film.

When I walked into the library it was so quiet and warm that it was almost like the place was sealed against the outside world. The strip lights hummed. Somewhere a child shouted for his mother and was immediately hushed. I walked to the counter, my shoes heavy on the wooden floor. My trousers were too hot; the nylon was rough against my kneecaps.

She wasn't on the phone. Or by the filing cabinet. Behind the desk, an older woman in a cardigan sat reading a book, and didn't look up as I went by.

Just wait until she comes, I told myself.

I walked towards my usual seat below a window, at the end of the gardening section. Selecting *Roses – an Expert's Guide* by Geoffrey Smith, I sat down. I'd seen him on the television, and didn't quite trust his easy manner. The book left a grubby film on my fingertips. Every book in the library seemed to smell of other people's hands. The flyleaf had a photograph of Geoffrey holding a rose in his red scrubbed fingers, a fine layer of dirt beneath his nails. I supposed that I was meant to find that comforting. I wondered if Kathryn would like to see a layer of dirt beneath my fingernails, if that would convince her I was a man worth taking a chance on. A capable, outdoors sort of a man.

The pages of the book were thick and soft. The spine creaked as I balanced it on one knee and turned each page. Burning dust from the overhead fan heater hung in the air; a warm blast agitated the hair on the back of my head. It was going a bit, even then. Mum pointed it out to me soon after my twenty-fifth birthday. 'Your grandfather was bald at thirty, Howard,' she said. 'Mind you, you've got your father's hair. Thick and sandy. He had it all over. And I mean everywhere.'

I turned a page.

'Good evening, ladies!'

The voice of the man with the four carrier bags travelled across the library. Every Thursday evening he was there. Usually he was the only other man in the place. He wore a flat cap and a raincoat, buttoned right to the top, and a long blue scarf. Once I followed him as he stormed upstairs to the reference section. He dumped his carrier bags in the middle of the room and began spinning through the catalogue, the cards thudding against his fingers.

Kathryn was never upstairs. She wasn't a reference librarian. Nevertheless, he seemed to know her.

'Ah, the lovely Kathryn! When are you going to stop shelving and let me read you the first volume of my memoirs?' His voice boomed out over the shelves, and I heard her high-pitched laugh.

So she was here.

I turned another page.

Then there was a squealing sound. I leant forward, the back of my neck taking the blast from the fan heater. Yes, there it was, a squeal followed by a series of clicks, surprisingly definite. Click-clack, click-clack, squeal. Click-clack, click-clack, squeal. Kathryn was wheeling the shelving trolley in my direction, her heels tapping on the wooden floor.

The squeals stopped and I knew she was in the aisle next to mine. I turned my head and glanced through the space between the shelves. The fabric of her red blouse bulged slightly as she reached for a book. She made a sighing sound, and I knew she would be blowing a rush of air up towards her fringe. I'd watched her do it while she was on the phone. A difficult caller, probably. Her jaw would stick out and she'd blow up. Maybe roll her eyes.

Her hand was on a book not more than ten inches from my ear.

I looked back at *Roses – an Expert's Guide*. Chapter Five. There was an illustration of a Gertrude Jekyll, its petals pink and giving. *An excellent all round rose*, read the caption. *Good scent and even blooms*.

Kathryn's knee clicked as she knelt to a low shelf. I wondered if she could see my sock through the gap, and I tried to remember which pair I had put on that morning.

She sighed again and stood up, then selected another book from the trolley. I looked through the gap in the shelves. As she reached for the top shelf, her blouse lifted above the waistband of her skirt and revealed a section of rose-patterned petticoat. It was black and lacy; big petals and leaves curled up her side. Through the lace, the whiteness of her skin was just visible.

I stared at these white patches of flesh until she stepped back on her heels and the blouse settled against her waistband. It can only have been a few seconds, that time I had with Kathryn's side right there in my eye line, but I remember every detail of that lace, the way the rose stretched as she stretched, its holes expanding over her skin and sighing back into place.

The squealing started up again. I looked back at my book. *Blooms guaranteed throughout the summer, if you treat this species with respect.*

Click-clack, click-clack, squeal. She turned the corner and then she was right in front of me, standing beside the trolley. The air around us seemed to sway slightly as she breathed in and out. She selected a book on tulips and clutched it to her chest.

She stood there for a while, gazing over my head. I looked at her hand, the way each finger stretched over the big red bloom on the cover.

Then she spoke. 'What's that you're reading?' Her voice was small but firm, each word clearly pronounced.

I looked down at the book, then back up at her. Sweat prickled on my forehead. Her eyes were on my mouth as I forced out a word. 'Roses.'

She nodded. 'My dad grew them. All along the front of our house.'

'I know.'

She looked surprised.

'I mean, I remember.'

Above us, the light hummed.

'Do you have a favourite?' she asked.

'Favourite?'

'Rose.'

I searched for a name. She began to drum her fingers along the tulip. I noticed that she still wore her wedding ring.

'Gertrude Jekyll's very good.' I took a breath. 'It's the best all round rose. Blooms guaranteed throughout the summer. Easy to care for. But the best thing about it, of course, is that it's very, very beautiful.'

'Hmm.' She began to smile. 'A bit pink for me.'

'You know it, then?'

She nodded. 'My dad had them all over the place. Flirty Gerties, he called them. But red's my favourite.'

I looked at her blouse. 'I thought so.'

She looked away then, and I wished I'd said something else.

As she reached up to slot the tulip book into place, her blouse lifted again. She would have down on her skin there, on her belly and perhaps her side. Fine down, almost invisible, but I would know it was there.

'Do you have your own garden?'

I shifted in my seat. 'I'm getting one.'

'And will it be all roses?'

'Oh no. I have plans. Tall wild flowers growing in between the roses. Maybe an archway. Box hedges lining gravel pathways. Nothing straight, but everything in balance. The thing with gardens is you have to have vistas. Something you can look through.'

She laughed. 'You sound like you're going to open it to the public.'

'Maybe I will.'

We looked at each other.

'Better get on.' She grabbed the trolley handle with both hands.

'Just a minute,' I said.

Her fingers loosened their grip, but she remained stooped over the trolley.

'I want to ask you something.'

She looked at me, both eyebrows raised and her lips slightly open. The fan heater blew a strand of hair across her cheek and she jutted her jaw forward and blew upwards.

'I have to ask you something.'

'Yes?'

As she waited for me to speak, she stroked the spines of the books on her trolley, letting her fingers trail loosely over the titles.

I cleared my throat.

'Do you like climbers or trailers best?'

For a minute she didn't respond. She continued to run her fingertips over the books as she watched me. Then she said, 'Why?'

'Because I'll need to know. I'll need to know which one to buy for you.'

'That Kathryn Welch is one of them.'

I was late getting to the power station canteen. I missed my usual seat by the window, so I had to sit at the end of a long table right next to the tea urn. The hot metal was at my back and men kept brushing my shoulders as they queued up with their mugs. Steam spurted around me as I stirred my tea.

At first I thought it was my imagination; I thought that I was hearing Kathryn's name only in my head, just as I was somehow expecting her to telephone or leave a message, even though she didn't know where I worked.

'Tweed knickers, but I'd like to get them off her.'

A big laugh broke over my head. I stirred my tea faster.

'She's a lovely one, eh, Howard?'

I turned round in my seat. Derrick Pearce shot a jet of steam into his mug. He held it high in the air and examined it before taking a slurp. Then he looked over at me. 'You got that tea stirred? You'll wear the bloody spoon out.'

I tapped the spoon three times on the rim of my mug before letting it rest on the table.

'She told me you're keen.' Derrick's voice was softer. He smiled.

I scraped my chair back and stood up. Derrick's face was wide and red, and he breathed out a stream of cigarette-and-tea-smelling breath. I noticed he had one collar inside and one outside his jumper.

I stepped round him.

When I got back to my desk in the control room, I ripped out the notebook page on which I'd written

Kathryn's name. I tore it into lengthways strips, and then I folded the strips and tore them horizontally. Then I tore each one again and let the pieces flutter out of my hands and into the wastepaper basket, where they lay in a mound of paper dust.

I managed to stay away from the library for the next month. I didn't go into Darvington at all until I had to take Mum to town for a doctor's appointment. While we were there, she took a fancy to borrowing a novel.

'It will help me kill the hours while you're at work,' she said.

I hung back outside as she pushed the door open. It was Saturday morning and I knew it would be busy in there. Probably Kathryn would be overwhelmed by phone calls, filing and shelving.

'Are you coming in?'

The wind blew a pile of leaves around the door; I traced a line through them with my foot.

'Don't just stand there, Howard,' Mum called to me, 'come out of the wind.'

The door closed, sealing us inside. Blown-in leaves had been trodden down to soft streaks on the doormat. I stepped over them and tried not to look at the counter.

'Isn't that Kathryn Welch?'

Through the Saturday shoppers and the families taking their children on their weekly library outing, Kathryn was walking towards us. She was wearing a short blue dress which fell into and over the curves of her body.

Mum nodded towards her. 'That's a very short frock for a library.'

I stood there, looking at that blue dress. Then Kathryn's eyes met mine and she held my gaze for a second before walking away.

I put a hand on Mum's shoulder and said, 'Aren't the novels over there?'

I glanced round the library. The man with the four carrier bags was nowhere to be seen. A dampness was creeping under my armpits, so I removed my jacket.

A branch was blowing against the window I usually sat beneath, but it made no sound. It swayed silently, its leaves pressing flat against the glass for a moment before springing back to life in the wind. The humming of the strip lights was all I heard as I made my way over to Kathryn. The phones, the children, the thud of books being stamped all faded. I walked through the hum towards her.

She was staring at the spines arranged on the top shelf of her trolley. Part of her dress was pulled up slightly against her thigh where she leant on the wood.

'Hello,' I said. And without thinking about it, I added, 'I've missed seeing you.'

She stuck her jaw out and blew up into her fringe. She didn't look at all surprised. 'Good,' she said.

I think Mum guessed there was something going on from the frequency of my library visits, but she didn't question me, even after she'd seen Kathryn there in her blue mini-dress. I suppose I started to come home looking pleased with myself after that. I'd spend at least an hour in the library with Kathryn, following the trolley as she wheeled it round the aisles, sitting down and chatting to her as she reached up to those high shelves, watching for any glimpse of the white skin of her side.

I decided to ask her to the power station dance. I'd been visiting her for at least a month, but I wasn't sure if she would be ready to say yes. Our conversations had been about my plans for a garden, her father's roses, the forthcoming library extension, the books Kathryn liked to read. She would recommend things to me but I didn't take them out as I knew novels weren't my thing. Once I had *The Mayor of Casterbridge* by Thomas Hardy in my hand all the way up to the counter, thinking it would make her smile and nod if she stamped it for me. But at the last minute I deposited it on the trolley. I knew I'd never read it, which would mean I'd have to lie to her when she asked me.

So there had never been any mention of anything personal. I had not questioned her about her dead husband. She had not enquired if I was courting any girl.

On the day I decided I would ask her, I spent the bus journey from Calcot to Darvington forming different ways of putting my question.

Would you care to join me at the power station dance? I asked the trees that hung over the river.

There's a dance on Saturday night. Do you fancy it? I asked the bus stop just after Darvington Bridge.

Want to join me at the dance on Saturday? I asked the posters in the Co-op window.

Should I just go straight to the desk and come out with it, leaning urgently on the counter? *Kathryn. I want you to come to the dance with me.*

Or wait until she was alone in the literature section and spend half an hour building up to the subject? Perhaps there would be some novel I could enquire about that had a big dance scene in it. Something like Jane Austen. Not that a power station dance would be anything like that.

Or perhaps I should start with a compliment.

You look like you'd enjoy a good dance.

No, that sounded slightly obscene. That was what some of the men at work would be saying to their women down the Barley Mow. *You look like you'd enjoy a dance love. And the rest.*

By the time I arrived in the warmth of the library, my mind was blank. I couldn't see Kathryn anywhere. I even went upstairs to the reference section. The man with the four carrier bags was thundering through the card catalogue. But Kathryn was nowhere to be seen.

I walked slowly down the stairs, listening for the click-clack of her heels. And as I reached the final step, her voice was suddenly there.

'Howard. Hello.' She was stroking the spines of the books on her trolley. 'Isn't there a dance at the power station on Saturday?' she said.

So later that evening I probably came in whistling.

'I'm beginning to think you've got a fancy woman,' said Mum.

Nothing else was said until the Saturday morning before the dance. Every other Saturday I would take Mum to the covered market in Oxford to buy what she called 'some real meat'. She didn't trust Hughes's in Darvington. 'It's too cheap,' she said. 'And it's all wrapped up, ready. I don't trust that. You don't know what it is. I want to see it on the counter. I want to see him cut into it.'

But that Saturday I had to buy some new trousers for the dance. I knew that none of the trousers I usually wore would be acceptable. They were not what young men wore. They were the sort of trousers worn by men in banks, in schools, in offices. I needed something that would show Kathryn I was a worthy dancing partner for a woman in a blue mini-dress.

So I'd have to say something to Mum. I was twenty-eight years old. This was the first time I'd wanted to tell Mum about any girl.

That morning she cooked us bacon, eggs and fried bread, like she always did at the weekend. I cut into my egg and the yolk leaked into the bacon fat.

'Into Oxford today,' I said.

Mum folded a rasher onto her fork. 'I'm beginning to wonder if that market is worth it.'

'Maybe it isn't. It's quite expensive. You could try somewhere else. Somewhere closer.'

'I can't buy the meat in Hughes's, Howard, if that's what you mean.'

'But like you say, it is expensive. In Oxford.'

She nodded and continued to eat.

I put down my knife and fork.

'You're not making much of a dent on that bacon, Howard.'

'The thing is,' I said, 'the thing is, I'd like to go on my own today.'

She didn't stop chewing as she stared at me. She swallowed, dabbed the corner of her mouth with her apron and picked up her teacup.

'I see. Well, you can do as you like. You're not my little man any more. You're grown now.'

She blew loudly into her tea. Then sighed. Then blew loudly again.

'Mum – '

'It's all right, Howard, really.' There was a little laugh in her voice, and she arranged her mouth in the way she always does for photographs: lips turned slightly up at the corners. 'You go and do what you have to. Whatever that is. I won't stop you.'

'Mum – '

She put up one hand. 'I mean it.'

'It's just that I'm taking a girl out tonight.'

Slowly, her hand came down and rested on the top of her cup. All her fingers curled around the rim, as if she was afraid that something would fall into her tea. She stared at her hand.

'She's a lovely girl, Mum. She works in the library.'

She nodded, keeping her head bowed over the teacup. I noticed that her grey roots were beginning to show.

'In fact, you know her. It's Kathryn Welch.'

She took a breath. 'Howard. You don't have to tell me. What I mean is, I don't want to know. Unless – ' she clenched the tea cup tighter – 'unless I really have to.' She looked at me, her grey eyes small and frightened. 'Do you understand, son?'

On our first date, Kathryn wore a pink outfit. It made her look like a rosebud.

We sat at a table, staring at our drinks. I remember watching a bead of moisture slip down her glass of gin and tonic. Every time she reached forward to pick up her drink I thought I'd be able to touch her hand. It would be easy: I'd just reach out and fold my fingers around hers. And she'd look up and say my name. *Oh, Howard.*

But she kept on sipping, and my hand stayed cold around my pint.

Derrick Pearce looked over from the bar. He wore a bright purple shirt and tie, and pointed shoes.

I got up to go to the toilet, and when I came back, Derrick was in my seat, leaning over Kathryn, whisky glass in hand. She was smiling, and her hand was at her neck. 'Why don't you come and dance, love?' he was saying.

Kathryn looked up at me.

'Just one dance,' said Derrick, twisting round to give me a wink. 'Howard won't mind. Will you Howard?'

Kathryn's eyes searched my face as she took a sip from her gin and tonic.

'I would mind, actually, Derrick.' I tried to smile at her. 'I would mind a great deal. But it's up to Kathryn.'

She put down her drink and, without even looking at Derrick, she stood up and led me to the dance floor. We danced together all night, my hand resting in that warm little hollow at the bottom of her back.

two

Spring, 1966

The film's sharp edges scratched at my hands. I held its end up to the light and looked through the perforations along the top before tucking it in the slot. Soon Kathryn's image would be there, captured on my film.

I'd bought a camera in Ivor Field's Photographic Supplies in Darvington. An Ilford Sportsman. It was second-hand but looked as good as new; they'd thrown in a black leather carrying case for nothing. The man in the shop, who called me 'Young Man', showed me how to unscrew the case from the camera's bottom. But, as he pointed out, this wasn't really a necessary skill, as you could easily take as many pictures (or 'shots', as he called them) as you liked with the strap still safely hooked around your neck. You need never risk dropping it.

The case was new leather. I brought it to my nose and inhaled: it smelled fresh, a bit like the earth I'd dug round my new roses the day before. I loved the sound the button made as you pressed it to take a picture ('a firm touch is what's needed, Young Man,' said the man in the shop, 'as I'm sure you know'). A definite click, no going back. There were dials around the lens, with numbers marked on. I had a booklet which told me all about what they meant. As long as I could focus, the man said, I could take a picture. It was just a matter of getting Kathryn within the central square, framing her, and closing the shutter. Click.

It was a Sunday afternoon in early spring. Kathryn and I had been courting for a few months, but this was the first time we'd arranged to meet at my house.

I remember the light coming through my curtains that morning; how I knew it would be warmer that day from the way the sun seemed to penetrate right through the material.

As I watched for Kathryn from my bedroom window, the glass became wet with my breath.

Eventually she came into view. She was wearing a yellow dress and cardigan. She'd come out without her coat, but was carrying a yellow umbrella. She frowned as she walked; the little nick in the centre of her forehead deepened as she examined each of the houses along our road. It was as if she'd never seen them before, although she'd lived here all her life.

I thought about opening the window, leaning out and snapping her right there and then, framing her little frown in my central square. Click.

'Howard. She's coming.'

Mum must have been watching, too, from the living room window.

'I'll get the door,' she called, before I could make it half-way down the stairs. I ducked into the living room so that I wouldn't be waiting behind Mum when Kathryn came in.

Then I realised I still had the camera around my neck, so I took it off and placed it on the nest of tables. I clicked the case shut and arranged the strap so it curled around the case.

I stood by the fireplace. Placing one hand on the chimney-breast, I attempted to lean against it in a relaxed manner. I wished Mum didn't have that photograph of me in my school blazer on the mantelpiece. 'You loved that school, Howard. I couldn't drag you away from the place,' she always said when she caught me scowling at it. 'I loved the blazer,' was what I wanted to reply. The feel of the silk embroidered badge on the breast pocket. The shiny buttons on the cuffs.

'Do come in, dear.'

I took my hand away from the chimney-breast and put it in my pocket.

Kathryn stood in the doorway, her shoulders slightly hunched. She looked all round the room, that nick still in her forehead, before she looked at me.

'Go on in, dear. Howard's been waiting for you.'

Kathryn stepped forward. Mum edged past her into the room. 'Well, this is nice,' she said, standing by me, pulling her face into a smile.

'What a lovely photo,' said Kathryn, gesturing towards the fireplace.

'Howard loved that school.'

Kathryn raised her eyebrows.

'Have you got the camera all ready, son?' Mum asked.

Kathryn looked at me. I nodded towards the nest of tables. 'I bought it. Yesterday.'

'I expect he'll want to take some snaps of you, dear. All dressed up in your nice clothes.' Mum's smile didn't move as we stood in silence, staring at the camera.

'Shall we go?' I suggested.

'We can't drive on a day like this,' said Kathryn, looking up at the sky.

The front path glowed in the sunshine. I decided to sling my jacket over my arm.

Kathryn stopped and stood at the gate. A tulip brushed her leg as she swung round to face me. 'We should just walk, don't you think?'

I had put a new blanket on the back seat of the car.

'Just walk?'

'It's such a lovely day. It's a shame to waste the sunshine, sitting in a car.'

I'd spent all yesterday afternoon brushing out the upholstery and polishing the dashboard and the mirrors. I had removed Mum's Mills & Boon novel from the glove compartment, replacing it with a new bag of barley sugar. I had imagined unwrapping them for Kathryn, feeding her sweet morsels as we drove.

'Come on,' said Kathryn. 'I know where we should go.'

We walked through the village in silence, swapping the odd small smile, until we reached the church. I thought about asking Kathryn if I could snap her in front of the yew trees in the graveyard; the daffodils were out and with her yellow outfit it would have made a pretty picture. But instead I asked, 'Where are we going?'

'Not far.'

We took the lane around the side of the church. Kathryn led the way, her hand trailing along the old stone wall. I walked behind, watching her skirt sway slightly with each step.

'I enjoyed the dance, Howard.'

'Do you know Derrick Pearce?'

She twisted her umbrella in her hand. 'A little.'

'He mentioned you, at work. Before the dance.'

'Did he?'

'He mentioned that he'd spoken to you.'

'Really.'

I waited for more.

'I think he was keen on me for a while,' Kathryn said.

'I see.'

'I don't like him much, though.'

'No.'

The lane smelled of rain and earth. It had become warmer and my toes rubbed together in my shoes. I would have to choose thinner socks tomorrow.

'I've been planting some more roses.'

'Oh yes?'

'I've bought a yellow one. It's the colour of your dress.'

She turned and gave me a quick, bright smile before continuing down the path. The lane became thinner and darker. Blossom hung over our heads; a few petals were already floating to the ground.

'How do you know Derrick?' I asked.

'I don't *know* him, Howard.'

'I thought you did.'

Kathryn stopped walking and looked into my face. 'He came into the library. Like you.'

I laughed. 'Derrick Pearce, in a library?'

'What's funny about that?'

'I didn't have him down as a library man, that's all.'

'I didn't have you down as a library man, Howard.' She carried on walking, twisting her umbrella in time with each step.

We came out of the lane and into the fields behind the power station.

'I haven't been down here for a long time,' Kathryn said.

From where we stood, I could see the cooling towers of the power station on one side, and the pools – the disused gravel pits – on the other. The power station pumps its surplus ash into these pits. They're really the best place for it. Things seem to grow down here, whatever happens.

The closest pool shimmered in the sunshine, its surface

glinting through the leaves as if there was nothing beneath. At that moment, it looked as if it was a real lake, not a man-made, oversized puddle.

Steam rose from the cooling towers into the sky. People often think there are burners or something sinister inside them. When the power station was first built, Mum thought the village would be choked by smoke. 'My washing will be black,' she said. But I explained to her that each tower is actually a hollow concrete shell. They're just for cooling the water from the power station. It's not smoke coming from the towers; it's condensation.

'I swam here once.' Kathryn had made her way through the trees and was standing at the edge of the first pool, grasping the elderflower bushes on either side of her, peering into the water.

'Be careful,' I said, following her. 'There's a sign here somewhere. Deep water leading to possible entrapment.' I tried to make my voice light.

She leaned over a bit further, making the branches sway. 'It was so cold. Even though it was the hottest day I can remember.'

I undid the camera case. 'Look at me,' I said. She looked back and I pushed the button. Click.

She blinked. 'I wasn't ready.'

I snapped the camera case shut. 'When was that?'

'What?'

'When you swam.' I worked my way to the edge of the bank where she stood.

'A long time ago.'

I put my hand on her shoulder and squeezed, and was surprised by the hardness of the bone there. 'We could swim here, if you like.'

'I don't think I'll ever do that again, Howard.' She circled the tip of her shoe in the mud.

After a minute, I asked, 'Can I take another picture?'

As I positioned myself a few feet from the bank and tried to get Kathryn in focus, she glanced up at the cooling towers behind me.

'I hate those towers.'

I turned the dial until her edges became crisp.

'The way you can't escape them.'

'Smile.'

'They're so… overwhelming.'

I clicked. 'You didn't smile. I'll have to take more if you don't smile.'

She continued to gaze over my head at the cooling towers.

'They're my work, Kathryn.' I closed the camera case.

'I know. It must be worse for you.' She walked back up the bank towards me, her feet slipping slightly in the soft earth.

'Not really. I like seeing them again. If I've been away.'

She stumbled a little then and caught hold of my arm to steady herself. 'Really?'

'Yes. Six towers. Six towers means I'm home.'

The sun was getting lower in the sky and the afternoon light was softening around us. Kathryn put her hand up to my cheek and ran her finger along the length of my nose. 'Six towers,' she said. 'Funny. I've never counted them.'

I smiled at her. 'But I know everything about them, you see.'

'Oh yes?'

'Yes. I know what they're for. Why they're important, *necessary*. And you don't. Which is why you don't like them.'

She laughed. 'Is that right?'

'Each one of those towers cools the water from the power station condensers, using the natural updraught of air. And that's necessary every time you switch a light on. Those towers are a miracle, Kathryn. They help keep Calcot illuminated. They keep the whole county illuminated. And warm. They keep everything running.'

She twirled her umbrella. A bird skimmed over our heads and across the water. 'There's other things, though, that we need,' she said. 'To keep things running. Apart from heat and light.'

'Not much,' I said.

She wrapped her arms around my waist and I smelled the warmth of her thick hair. 'No,' she said. 'No. I suppose not.'

It was a quiet wedding. Kathryn carried red carnations; I remember thinking that with all those frilly edges they weren't quite right for her, but they suited the registry office with its green leather armchairs and photos of local councillors on the walls. When we signed the register Mum's hand rested on my shoulder, and Kathryn stared as I wrote my name with the fountain pen. 'Your signature,' she said. 'It looks different from how it did in the library.' I gave Mum my camera to take some pictures, but none of them came out very well. I still have the one I took, of Kathryn just after the ceremony, standing in the doorway of the town hall, looking off to the right, holding her bunch of blooms down by her thigh, the fleshy tip of her nose slightly pink from the cool spring day. On the back of the photo I wrote, *Mrs Kathryn Hall.*

The house was a surprise for my wife. We'd been living with Mum for a few months after we were married, which I didn't mind, but Kathryn was keen to move for obvious reasons. So I'd been to the council and put our name on the list, and this place had come up in Totleigh Way. It was just down the road from Mum's and it had gardens back and front, so I took it immediately.

It was a hot day when we came here; the grass out front was scorched, and there was dust all over Kathryn's new shoes by the time we made it to the door.

'It doesn't look too promising from the outside,' I said as I pushed the key in the lock. Kathryn squeezed my hand. 'Our new house!' she whispered.

I thought afterwards that I should have carried her over the threshold, but she was in the door and up the hall before I could say anything.

We stood in the hallway in silence. It was cool in there even though the sun was blazing outside, and the smell of damp rose up like rotten fruit.

We walked through the downstairs rooms, Kathryn leading the way, her heels clacking on the bare concrete floor. The walls in the hallway were covered in green paint that was so thick it shone. Kathryn ran a finger along the paint as she walked, tracing each bump.

She opened the door to the kitchen, looking back at me uncertainly before entering.

We stood in the middle of the room and looked around. I knew that her eyes would be registering every detail, and I noticed, with a sudden, sharp clarity, all the things she would be noticing. I don't think the walls had ever seen plaster. They were painted white, but had gone yellow long ago. On one wall there was a brown outline where the cooker must once have been. The smell of ancient chip fat hung in the air.

I knew these were all merely surface things, things I could fix. But my wife felt differently.

I watched as her face fell.

'Let's go upstairs,' I said, before she could speak. 'Bound to be better in the bedrooms.'

When Kathryn stepped into the room that was to be our bedroom, she started to cry. There was mould all up the wall around the window. A sheet of wallpaper hung down like a strange curtain.

'It's not that bad,' I said. 'Look at that lovely big window. The light it lets in.'

She sniffed.

'We'll get it sorted in no time.'

'I can't live here. Look at it.'

'You're not seeing it, though; you've got to trust me. I can see how it will look – when I've finished.'

'I can't live here, Howard.'

'Wait,' I said. 'Wait here a minute.'

I'd had a feeling that she'd react like this, so I'd bought her a little gift, in preparation. I fetched it from the car and ran back up the stairs to her.

'What's that?'

'I thought you could help me plant it. In our new garden.'

She looked at the gnarled stump of a rose that I'd placed in her hands, and was silent.

'It's for you, Kathryn.'

She put the tub down and embraced me, her arms tight around my shoulders.

'Thank you, Howard,' she said, but I felt the wetness of her tears on my neck.

I didn't stop Kathryn working at the library, even though Mum mentioned it every time we went there. 'And you're still working at the library?' she'd ask as she poured the tea or handed round the biscuits. 'Yes,' Kathryn would reply, with a look at me.

'Full time?' Mum would add, and I'd have to say, 'Mum, you know Kathryn's full time,' and attempt to change the subject. On bad days, Mum wouldn't let the subject change, and she'd quiz Kathryn on how she had the time to prepare my dinner and keep the house clean. Then Kathryn would be silent with me on the walk home, and I'd have to go out in the garden and stay there, whatever the weather, until she called me in or came out and put her hand on my shoulder, which was the signal that I was forgiven. Then I'd lead her round the flower beds and show her what I'd planted, and what was doing well, and she'd listen to it all, nodding and smiling, and usually she'd spot a weed.

'You've missed a bit,' she'd say, pointing and laughing.

Sometimes when I was out there she'd bring me a cup of tea. 'You never drink enough,' she'd say, handing me the cup and saucer, her eyes squinting against the sun, and then I'd want to call Mum round to the house immediately, to show her what a good wife Kathryn was.

One Saturday she came home from her morning's work at the library with a packet of seeds she'd bought in Woolworths.

I knew she'd been seduced by the photograph on the packet (people always are): glossy red poppies, a whole field of them.

Now, poppies are not what I'd call a stylish flower. They look lovely in their place – a farmer's field, at the side of the road – but in a garden they all too often end up looking sad and scraggy, their stems sticky with blight, their flowers over in a jiffy, leaving the seeds to blow all over the place so you just don't know where another one is going to pop up next year, or the year after that.

But Kathryn was keen on poppies.

I was sitting down with the newspaper and a fresh pot of tea (I knew she'd be back by one thirty, so the kettle went on at one twenty-five, and I was usually pouring by the time she opened the front door). She stood in front me and waved her packet of seeds; her dark hair shook around her shoulders.

'Look what I've got.'

'Do you want tea?' I asked.

'What? Oh, yes. Thanks.' She sat opposite me and held out the packet of poppy seeds before her.

'They're so beautifully red. And yet so delicate.' She seemed pleased with that thought. 'Don't you think so, Howard?' she asked. 'Isn't it strange how a flower can have such a strong colour and yet be so vulnerable?'

I looked up from my newspaper. 'Where are you going to plant them?'

'I thought I'd just scatter them. You know. Be a bit free-spirited about it.'

I laughed. 'You can't just scatter them. I've got to know where they are. For watering.'

'But you water everywhere,' she said. 'Anyway. There's no need to worry. I'll look after them.'

'What do you know about gardening?' I asked, reaching out to take the packet from her.

'What do I need to know?' She snatched the packet back. 'You shove them in the ground and hope for the best. Then you spend hours out there, watering, trimming, hoeing and picking out the bits you don't want, and – Bob's your uncle – you're a gardener. Apparently.'

We stared at each other.

'Well. You'd better plant them, then,' I said, opening the back door and stepping outside. I had box to trim, dahlias to dead-head. Plenty to keep me busy.

About an hour later, I stopped and looked up at the back of our house. Kathryn was standing at the bedroom window, staring out at me. I waved, and she opened the window.

'I'm going to plant them,' she called. I glanced over my shoulder to make sure the neighbours weren't in their gardens.

'Oh yes?'

'Watch me.' She leant out and shook the open packet. The wind must have carried most of the seeds over into next door's garden, but I felt a few of them brush my face as they fell to the earth.

'That's what I call gardening,' she said, and she closed the window.

three

Autumn, 1968

I knew there wouldn't be any sweets in the sweetie tin, but I opened it.

About a year after we'd moved into our own house in Totleigh Way, I was looking in Kathryn's drawer for a bar of soap. She kept soap in her underwear drawer for the fresh smell.

But instead of soap I came across an old sweetie tin. On the outside, there was a picture of toffees in all kinds of wrapping.

Inside was a small pile of photos – there couldn't have been more than twenty – held together with a piece of white lace. I slipped the lace off. It was soft and wide, with a blue bow on it, and it was threaded with elastic.

It wasn't until afterwards that I realised this was a wedding garter, and that Kathryn hadn't worn a garter on our wedding day.

The top photo was of Jack, smiling, on a motorbike, both feet firm and flat on the ground. I recognised Kathryn's house behind him, the neat hedges that her father always kept so well. Jack was wearing wide trousers, with a sharp crease down each leg.

I let the photographs fall on the eiderdown.

'What are you doing?'

I tried to scoop the photos back up into the box, but my fingers seemed to have jammed in one useless position.

'Howard? What are you doing?'

Kathryn snatched at the photos and turned away from me. 'You're getting them in a muddle!' She began to sort them, placing each one out on the bedspread so she could survey them. 'What were you thinking?'

I stood behind her and watched her shuffle the photos. She was careful not to touch anything but their edges. 'What a muddle,' she kept saying.

She slipped the garter back around the photos. I had an idea then that it looked like one of those fancy ribbons people tie round the necks of poodles and other silly dogs.

I reached out and tried to draw her to me, but she kept her arms rigid at her sides, holding the photos in one hand.

'Please don't touch them again,' she said. 'They're all I've got.'

For the next month, I stopped myself from opening that sweetie tin. Every Saturday when Kathryn was at the library and I was alone in the house, I made myself go into the garden and away from that drawer. I told myself that I must not invade her privacy, that to peek would be unforgivable, that anyone with an ounce of integrity would leave the photos to lie there in their ribbon, wrapped and safe and in the past, just where she left them.

But I kept seeing the image of Jack on the motorcycle, his feet so steady, his smile so wide. And I kept imagining what would be on the other prints: Kathryn and Jack smiling in all the local beauty spots, Hepton Lock, Whitley Clumps, Shotton Hill, Bradley Woods in the springtime, for the bluebells. I had to look to see if it was as perfect as I imagined it to be. To see where he'd taken her so I could avoid going there. To see how I could take better photographs than him.

So the next Saturday morning, not a minute after Kathryn had left to catch her bus, I was upstairs. I stood in front of her underwear drawer for a few minutes, listening to my own breath and knowing I was going to look inside the sweetie tin.

I delved my hands into her piles of knickers. My fingers trawled through cotton and elastic until I felt the hardness of the tin. I dragged it out. A pair of pink knickers that I hadn't seen before came with it and I flicked them back into the drawer.

I sat on the bed, opened the lid and slipped off the garter. My fingers were trembling, the tips wet with sweat. I was sure I'd mark the garter, sully its whiteness.

I fanned the photos out in my lap.

As I picked up each one and examined it, the thing that struck me was that you could tell there was no one else in Jack and Kathryn's lives, because no one was ever around to snap them. There was only one photo of the two of them together. In all the others they were alone, but in the same location; there'd be one of Jack standing there, posing, and then another of Kathryn in exactly the same pose, in exactly the same place. Like they were mirrors of one another. As if they couldn't bear to do anything differently.

Kathryn on Jack's motorbike, her bare legs against the metal, her black eyes squinting against the sun. Kathryn on a picnic blanket, her thick hair curled up on the top of her head, holding what looked like a chocolate éclair to her open mouth. Laughing.

It seemed that in all the photos her mouth was wide open, her lips pulled back over her teeth. I didn't remember ever really looking at her teeth before, but now here they were, bared. And her chest was pushed out into the air; each breast seemed to be showing itself somehow, showing itself to him.

A couple of the photos were on a beach. I guessed from the new-looking pier that it was Bournemouth. One of them showed a flat expanse of sand, with KATH LOVES JACK scraped into it. It was the capitals I hated. So definite. The sun must have been low behind him when he took it, because I could see his long shadow in the corner, spreading over her letters.

There was only one photograph of the two of them together, in front of one of the pools by the power station. They must have stopped some stranger and asked for a snap, Jack smiling, handing over the camera, explaining how it worked, no doubt, while Kathryn stood waiting and laughing in front of the pool, one hand on her skirt to stop it blowing up too much in the breeze.

In this photo Jack was leaning forward, grinning, and Kathryn looked so small beside him you might have thought she was his little sister. She had both arms flung around his middle, gripping him, and her head was squeezed into his armpit. Behind them, the pool looked black, wide and bottomless. I studied Jack, his confident pose, the way his hair stood up off his forehead, the way his clothes seemed just that little bit too large for him. He looked like he had room. His big body had room for manoeuvre.

Then there was one of Kathryn alone. This one didn't have a mirror image with Jack in the same pose. And it was the only photograph that was taken inside.

She was lying on a double bed. On the wall behind her was a painting of the sea. A lamp with a tiny fringed shade was in the corner. I guessed it must be a Bed and Breakfast room. We'd never stayed in such places.

She was lying on the bed in her underwear. Jack had taken a photograph of Kathryn in her underwear. Her bra was black and lacy; the pattern swirled around her breasts, and I remembered the lace of her petticoat, the one I'd seen in the library that day, and I thought of how I hadn't seen it since. Again, her chest was pushed forward. Her knickers were pushed down over her hips so you could see her white stomach bulging just slightly over the top of them.

And she had her make-up on. Her eyes were the blackest things in the photograph. I had never seen Kathryn with make-up on in bed.

I looked at that photograph for a long time, wondering who the woman in it was.

I cut open the steak and there was blood, just as I like it. Kathryn speared a piece of cheese omelette.

I couldn't taste anything, so I reached for the salt.

'You should watch your salt intake, Howard,' Kathryn said, swallowing her omelette. 'Dr Webb was in the library today and he was telling Audrey about the dangers of high blood pressure. Apparently her husband – '

'Did you tell Jack what to put on his chips?'

'I beg your pardon?'

'Did you tell Jack what to put on his chips?'

She put her knife and fork down.

'Don't say his name in that way.'

'I asked you a question. Did you tell Jack what to put on his chips?'

Kathryn was holding on to the edge of the table as if it might blow away at any moment. Her hair was clasped at her neck with a gold clip, which seemed to pull her cheeks tighter. 'Don't say his name in that way,' she repeated.

'How am I supposed to say it? Tell me, Kathryn. How do you say it?'

She stared at her plate.

'How do you say it? Because I've never heard you say it.'

'I won't have this,' she whispered, still gripping the table.

I stabbed my fork into the solid meat of the steak.

Kathryn stood up. 'I can't have this, Howard.' There was a tremble in her voice.

I took a big bite of meat and chewed on it.

'You have no right.' Her mouth was twisted. She reached up and touched her hair clip.

I could see she was close to tears but I carried on chewing for a while. Then I swallowed. 'I think I have a right to know.'

She said nothing.

I shook more salt on my chips. A few of the hard crystals bounced across the tablecloth.

'I have a right to know, Kathryn.'

'Why?'

'Because I'm your husband,' I said. 'For Christ's sake. I'm your husband.'

I did everything I could to be near to her. I liked to walk with her so I could lead her by the arm. If she was going up the shops I would go too, just so I could touch her sleeve, steer her by the shoulder, and then, when we were in the shop, I could place my hand flat against the small of her back as she paid for half a pound of bacon, and everyone would know that she was my wife. That she was my Kathryn.

After I saw the photograph Jack had taken, I thought about her in her black underwear, the little bulge of her stomach shelving suddenly down into the top of her knickers. I thought about the lacy pattern of her bra, the dark shadow of her nipples blooming beneath it.

When I held her in bed before we slept, I worked out the words in my head. I would say, 'Why don't you come to bed in your underwear?' Or, 'I'd like to see you in your bra and knickers.' But these were words I'd never used in front of my wife. *Bra* and *knickers*. They were women's words. Like *period* and *pregnancy*.

The closest I came was one night after we'd been to the pictures to see *The Graduate*. Kathryn knew about these things, what films were on and where and what they were about and whether they were any good. I just went along to have a look, and usually enjoyed them, whatever they were.

We were sitting there together in the dark and I could smell the new perfume I'd bought her. It was strong and acidic, and it made my nostrils itch a bit; but the fact that she'd sprayed something I'd bought on her bare neck and her upturned white wrists pleased me.

When Mrs Robinson removed her clothes and shut Benjamin Braddock in the bedroom, Kathryn put her hand on my knee and squeezed. I closed my fingers over hers and she didn't resist when I moved her hand further up my thigh.

I don't remember the rest of the film.

Outside the night was clear and cold; a sparkle of frost was just visible on the road. We stood under the lights of the foyer and kissed. I reached my hand up into the heaviness of her hair. She held onto my fingers as we walked to the car, and though her hand was cold I felt I had enough warmth for both of us.

I drove too fast on the way home. Kathryn didn't say anything; she just sat there smiling in the seat next to me.

'I enjoyed the film,' I said, changing into fourth as we

hit the Darvington road.

'I thought so,' she said, with a look over at me.

'We should go more often.'

'Yes, we should.' She squeezed my knee again.

I pulled up outside the house and jumped out to open Kathryn's door. It stuck a little and I spent a few moments laughing and tugging at the handle.

She stepped out, her high-heeled shoe making a crunching noise on the frosty pavement.

'You treat me like such a lady, Howard,' she said, and I thought I heard a little sigh in her voice.

I followed her inside. The house was warm and I was pleased with the way I'd decorated the hall and the living room to match. The lights were just right, big paper globes that softened the glow. Kathryn had chosen them and I'd fixed them up for her. I'd spent two weekends sanding down the woodwork, undercoating and painting three thin coats of white gloss on. Now the doors and the skirting boards shone, and the embossed wallpaper she'd chosen for the hall hung flat and bubbleless, all the patterns matched up at the joins. I'd enjoyed flattening out that paper and wiping it over with the soft brush. Afterwards, Kathryn had stood with her hand on the wall and said, 'It looks so much warmer.'

'Let's just go straight to bed,' she said now, climbing the stairs.

I sat on our bed, waiting for her to finish in the bathroom. She'd bought a table lamp with a pleated silk shade in Woolworths. It was a dark pink, like the roses we'd decided on for the wallpaper. I didn't know how to lie on the bed as I waited. Every position seemed too obvious, too lewd. So I sat on the edge and looked at the pink shade. Particles of dust played in the air above the bulb.

Water screamed in the pipes as Kathryn washed. Taking

her make-up off. Then the light in the bathroom clicked.

I sat on my hands so they wouldn't be too cold when I touched her. I would just ask her. I would ask her about her underwear. No, I would tell her I wanted to see it. I wouldn't make it a question. She would respond to my demand. I was her husband. She would do this for me.

When she came in she already had her nightie on.

'Where's your underwear?'

That wasn't right. That wasn't right at all.

'In the laundry basket, you ninny. Where it belongs.' She walked over to the dressing table and started dragging a brush through her hair. Crackles of static sparked around her head.

I sat staring at the shade.

'Are you all right, Howard?'

She sat down beside me. Her nightie was pink with a lace trim around the neck and the hem. It had little puff sleeves and a bib of lace at the front.

'I want to see you in your underwear.' I looked at the roses on the wall in front of me as I spoke. The heat from the lamp made my cheek hot. That lamp made the whole room pink, I realised. Like a girl's bedroom. I was sleeping in a girl's bedroom.

She caught my chin in her hand and turned my face towards her, her nails sharp against my jaw. 'Is that what you want?' she said, the nick in her forehead deepening.

I reached one hand out and flicked the lamp switch off. Kathryn let go of my chin.

We sat in the darkness. I kept my thumb on the lamp switch. She didn't move. I didn't move. Although our thighs were close, they didn't touch. I thought about touching her in the darkness, but the hand on the light switch felt cold and heavy, and the hand beneath my thigh seemed to have died.

'Howard.'

'Yes?'

'Is that what you really want?'

I flicked the switch on again and looked at my wife. I studied her unblinking brown eyes, thinking that if I could only see deep enough I would know. I would know the strength of her feeling for me, whatever that feeling was.

I pressed the switch again and spoke into the darkness.

'I want to see you in your underwear.'

Then she went so quiet that for a moment I thought she was holding her breath.

The mattress gave a sudden bounce as she stood up. I heard Kathryn's feet padding on the carpet and over to her chest of drawers. I could hardly keep track of her shape as she moved, a black ghost in our bedroom.

I thought of all the women's underwear I'd ever seen. Underwear actually on a woman's body, with flesh inside it. There was Susan Lively, a girl with long ginger curls at school. She'd done handstands so her skirt fell over her head and all the boys could see her white pants. She'd hold them for quite a while, too. At the back of the playground, by the wall of the orchard. There'd be bruised apples on the ground, holey from the worms, and Susan's legs flashing up into the air. One sock scrunched down around the top of her ankle strap. I remembered the neat frills around the tops of her legs, the way her thighs spilled out of the elastic, and the way that lovely bone stuck out and then curved into a hollow.

'Brazen hussy,' the teacher called her. 'Susan Lively you are a brazen hussy, get inside now. And you boys should be ashamed of yourselves too.'

And Mum, that time I walked in on her getting dressed in the kitchen. I must have been twelve. On winter days it was so cold in our house that she would go down in the morning and light the gas stove, then leave the oven door open all day. She'd dress down there, on the mat by the sink. I knew she was in there, and that I wasn't supposed to open the door. She was stooped over, gripping the enamel of the sink with one hand while she adjusted her stocking with the other. White spongy flesh hung between the top of her stocking and the bottom of her bloomers. When she saw me she said nothing, just walked over to the door and closed it. And then when she came out of the kitchen, fully dressed, it was like nothing had happened. She looked at me, sitting on the stairs, hiding my red face in my hands. 'Aren't you at school yet?' she said, with a gentle shove on my shoulder.

When she hung her knickers out to dry they blew in the wind like shopping bags; only after that they weren't like bags at all, because I knew that Mum's flesh had been inside them, spilling out of the sides and warming the cotton.

Over by the drawers, Kathryn stooped down and hooked the hem of the nightie around her fingers. I could just see the outline of her now. Her curvy hair and body. The tips of her breasts moving slightly as she pulled open the drawer. She sighed as her fingers rummaged through its contents. I thought how hard it must be to tell what was what in this darkness, wondered how she would choose the best pair. But I didn't turn the light on.

She closed the drawer, letting her hips fall against it to shut it fully. I thought of the way she'd slammed the library filing cabinet closed as I watched her. Swing and slam. But this wasn't like that at all; it wasn't nearly as definite. She held the knickers out before her and stepped into them, one leg at a time, wobbling a bit. Then she reached into the straps of a bra and hoisted herself into it. It took a minute for her to hook herself up.

'What about your legs?'

'What?'

I tried to think of a word I could use that wasn't stockings. 'Wouldn't you usually put something else on?'

She put her hands on her hips. 'Howard – '

'You would usually be wearing something else.'

I heard her blow upwards into her fringe, as she had done on that day in the library. 'OK,' she said. 'All right.'

She sat down on the opposite side of the bed as she rolled up the stockings. The mattress bounced as she leant over and came back up again, smoothing each leg with her hand, the hardness of her wedding ring rasping along the sheer fabric.

'Bugger.' She turned round to face me. 'I think I've got a ladder.'

'It doesn't matter.'

She blew up into her fringe again. 'I can change them.'

'No. Don't do that.'

We sat on our opposite sides of the bed. I kept one cold hand on the light switch; the other lay dead under my thigh. She drummed her fingers lightly on the mattress. She was in her underwear, as she had been for Jack. I wanted to see her, but I knew that I wouldn't be able to turn the light back on.

'I'm getting cold,' she said. 'I've got to get into bed.'

'Yes. Don't get cold.'

She pulled back the covers and slid into the bed. Shivered.

I stood up and undressed.

We lay in bed together. The sheets felt hard, frozen. I thought I wouldn't be able to move under the cold weight of them, but then Kathryn's hand caught my fingers and led them over the cold expanse of the mattress and onto her breast.

I let my hands run over the pieces of fabric that covered those parts of her body, my fingers pulling on elastic, the tips of them feeling the roughness of lace, the flimsiness of nylon. She lay there, quietly breathing, as I removed it all, piece by piece, and she didn't help me when I struggled with the hooks of her bra and her suspenders, she just let herself go loose in my arms so I could turn her whichever way I wanted and I knew she wouldn't break, or even make a sound, as I pushed my fingers into her and called her my wife.

four

April, 1969

It was one of those cold, bright spring Sundays that's perfect for pushing the mower back and forth, working up a glow, then going into the house smelling fresh, like the grass. But we were at Mum's, for tea.

Mum handed round a cake she'd made. She spent every Sunday morning baking, ready for our arrival.

'It's too dry,' she said as she cut into it with her silver cake knife. 'I know it's too dry.'

It was coconut, and there was a coating of that chewy desiccated stuff on the top. As I picked a piece up a lot of crumbs fell back onto my red spotted plate.

'It's lovely, Mum,' I said.

'Bless you, Howard, for your charity. It's the coconut. Difficult not to make it too dry.'

We were sitting in the living room. In front of Mum was the second largest of her nest of tables, upon which was the coconut cake, and the silver cake knife that was part of Mum's set of Good Cutlery. That knife came out every Sunday, but I had never seen any other item in the set of Good Cutlery.

Mum poured the tea into the iris-patterned cups. 'I love irises,' she said. 'I think blue is my favourite colour. For flowers.'

Kathryn had been quiet all day. I could tell she felt cold because she had her hands clasped around her knees and was hunched forward. Mum tended not to have more than one electric bar on unless it was completely necessary.

Mum eyed Kathryn's posture. 'Is she cold?' she mouthed to me.

'I'm fine,' said Kathryn.

Mum took a bite of cake, chewed and swallowed. 'Isn't Kathryn having any?' She waved a plate in my wife's direction. 'Come on, tell us what you think, Kathryn. I think it's better than shop bought, at any rate.'

'I'm sure it is,' I said.

Kathryn bit into the cake.

'Of course, not everyone has time for baking,' said Mum. 'I'm one of the lucky ones.'

I looked over at my wife. She put her plate down on the arm of her chair.

'It is a little dry.' She spoke very quietly, hunching her shoulders up higher and fixing her gaze on the corner of the table.

Mum's cuckoo clock ticked loudly.

As she put her cup and saucer down, Mum's eyebrow began to twitch. She shifted in her seat and said, 'Well. Well. Well.' Then she stood, nearly toppling the second largest of the nest of tables, swooped an arm down to pick up Kathryn's plate, and marched into the kitchen, pleated skirt swirling behind, plate held out in front.

I looked at Kathryn. 'What did you say that for?'

'She's the one who said it, Howard. I was just agreeing with her.'

'She always says that, though. She always says those things.'

'What do I always say?' Mum had re-entered the room and was standing behind me with a big plate of Gingernuts in her hand and an even bigger smile on her face. 'I thought Kathryn might prefer a biscuit. Seeing as she doesn't care for cake.'

'Look. I just agreed with what you said.' Kathryn's voice was suddenly loud, and she put her hand up to her throat as she spoke. She looked over at me. 'That's all I did.'

'Coconut cake is meant to be a bit dry, surely – '

'It's all right, Howard,' said Mum. 'You don't have to try to make it better. Kathryn's quite right. The cake was dry. I don't know how anyone could eat it.'

The three of us were silent for a moment. The cuckoo clock kept ticking. Then Mum leant over Kathryn and for a minute I thought she was going to grab her by the neck, but she just placed the plate of Gingernuts in her lap and said, 'Have a biscuit, dear.' She looked into my wife's face. 'Go on.'

Kathryn took a biscuit and began to chew as Mum watched.

'The cake's wonderful. Really,' I said. 'Wonderful.'

Mum straightened up. 'I think I'll put it in the bin.'

She snatched the cake from the table and marched out again.

Kathryn and I sat in silence, listening as Mum scraped the cake into the bin, the knife screaming on the china.

After a moment, I spoke. 'Get your coat on. I'll meet you outside.'

By the time I'd left Mum's, Kathryn was halfway down the road. She walked with her head on one side and a little swing in her hips. She walked like she wasn't in any hurry, one foot stepping deliberately in front of the other, her arms swaying a little, her hair swaying a little.

Even then, I wanted to touch her.

Behind branches just coming into bud, the sun was low in the sky. As I followed Kathryn out of the gate and along Totleigh Way, the sun hit me full in the face. I stood still for a minute, blinded by the bright orange light, and I felt my hands and feet go warm. I closed my eyes and breathed deeply.

Kathryn could wait. Mum could wait.

'I'm expecting a baby.'

I opened my eyes and squinted against the sun. She must have stopped and walked back towards me, because she was facing me now.

'Howard. A baby.'

Her coat was unbuttoned and I could see the whiteness of her throat.

I stepped forward and slipped my hands inside the rough wool of her coat and pulled her towards me. There was a slight smell of bacon fat on her collar; it mingled with the sweet hairspray scent of her hair. I held her closer.

We stood in silence. It was so warm there in the sunlight that her forehead was slightly moist when I kissed it.

I looked around me. There was nothing but that strange orange light.

Kathryn put her arms around my shoulders and rested her head on my chest. Her hair tickled my neck as she spoke. 'Are you pleased?'

I wanted to shout out in the street, to run back to Mum's and tell her, to pick my wife up and carry her home, but all I could do was say yes, yes. Yes.

I had no idea you could get so ill just from that, from expecting a baby. It was like every part of Kathryn's body was against the idea. Bits of her that I thought might have just yielded to the situation swelled up, bruised, bled and even split. Every month her body seemed to resist that little bit more. And all the while, he was in there, growing stronger and stronger.

By the seventh month, her legs were like thick branches. Her curves were swelling, bending the wrong way.

One morning I kissed her in the kitchen and left for work as usual. But when I stepped outside it was colder than I'd thought, so I popped back upstairs for my jumper, and there she was, naked, standing in front of the mirror, a hand on her belly, looking herself up and down. She'd slipped off her dressing gown, and it lay in a red Kathryn-shape on the bed behind her. It was as though she was standing in front of one of those distorting mirrors you get at the fair; she was a strange reversal of her usual shape, her flesh now solidly filling the spaces where her curves had once dipped in and out.

She turned and saw me standing in the doorway.

I looked at the floor. 'My jumper – ' I said, 'it's a bit chilly out there.'

I knew she was staring at me.

'I'll leave it.' I began to retreat. 'Sorry.'

As I was closing the door behind me, she called my name. I hesitated on the landing before answering, to give her time to put her dressing gown back on, then I spoke into the small crack in the door. 'I'd better get to work.'

'Come back in.'

'I'll be late.'

There was a silence before she said, 'Please.'

I stepped into the bedroom. She was still standing in front of the mirror, one hand on her rounded belly. The dressing gown in the Kathryn-shape remained splayed out on the bed behind her.

'Do you want to feel the baby?' she asked.

I looked at her. She wasn't smiling but her eyes were

soft. I lay my jacket on the bed beside her dressing gown, put down my briefcase, and shut the door carefully behind me before approaching. She watched my reflection in the mirror as I moved towards her. I noticed that her breasts had spread out across her chest and the nipples were so dark they looked like flattened poppies.

'My hands are cold,' I said.

'It doesn't matter.'

There was a streak of talc running from the top of her thigh to her knee and I wanted to reach out and rub it away, but she led my hand to her stomach. Even her fingers were softer and rounder; as her hand clasped mine, I thought of plunging my fingers into warm earth.

'Can you feel it?'

I waited. Her stomach was hot, and my hand was heating up.

'Not yet.'

'There. Did you feel that?'

All I could feel was the heat, and I kept thinking of the talc on her thigh. 'Aren't you cold like that?' I asked.

'Like what?'

'I just thought you might want to put your dressing gown on.'

'There!' she said. 'Did you feel that?'

There was a pulse beneath my hand. I waited, and then there it was again, something pushing through Kathryn's skin and into mine.

'I felt it,' I said.

'I knew you would,' said Kathryn. 'Eventually.' She smiled up at me, and I let out a laugh as our baby kicked again.

She brought him home from the hospital wrapped tightly

in a yellow crocheted blanket that Mum had kept from when I was a newborn. It was trimmed with satin, soft from so much washing. I worried that the car wouldn't start in the cold, but I turned the key in the ignition and we were off first time.

We drove home on icy roads. I took each corner very slowly, changing down into second in plenty of time. The sun was out, despite the cold; puffs of steam from the power station cooling towers were full and white as we came into Calcot. Kathryn opened her own coat and folded the bundle of our baby inside, close to her chest. As I drove, I left one hand on the gear stick so Kathryn could hold it.

She carried him into the house. Wrapped in his blanket, he was a bundle of yellow wool with a tiny pink nose sticking out. I kept looking over her shoulder to see his face, but I couldn't find him in his woollen nest. So I asked her how he was, and that was the first time she put her finger to her lips to shush me. I thought of how I had never seen her do that in the library, even though that's what librarians are supposed to do. One finger pressed down over both lips so they bulged a little beneath it.

'Shush, Howard. Baby's sleeping.'

She held him closer, gathering his blanket around him, and he woke with a yell.

Baby's sleeping. It became her catchphrase. *Be quiet, Howard, baby's sleeping. I can't do that, Howard, baby's sleeping.*

He slept in his carrycot next to our bed. Every night I would wake several times to the sight of Kathryn bent over in her nightie, checking on him, and I knew she was resisting the temptation to touch his face, just in case, to listen for his tiny heartbeat, just in case, to bend her head to his mouth so she could feel his breath on her cheek, just in case.

In fact he was a good sleeper, right from the first. He even snored a little, his lower lip gently puffing away, bubbles of spit blooming.

When I looked at him I saw my own mouth, big and unwieldy, pouting back at me. And when I lifted him from Kathryn's arms as she went to fetch his bottle, it was my mouth I saw open, the lower lip dropping drastically so he looked like a little clown with drawn-on downward lips. His hair swirled at his crown and stuck up in a tuft at the back of his head. 'Just like a cockatoo,' I said. 'You've got a cockatoo touch,' I whispered to him, holding his face to mine and feeling the hot dampness of his cheek as he cried and cried.

When he was a few months old, I came home from work and said her name, but there was no response.

'Where are you?' I called down the hall. 'How's Robert?' I removed my scarf, gloves and coat. As I bent down to unlace my shoes, a smell reached my nostrils. It was sweet, horribly sweet, and slightly musty.

'Kathryn?' I said, but again there was no response. Leaving my shoes on, but unlaced, I pushed open the living room door. The smell became stronger. Burning. Something was burning.

She was asleep on our new three-seater sofa; Robert was in his carrycot at her feet, and his baby blanket was scalding by the gas fire.

I picked up the carrycot, removed the scalding blanket, and switched the fire off. I looked at my wife, at the blackness beneath her eyes, at the hair that was stuck to her cheek. She was fast asleep, her mouth hanging open, her head slumped down to her chest. I didn't want to wake her. I wanted to let her sleep. So I opened the window a little and I left her there on the sofa.

I carried my son up the stairs and he didn't stir. I opened the door to his room, and I put the carrycot down on the floor. I reached down and fished him out of his blankets. His hair, dark brown, was like a fine cap, tight to his skull. The skin on his legs and arms looked tight, too, filled to bursting point with flesh. I smelled his head, feeling the wispiness of his hair tickle my nose, and he smelled of Kathryn. He didn't smell of baby powder or of any sweet smell of his own, but of Kathryn's mixed odour of rose talc and gingery sweat. I inhaled the smell deeper, and then I put him down in his cot and covered him with his new Sooty eiderdown.

'Where's Robert, where's my baby?' Her voice reached me before she did.

When she came into the room, her face was bright red and still skewed from sleep; her eyes looked odd, as if they were staring in different directions.

'Where is he?'

'He's here. Look.'

She rushed to the cot and gripped the bars. 'What happened?'

'It's all right.'

She reached into the cot, but I put my arms around her and turned her towards me. 'It's all right.'

'Howard, what – '

'Shush,' I said, as I held her. 'Baby's sleeping.'

five

Summer, 1974

It was a lovely caravan park, Rockley Sands, and it was one of those weeks where the sun doesn't stop shining and you wonder whether there could be anything better in the world than strolling through Bournemouth pleasure gardens, the band playing, your wife with her hand in yours, your son running on ahead.

I had the MG Magnet by then; Kathryn liked the leather seats. They didn't get too hot in the sun, and that week the sun seemed to pour in every window, heating every surface. Each day we went on an outing in the MG, taking a picnic lunch with us. Robert was four years old.

Kathryn would make the sandwiches in the caravan kitchen, which was really a shelf and a hob in the living room – which was really a corner of the caravan with a cushion running beneath the window – but we liked it. When we arrived, Kathryn commented that the caravan was more modern than our house. 'Look at that hob,' she said. 'Wipe clean. Electric. Lovely.'

'You can't control electric,' I said. 'Not like gas.'

'And you'd know about ovens?' she said, with half a smile.

'I know about power supplies,' I replied, but she was

busy telling Robert not to run around the caravan.

He was exploring, which was something he liked to do – indoors. Opening cupboards, looking beneath cushions, swishing the curtains back and forth. Kathryn raised her eyebrows at me as he rushed into the toilet, looked under the seat, and made a close examination of the toilet brush. He liked to know the details of everything. 'The toilet's got a lock!' he said, flipping it so the little sign went from 'vacant' to 'engaged' and back.

'Robert, are you all right?' Kathryn knocked softly. 'You can come out now. We're going in a minute.'

Moments after we'd made the sandwiches, packed the picnic bag and got our sandals on, Robert disappeared into the toilet.

'I'm coming,' he called, as sunny as you like, but then he stayed in there for another five minutes while we tried to remain unconcerned. I picked up the MG keys and the picnic bag. Kathryn and I stood together outside the toilet door, waiting.

'You try him,' she said.

'Are you all right, son?' I called, rapping hard on the door but trying to keep my voice light. Most likely he'd broken something in there and was trying to hide it.

'Yes.'

'Come on out then, will you?'

Kathryn watched me with wide eyes as I leant against the door and listened for him. 'What's he up to?' she hissed.

'Robert. We're going to go in a minute.'

'Coming,' he sang out.

But the door didn't move, and there was no sound. 'This is why we don't have a lock on at home,' I said.

'Perhaps we should just leave him. He'll come out when he's ready.'

'Right, Mum, let's go,' I said in a loud voice, winking at Kathryn. 'Have you got the picnic?'

Kathryn looked blank.

'We'll see you later, then, Robert,' I called as I walked to the door of the caravan, opened it and closed it again, shushing Kathryn before she could say anything.

We stood in silence for a moment before she said, 'This is silly,' and began to bang on the toilet door with her fist. 'Robert!' she shouted, 'Mummy's worried about you! Come out now! Robert!'

He came out then, his coarse hair sticking up at the back of his head, and rushed into her arms. At that moment he looked just like her, with his big eyes and curvy lips.

'What were you doing in there?' I demanded.

He buried his face into her waist and she stroked his head.

'Robert?'

He spoke into Kathryn's stomach. 'I like it.'

'Whatever can you like about a toilet?'

He didn't reply.

'Why don't we sit down for a minute?' suggested Kathryn.

'But we're going to Brownsea.'

'There's no rush, Howard.' She led Robert over to the ledge of cushions beneath the window and sat him on her lap. He was wearing his T-shirt with a picture of the power station on the front. I'd bought that for him at the last open day. The picture had cracks running through it from so many washes; the towers were beginning to fade.

I stood at the window, the picnic bag still in my hand. 'You had us worried.'

'He's sorry,' said Kathryn.

Robert's knees were pale and smooth, unnaturally so for a boy of that age, I thought. I was sure I'd had scabs and grazes at four, although I didn't remember how I got them. I just remembered the pleasure of peeling back the congealed flap of blood, uncovering the fresh pink flesh beneath. 'Don't pick at it or it will never heal,' Mum would say, offering a thick fabric plaster.

'It's all right,' I said. I reached into the picnic bag and searched for a caramel wafer. 'Is the toilet really your favourite room?' I asked, handing him the wafer.

He nodded. I put the picnic bag down and knelt before him, placing my hands evenly on his knees.

'Why is that?'

He shifted on his mother's lap.

'Robert? I'd really like to know.'

'It's got a lock on the door,' he answered, biting into his biscuit.

It must have been around eleven by the time we boarded the ferry, and Robert had let go of his mother's hand. The ramp clanked into place and grey smoke pumped out over the water. Kathryn said she would go and sit indoors, out of the sun. Gulls barked overhead and the salt in the air misted my sunglasses. I took them off and, squinting in the bright light, looked around for Robert.

He was sitting on deck with another boy. The boy wore a pair of red shorts, and his bare chest was darkly tanned, but he was smaller than Robert. He'd emptied a blue plastic bucket onto the wooden boards and they leant together, counting shells, their fingers sorting through the ridged lips. I remembered a shell I'd kept as a boy, how it had glinted on the beach, and how dull it had looked on the shelf back home.

'Can I have a look?'

Neither one spoke.

'Here.' Kneeling by the bucket, I picked up a large mollusc. It was the wrong shape, but I held it to my ear anyway, tilting my head and closing my eyes.

'Daddy – '

'Shush. I'm listening.'

The two boys looked at each other, Robert screwing his face up against the sun.

Reaching over to shield my son's eyes, I said, 'I can hear the sea. In this shell.'

'Let me,' said the boy in the red shorts. I handed the shell to him; he clamped it to his ear and shook his head. 'I can't hear anything.'

'Let Robert try,' I said. The sun was warm on my shoulders, and the sea air seemed to have cleared my head of all memory of this morning.

But the boy ignored me, threw down the shell and sorted through the others in his collection, balancing them, one on top of the other, in little piles.

I handed another shell, almost as big as the first, to Robert. 'Try it.'

He took it and held it briefly by his ear before shaking his head.

'Closer,' I said. 'You have to hold it closer. Or the sea won't reach.'

Just then, the other boy upset his piles of shells. They clattered on deck and the boy began to wail.

But my son didn't move. He kept the shell to his ear while I shielded his eyes and watched him.

'I can hear it,' he said.

The boat chugged beneath us; the sea was a calm pond.

Brownsea was sandy, full of gorse. The rich smell of the shrub rose up in the heat, mingling with the sweat of hundreds of families searching for shade. Many of them, denied the use of cars, had flopped out on the nearest strip of grass by the harbour, and I knew they would still be there when we returned to the ferry.

But we would walk further. As we walked, we passed shirtless men in shorts, lying on what was left of the scorched grass. Women rested their heads on their husbands' naked thighs, chests or stomachs, and stroked their exposed skin. Couples smiled and sweated together as their children played somewhere within earshot, their shouts softened only slightly by the fierceness of the sun.

I had read that the most beautiful part of Brownsea was the north-east beach, and I intended to take Robert and Kathryn there – it was about a thirty-minute walk – although I hadn't yet mentioned it to them.

After ten minutes of walking along the gravel trail, Kathryn said, 'Shall we stop here?'

'Can I have an ice cream?' asked Robert.

'We're not there yet.'

'I'm hot,' said Robert, and his mother knelt before him and wiped his forehead with her hand.

'I'd like an ice cream, Howard,' said Kathryn, standing up and touching my arm. 'I think I saw a van back there.'

'All right.' I smiled. 'One each, then.'

Kathryn had a Midnight Mint. It was her favourite, dark chocolate encasing cool white ice cream. She ate it carefully, as she always did, nibbling off a section of chocolate before licking out the ice cream within.

I had a 99 cone, as did Robert. When I asked him if his was good, he nodded without bothering to stop licking.

'Let's sit for a while,' said Kathryn, pointing to a grassy area beneath some trees.

Kathryn sat with her head in the shade and her legs in the sun. I propped the picnic bag against the trunk.

'Can I have a sandwich now?' asked Robert.

'You've only just had an ice cream,' said Kathryn.

He contemplated this for a moment before touching me on the leg. 'Would you like a sandwich, Daddy?'

Just then a high screech seemed to bounce right round our heads and back again.

'Did you hear that, Robert?'

'Can I have a sandwich?'

The cry cut through the air again, clear and loud, and then I knew exactly what it was.

Robert reached for my hand. His fingers were sticky and hot.

'Shall we go and see what it is?' I said.

He hesitated for a moment, looking in his mother's direction.

'You two go,' she said, with a nod and a smile. I thought how beautiful she looked then, with her bare legs stretched out on the grass, and her face calm and cool in the shadow of the branches.

We walked towards a clearing. Robert kept up with my step, his fingers almost glued to mine with ice cream and sweat. Then we heard the cry again.

'Look at that, Robert.'

A peacock was standing in the middle of the dusty grass, feathers shivering in full sunlight. That bird made everything around it look bleached-out and tired. A fan of blue and green and purple spread out from its back and shook once, twice, three times. Its head glinted as it darted from side to side. I immediately wished that Kathryn was there to see it, too.

'Isn't it lovely, Robert?'

But he was looking off to the right. Peeling his fingers

from mine, he pointed. 'What's that man doing?'

A man was crawling towards the bird on his hands and knees, open palm outstretched. His jeans were baggy, and with every shuffle forward they seemed to work their way that bit further down his backside. A streak of sweat darkened the back of his T-shirt.

'What's he doing, Daddy?'

By this time, a little crowd had gathered behind the crawling man. He managed to stay perfectly still as the bird shook its feathers again and took a step towards his open hand.

'He's feeding the peacock,' I said.

'Can we watch?'

'Just for a minute, then.'

A few people had come to stand behind us, waiting to see whether the bird would take the bait. I held Robert's shoulders as the man edged closer, his hairy arm stretching towards that little jerking head.

Then something else caught my eye. Beyond the bird I saw what must have been his wife and their child, a little girl. The wife was kneeling down, pointing and smiling, and the girl was watching, entranced. She wore a floppy sunhat just like her mother's, and their teeth were very white in the sun.

When the bird's beak finally dipped into the man's palm, mother and daughter began to clap, and, hearing this, Robert joined in. Of course, this caused the bird to take fright and hurry away over the parched grass, feathers bobbing. But Robert was smiling so much and clapping so hard, that I, too, began to applaud; together we clapped for at least a minute as we watched the peacock disappear into the trees.

'Can you do it?' Robert asked, grabbing my leg and looking up at me.

'Can I feed it?'

He nodded. His eyes were bright and wide.

I crouched down and looked into his face. 'I've got a better idea,' I said. 'You can feed a peacock. When we get to the other part of the island. The best part.'

'Can I?' Robert looked at me with a little frown, not quite believing it.

'Yes,' I said, lifting him up onto my shoulders and carrying him away from the clearing, back to his mother. 'You can feed as many peacocks as you like.'

'They might bite me.'

'They won't. I'll make sure.'

We never made it to the north-east beach, but I didn't mind because, towards the end of that afternoon, two peacocks found us.

Kathryn spotted them first. I'd thought that perhaps I wouldn't be able to keep my promise to Robert, that I'd have to tell him we'd feed some birds on another day, but just as we were about to pack up our picnic things and head back for the ferry, my wife nudged me.

'Over there.'

Robert was standing up, stretching and rubbing his eyes. It had been a long, hot day; he was tired, and I expected some trouble – perhaps a few tears or a little tantrum – soon.

I caught hold of his hand and drew him close to me. 'Look,' I whispered. 'Look.'

They were just as magnificent as the first bird: their tiny heads made me think of clusters of precious gems, winking in the late afternoon light.

'Do you think they'd like some sandwiches?' I said.

Robert gave me a big smile.

Kathryn sat and watched as I ripped up the last of our crusts and handed them to Robert.

'Quietly,' I said. 'Just let them come to you.'

Moving as slowly and carefully as I could, I scattered a line of crumbs along the grass, starting from a spot close to the birds and ending at the point where Robert was crouched, ready.

We waited. Robert licked his lips; his face settled into a determined frown. He stared and stared at those peacocks until, eventually, one began to strut towards him, following the trail of bread. Its beak stabbed the ground repeatedly, and Robert studied its every move as it came closer.

'Do you think he'll be OK?' Kathryn hissed.

'He'll be fine,' I whispered.

When the bird was almost close enough to take the bread, Robert looked back at me; I simply nodded to him, and he resumed his position.

He remained absolutely still as the peacock bent its head to his palm and took the food. He watched that bird with wonder, his mouth gaping and his eyes wide, but he didn't make a sound. Only when the crumbs were all gone did he straighten up and let out a squeal, which made the bird scurry away on its spindly legs.

But he'd done it.

I looked at Kathryn. 'You see?' I said. 'He's tougher than we think.'

On the last night we decided to treat ourselves. We'd leave him asleep in the caravan for an hour while we went to the park club for a drink.

Gin and tonic for Kathryn. I had a Mackeson. I couldn't remember the last time we'd been out on our own like this. Kathryn's flowered sundress showed the curve between her breasts, which glowed a little pink; her cheeks were brown from the sun, her lips full with lipstick, her hand rested on my knee. I kissed her there and then, sitting on our squat velvet-covered barstools, the smell of old beer all around us.

The jukebox was playing the oldies, The Miracles, Roy Orbison, things we heard before we were married.

I don't remember speaking at all, I just remember the kisses she gave me, which were full and open and in front of everybody. We sat there together for over an hour, and I kept buying the drinks; the Mackeson's dense brown liquid was both savoury and sweet as I glugged it back, and she didn't say anything to stop me.

As we walked to the caravan we must have been a little drunk, because Kathryn took off her sandals and wandered barefoot in the grass. I watched her as she meandered between the caravans, swinging her sandals by their straps.

'It's so cool, Howard,' she called. 'You can feel the wet between your toes. You should try it.'

Looking round to check no one was watching, I unstrapped my sandals and joined my wife on the grass. She took my hand as we walked together back to our caravan. Kathryn joined in with some Diana Ross song that was drifting across the site.

'Why did you marry me, Kathryn?' I asked.

She stopped singing.

'What sort of a question is that?'

I looked into her face. Her skin had taken so much sun that her teeth seemed to glow white in the darkness. At that moment, she looked like a new, exotic Kathryn. I waited for her answer.

Eventually she squeezed my forearm. 'Because I wanted to,' she whispered. Then she added, 'And you asked me.'

'I asked you?' I searched her face, but she was staring in

the direction of our caravan, and her mouth had fallen into an open 'O'. She dropped her sandals on the grass and pointed frantically towards our plot.

'The bloody door's open,' she shouted. It was the first time I'd heard her swear.

We ran to the caravan. There was nothing in his bed, and he wasn't in ours. Kathryn leant out of the door, her knuckles white on the frame, and called into the night.

'Robert! Robert! Where are you?'

I had to stop her because lights were going on in the other caravans.

'I'll never forgive myself, Howard, never,' she said, but I knew she meant that she would never forgive me.

Then I noticed that the sign on the bathroom door read 'engaged'. 'Kathryn,' I called, 'he's in here.'

Before I could stop her, she threw herself at the door, breaking the lock.

He was sat on the pan, asleep, his soft brown pyjama bottoms round his ankles, a silver line of drool hanging from his chin to his chest.

I carried him back to bed.

'Don't wake him,' I said, laying him on top of his crumpled sheets. But she held him so tight that he woke, and when he saw her frightened face, the tears came.

six

1976

I'd bought it for his sixth birthday, second-hand from Gregg's in Darvington. I had been going in there since I was a boy, inhaling the smell of rubber, listening to the bright ringing sound of new bicycle bells. They had whole drawers of bells at Gregg's.

I saw Robert's first bike straight away. It was a red second-hand Raleigh Spider, with white mudguards, red rubber handlebar grips and reflectors included. It was too big for him, but I could lower the saddle and handlebars right down, and that way he'd have it for a few years, at least. It had a little pouch beneath the saddle for a spanner and a puncture-repair kit. The only thing it didn't have was a bell.

I asked to see the selection.

'Is it for a boy?' the man behind the counter asked. His ginger moustache twitched. I had already selected a boy's bike, so I thought the answer was obvious.

'That's a shame. I've only got Minnies left.' He handed me a bell with a Minnie Mouse transfer on the top. That red bow was in her hair (how could mice have hair? I was sure that Mickey didn't have any hair), and those eyelashes curled up towards her ears. I weighed the bell in my palm.

'But it's for my son.'

'I might have some Mickeys in next month.'

Robert's birthday was the next week, and I wanted him to have the bell, to be able to warn people he was coming, to make some noise, to announce his presence. I wanted him to be able to do that.

'Perhaps I'll just take a plain bell.'

The man behind the counter frowned. 'All the kids have these ones. How old is your son?'

'He'll be six.'

'He won't mind, then, will he?'

I hesitated.

'I'll tell you what, I'll throw it in for free, with the bike.'

So he had the bike with the Minnie Mouse bell. The thing that puzzled me was, he didn't seem to notice the fact that it was Minnie, not Mickey. He just loved ringing the bell as hard as he could. 'I tried to get Mickey,' I explained, but he ignored me and rang the bell again. 'We can get you another bell. Later on.'

'Don't go on about it, Howard,' said Kathryn.

He rode the bike every day to school. He got on well with his lessons from the first, especially English and Art. When he came home with gold stars stuck in his spelling book, Kathryn ran out to the garden to show me. 'Look, Howard,' she said, thrusting the book between me and the dahlias, 'Robert came first.' We held the book out in front of us.

'He's going to get on,' she said. 'Really get on.' She kissed my cheek and laughed.

'It's early days,' I said, thinking that we shouldn't feel too proud. But I couldn't stop the smile that was spreading across my face.

Kathryn gave the book a shake. 'Gold stars. We should reward him.'

'We've only just bought him a bike.'

She gave my upper arm a playful pinch. 'Don't be such an old stick-in-the-mud. He deserves a little something. As encouragement.'

After a moment I thought of a suggestion. 'How about taking him to the power station?'

She frowned.

'As a reward,' I continued. 'I think he'd like it.'

'Would he?'

'Power. Cables and engines and trains – it's what boys like, isn't it?'

'I suppose.'

'I can show him what I do.'

'Do you think he'll enjoy it?'

'We'll go tomorrow.'

It's always breezier on the site. The wind cuts past the towers like a blade in the winter. But that Saturday it seemed to be warmer than it had been for weeks, and I let Robert unzip his anorak. His cheeks glowed. His thick hair, which his mother had allowed to grow too long, hardly moved in the wind.

I guided him around the bottom of the first cooling tower. Water roared as it poured down the concrete sides. We stopped for a moment while I explained how it worked. Every time he looked up at me, I thought he must be listening, but he didn't ask any questions until we were back on the road towards the turbine hall. Then he said, 'Why is there dust everywhere?'

I didn't notice that any more, the piles of soot that gathered along the kerbsides and made the puddles black. I didn't notice the way it caught in the back of your throat. I'd forgotten that when I first came to the power station I'd wondered why the snot was black when I blew my nose.

'It's from the coal.' I pointed to the black hill of coal dust. 'That,' I said, 'is what heats the water.'

He looked at it and frowned, but when I asked him if he'd like to go closer, he shook his head and reached for my hand.

'Are we going to see the fire?' he asked.

'Fire?'

'The fire the coal makes.'

I laughed. 'We're going to see where I work. I don't work with the fire.'

His fingers were moist as they tugged at my hand. 'I want to see the fire.'

Of course. He wanted to see the engine of the place. He was a young boy. He wasn't interested in buttons and levers. He wanted pumps and pipes and generators. He wanted noise and power, the hot centre of the place.

I decided I would impress him: I'd take him into the turbine hall.

'We'll go and see the fire,' I said, leading him into a side entrance and up the stairs to the viewing gallery door, 'but it'll be noisy. OK?'

He beamed.

Even on the stairs, there was a loud roar. I've never liked the noise of the turbine hall, the way it travels through you, making speech impossible. The men on the turbine floor seem to have developed some sort of sign language that I've never mastered.

Before we went in, I strapped him into a hard hat, making sure the visor wasn't too low on his forehead, and I handed him a pair of plastic safety goggles, which he let dangle from his fingers.

'You have to wear them, Robert. And earplugs. There's up to ninety decibels of noise in there.' I showed him how to pinch the foam earplugs between his finger and thumb until they were small enough to be jammed in his ears. Then I put on my own ear protectors and opened the door.

I could feel the noise through the metal grate of the walkway. It came up through my shoes, vibrated along the hairs on my legs. Robert reached for my fingers, his face turned to mine. His green eyes were wide open, unblinking. I squeezed his hand and smiled.

It was thunderous in there. The power station was never silent – there was always a hum or a whirr or a bell somewhere – but the turbine hall breathed noise. I felt a thrill, as I always did, at the size and power of the generator in that great hall: 2,000 megawatts of electricity were being created here, at this very moment. I often thought of the hall's long windows and elevated viewing platform as something like a huge theatre, with the generator as the star attraction.

But as we walked together along the viewing grid that ran along the top of the turbine hall, the sound swelling around us, I realised that I couldn't explain to my son what any of the tin boxes and lagged pipes and bright cables did; even if I'd have shouted at the top of my voice, he wouldn't have been able to hear a word. We had only sign language, and I wasn't sure what signs to use to explain the workings of the turbine. So we walked together dumbly while the generator roared around us and the men worked below.

When we were almost at the end, Robert let go of my hand and pointed frantically towards the roof. Following the line of his finger, I saw a pigeon flying upwards. Its wings were spread wide as it glided in front of the long window that stretched from floor to ceiling in that massive hall. Robert kept jabbing his finger in the pigeon's direction, grinning. I knelt beside him and we watched it together as it flew above the noise of the turbine, way beyond the heads of the men working below.

When we were out of the turbine hall, Robert pulled out his earplugs and said, 'Does the bird live in there?'

'Probably. They nest up there sometimes.'

'Why?'

'It's warm and sheltered, I suppose. No one can touch them up there.'

'But can he get out?'

I thought for a minute. 'Yes. The windows open at the top. Yes, he can get out.'

'He won't get burned, by the fire?'

'No. He's perfectly safe.'

But the truth was, I wasn't sure. Once it was in, would a bird be able to find that crack in the window again? Or would it spend the whole of its pigeon-life in the roof of the turbine hall, disorientated, deafened by the power of the place?

seven

Summer, 1979

It seemed there was no shade, even beneath the leaves of the lilac I'd grown all along the back fence. Its patches of purple froth were mostly over, and the tiny flowers were beginning to brown in the sun.

My garden was a glory in that June sunshine. We'd had nothing but good weather since May, and it was taking me an hour to water back and front every evening. I'd taken to watering in the early morning, too, before work. Six o'clock and I'd be out of bed, leaving Kathryn to sleep on for an hour. It was the most delicious freedom to me, padding out into the garden in my slippers, feeling the cool air edging through the gap in my dressing gown. As I worked my way around the garden with the can, the grass soaking my slippers, I saw the soil lighten and the petals begin to loosen as they warmed in the sun.

By then I was growing chrysanthemums and dahlias for show. I loved their pompom shape, the tight perfection of the petals. I loved the way earwigs hid inside the flowers, clinging on in their dark caves, even when you shook the stems. Kathryn said the chrysanthemums looked like soldiers wearing bright fur hats, they were so straight and striking when they bloomed. I had a whole bed, growing nicely up their canes. 'Golden Gem', 'Cecilia' and butter-yellow 'Hansel'.

Robert was nine. Whenever he went into the garden, even if Kathryn was there, I watched him. I heard my own voice become repetitive and scolding, but I couldn't stop the words coming. *Mind those seedlings. I've planted a shrub there, don't tread on it. Don't pick the leaves off my box.*

Kathryn had suggested I teach him respect for the garden by showing him how to love it. 'Teach him how to grow things,' she said.

So he'd chosen a packet of sunflowers, 'Teddy Bear' variety, which I expected to give us double blooms and good height, and I'd brought them on in the greenhouse.

Now it was Saturday morning, and, as Kathryn had started work again at the library, we were on our own until lunchtime. The seedlings were ready to plant out, and I wondered where I could find a place for Robert in the garden. It had to be away from the dahlia bed. In the end, I decided on a patch by the shed, where it wouldn't really matter what happened. Using the imprint of my boots in the mud, I measured out the plot. One, two, three, four. Turn, and the same again.

Then I marked four rows using wooden sticks and string. As I let the rough fibre run through my fingers, I remembered Mum finding me, aged eight, with a length of garden twine wound too tightly round my hand. I was sitting in our shed, staring at my cold fingers; they were pure white, like the dead skin you strip off your feet in the bath. I expected a scolding, but she unwound me without a word, and held my hand in hers until it was warm again.

When I'd marked out the plot, I told Robert to put some old clothes on.

'These are old.' He plucked at the leg of his shorts as if it wasn't worth touching.

'They don't look old to me.'

I heard him tut.

'Do you want to plant these or not?'

When he came back out, he hadn't changed his shorts or his sandals, but he was wearing an old T-shirt. It was far too small for him; his arms looked restricted by the tight little sleeves, and he kept hooking his hand beneath the front and pulling it down over his stomach, the outline of his knuckles bulging through the printed face of Mickey Mouse. I bought him that not long after the Minnie Mouse bell, as a sort of apology.

Music thumped over the fence and into our garden. The lad next door, Graeme, was playing his radio again. He always listened to the same radio station, just that little bit too loud, but not so loud that I could go round there and tell him to turn it down. And sometimes he sang along, in an out-of-tune voice, wailing when he didn't know the words.

I put a hand on Robert's shoulder and walked him round the plot, ignoring the beat that swelled around us. 'First of all, you dig a shallow trench. Water lightly. Then plant each seedling at even intervals. Bring the soil up around them. Water generously.'

He was gazing towards the fence.

'Shall we try it?'

Without looking up, he nodded.

When I came back with the trowel, Robert had left our spot next to the shed and was standing on tiptoe by the fence, trying to see over. I stood behind him and saw what he was looking at. Graeme was lying on a red towel on his concrete terrace. To one side of him was an oil spot from his motorbike, and to the other was another lad, also lying on a towel. Small swimming trunks and large sunglasses were all they wore. A bottle of suntan oil, its label stained dark from the grease, was upturned between them. A transistor radio blared by Graeme's friend's head. Neither of them moved a muscle as they lay there together, grilling in the sun.

'I like the music,' said Robert.

'Let's get this trench dug, shall we?'

I stood over him as he flipped the trowel in the earth. 'Can't you help me?' he asked.

'It's your patch,' I said. 'You dig. I'll help with the planting.'

I meant to go in and make a cup of tea, let him have a minute to get into it on his own, but I found myself standing by the fence again. The two lads' thighs were almost touching; Graeme had let his leg roll out to the side, showing the hairless place behind his knee. Their noses shone with sweat. Graeme tapped his stomach in time with the song on the radio, and the other lad moved his lips to the words of the song.

'Excuse me, lads.'

I'd spoken to Graeme only once before, when he'd looked over the fence and asked what year the MG was. Kathryn always said hello if we saw him in the street, even if he was wearing his motorbike helmet. 'He can't hear you,' I told her. 'He can see my lips,' she replied.

Graeme lifted his head and pushed his sunglasses down his nose to look at me.

'I just wondered if you wouldn't mind turning it down a bit.'

I thought that maybe he couldn't see me properly because of the sun, but then he reached out and placed a hand on his friend's shoulder. It wasn't a shove or a shake, it was a touch. 'Turn it down,' he said to him, and the other lad twisted the knob round. 'Sorry, Howard,' said Graeme, pushing his glasses back up his nose.

'Sorry, Howard,' repeated his friend.

They lay down and smiled at the sun.

The music was still low when I went back outside after fetching Robert an orange squash from the kitchen. Stooping over the patch, he was engrossed in his work, and didn't hear me approach. His coarse hair was almost like a hat on his head, and I thought that he must be hot under it. His jaw had dropped in concentration, and he was up to his elbows in dirt.

'You've planted them all.'

He looked up and nodded. The seed trays were empty, and there were two rows of plants in the soil. Not very straight, not evenly spaced, some of the leaves a little bashed, but they were in there. I crouched down beside him and put my arm round his shoulders. 'You've done a very good job.'

Then the music's volume increased. Only this time, one of the lads was singing along.

'Shall we water them in?'

The singing next door became louder and laughter bubbled up into the air. I ignored it. My son had planted rows of sunflowers, and he had done it on his own.

'Give them a good soaking,' I said, handing Robert my stainless steel watering can.

'Dad, I can't –'

Afterwards I knew that his fingers had opened with the weight of the water. I'd filled it too full, not thinking that his arms were a nine-year-old's, a little boy's arms. He dropped the can in the dirt, flooding the plants and engulfing his sandals in mud. There was a moment then, as we both stood there looking at the swampy mess, when I thought, if I can recover quickly enough, it will be like it never happened.

'It's all right – ' I began, but his face crumpled.

'That was your fault!' he announced, stamping his foot in the muddy ground.

The lads next door continued to sing.

'I'm sorry, Robert,' I said. 'I'm really sorry.'

Just then, Kathryn came through the gate.

'We were doing so well,' I said, watching my wife's frown deepen as she approached.

She put an arm around Robert and bent to look in his face. 'What's happened?'

'Nothing to worry about. A little accident.' I reached into the mud and dragged out one of the sodden seedlings.

'He's covered in mud, Howard.'

'I think we can salvage these.' Just a bit of drying off, that was all that was needed. 'I really think they'll be all right, son.'

Kathryn straightened up. 'What's that row?'

'It's the men next door,' Robert said. 'Dad told them to turn it down.'

Kathryn glanced at me. 'Did you?'

'Dad told them,' said Robert. 'And they turned it down.'

'Really?'

'There's no need to sound so damn surprised,' I said, picking up the muddy watering can.

Kathryn blinked back something like astonishment. 'No. No, of course not,' she said, letting go of Robert and touching my sleeve. 'Sorry.'

'Shall we plant these again, Robert?' I held out the seedlings.

He took one of them in his hand and gazed down at the soggy root.

'We can still plant them, can't we?'

He took another seedling from me and spent a moment examining it.

'No harm done. Let's give it another go.'

Then he lifted his head. 'All right,' he said.

Kathryn watched us as I led him back to our patch to start again. When I looked back at her, she was smiling. 'You'll make a gardener of him yet,' she called.

eight

January, 1982

I'd been pleased when I'd come home to another bike propped up beneath the kitchen window. 'Robert's brought a friend home,' said Kathryn. 'From school.'

I could hear the boys' laughter leaking down the stairs. Kathryn lifted a chop onto a plate. 'They're having theirs upstairs. I said they could.' She spooned out four slightly soggy potatoes, letting a small pool of water settle around them, then sat down to her cheese sandwich.

'That's all right with you.' She chewed her Red Leicester.

I wasn't sure if it was a question. 'Yes, of course,' I said. I sawed into the meat and watched the fat swirl into the potatoes, then thought to add, 'Just this once.'

Every night after that, a boy called Paul came. Paul's neck was already speckled with pimples. His fair hair was short on top but too long at the back, and often stuck out like a stiff brush where it met his collar. They played the same records over and over. *Tainted love, woah yeah.* The words to that one got stuck in my head.

Paul always seemed to be in my house. His bike (a racer, twelve gears) propped up beneath my kitchen window sill. His jacket (light grey, elasticated waist) slung over my banister. His shoes (white plimsolls, a star on each side) on the mat in my hallway. I thought I could smell his socks, see the sweaty imprint they were leaving on my stair carpet as he followed Robert up the stairs.

Within a month, it seemed, Robert had acquired the same jacket, the same shoes, and similar jeans to Paul's. I didn't tackle Kathryn about it, although I knew she must be supplying him with all these new items. Instead, I told her that I thought I could smell Paul in the house. A sharp, chemical smell. It reminded me of the smell in the turbine hall. She looked at me with a little smile. 'That must be Robert you can smell, Howard,' she said. 'I bought him some shower gel. Aqua Fresh, or something.'

'What's wrong with soap?' I asked.

'Nothing,' she shrugged. 'He just asked me to buy him this instead.'

We'd promised him a trip to London for his twelfth birthday.

I'd been to London once, with Kathryn, before Robert was born. I'd wanted to take her somewhere glamorous, buy her something to wear, maybe *take in a show*. But I didn't know where anything was. I only knew the words *Carnaby Street*.

I thought if we could just find Carnaby Street, we'd be bound to have a good time. We could do all the things I wanted to do there: the sun would be shining on the polished glass of the shop windows, and we'd stop somewhere for a coffee (which would be Italian, and would make a lot of noise as the waitress wrestled with the steaming machine). I didn't like coffee much, but in London it would taste different. We'd sit in a café window and watch the other young couples glide by. Pop music – something by Dusty Springfield, or even a black singer like

Sam Cooke – would be playing somewhere. And Kathryn would sip her coffee and look at me, and I'd squeeze her knee under the table.

But when we got there – after a three-hour bus journey – I couldn't work out where we were. It was all so loud, so grey, and so wet. The traffic splashed mud up Kathryn's new coat, and I felt every lump in the pavement through the thin soles of my best shoes.

In the end, we did find Carnaby Street. What I couldn't believe was that it was so short. Just one little street with a few shops on. There was a coffee bar, but it was crowded; we had to stand up, and the sugar shaker was sticky from all the greasy fingers that had been there before mine. There was a lump of crusty sugar stuck inside the nozzle, so the crystals couldn't shake out freely. I shook and shook, and all I got were a few yellow crumbs around my saucer.

Condensation ran down the windows, and everyone smoked. It wasn't Dusty Springfield or Sam Cooke on the radio, but the Rolling Stones. I've never liked them.

But Kathryn drank a coffee, and as she sipped at her foam, she slipped a damp hand into my pocket, and we stood at the counter together, steaming.

So I thought I must plan this trip for Robert's birthday with the greatest precision. I decided we'd splash out and catch the train. No three-hour coach journey via Sandhill, Wallingford and Henley-on-Thames for us – as diverting as those places may be. No stumbling off the coach feeling slightly sick, the streets swaying with the remembered rhythm of the coach. No. We'd sit back, Kathryn and Robert on one side, me on the other, and we'd relax as the countryside slid by; Sandhill, Wallingford and Henley-on-Thames would be nothing more than church spires in the distance.

Then Robert asked if Paul could come too.

I hadn't included Paul in my image of the train journey, hadn't pictured him walking next to Robert as we approached Madame Tussaud's, hadn't heard his voice in the Berni Inn restaurant I'd located. I'd seen only the three of us, Robert walking between Kathryn and me as we introduced him to the wondrous waxworks.

He was almost at my shoulder then; the year before, he'd suddenly sprouted. It was like he'd been elongated; everything about him was shooting up towards the sky. His arms and legs had extended.

'It's his birthday, Howard,' Kathryn said. 'It would be good for him to have a friend there.'

So Paul came.

His father dropped him off. He had a blue Rover that was so wide I thought he'd never get it in our drive.

Paul stepped out of the car and slammed the door. 'Hello, Mr Hall.'

Paul was always very polite. Mr Hall this, Mr Hall that. He didn't seem at all afraid of me, not in the way I remember being afraid of other boys' fathers. *And how are you Mr Hall?* he'd ask, as if he was an adult too. *And how's your wife?* That always seemed like a strangely intimate question for a young boy to ask a man.

'Hello, Paul.'

'How's your wife?'

'She's fine, thank you.'

I walked past him and over to the car. Resting one hand on the roof, I peered into the driver's window. Mr Kearney sucked on a cigarette. He wound down the window.

'He'll be safe with us,' I said.

Mr Kearney frowned as the smoke hit his eyes. 'Good stuff,' he said, starting the engine.

I managed to pat the roof of the Rover before he pulled away.

I successfully manoeuvred us through Paddington Station. Out on the street, we had to shout to make ourselves heard over the clatter of traffic and the chaos of bodies.

'We're going to McDonald's,' Robert announced. His eyes were on Paul, who was walking several paces in front of our group. I suddenly noticed how short Robert's jacket was. And his jeans looked much too tight.

'There's one just round the corner,' Paul shouted back at us.

'He's been there loads of times,' yelled Robert.

The two boys strode ahead, and I thought the better of protesting.

A man with a gold chain round his neck bumped into my shoulder and I had to step into the road to keep from falling.

Kathryn and I had to jog to keep up with the boys as they wound through the crowds, their heads bobbing together.

'Where is he, Howard?' Kathryn kept asking me. 'I've lost him again.'

'He's just ahead. Don't worry.'

'Where?'

I looked and for a moment didn't see anything but a wave of the wrong heads, ginger curls, blue hats, blonde wisps, black frizz – but then his wiry brown hair came into view, the back of his head a little flat, like mine. A swirl at the crown. His cockatoo touch.

Robert and Paul took a left through some bright red and yellow doors. I followed them with relief; it would be good to sit down and concentrate on a menu.

But inside was just as noisy as out. A great sound rose up from the floor of the restaurant. People yelled orders, gobbled food and shouted at each other; a kind of music – mostly a beat – blared over the tannoy.

At the far end was a long counter with photographs glowing behind it. It was like the meat counter at Tesco's, only not as ordered, because there was nowhere to take a ticket. And no one seemed to be in charge. The people behind the counter were dressed like garage mechanics, in brown dungarees and caps. There appeared to be no waitress. There was no queue, and nowhere to hang your coat.

Robert and Paul were already pushing into the throng of bodies around the counter. Kathryn stood on tiptoe and shouted in my ear, 'Why don't you let the boys do the ordering? We can find somewhere to sit.'

'Boys!' I called. Paul looked back at me, but Robert stared ahead at the counter. 'Boys!' I tried again, but Robert still did not turn around.

'Order whatever you want!' I shouted into the throng.

There was a long queue outside Madame Tussaud's. Loud foreign voices surrounded us. A group of Italian boys were in front, and they didn't stop talking for a second. They all seemed so excited, despite the fact that it had begun to spit with rain, and the entrance to the waxworks was still not in sight.

'Put this on.' I handed Robert the bright red fold-up waterproof we'd bought for him the year before. The hood had toggles and poppers at the chin. Kathryn opened her umbrella. I pulled my own blue waterproof over my head.

When I'd zipped my raincoat up to the neck, Robert still hadn't got any further than putting his arms in. He was punching the air before him, and marching with stiff legs for Paul's amusement.

'Prince Charming! Prince Charming!' trilled Robert, and Paul laughed.

The rain came down harder.

'You'll get wet,' I warned.

Robert stamped one foot and then the other on the pavement and fixed me with a stare. A couple of the Italian boys looked round at him.

'Prince Charming!' He marched towards me with a flourish. His eyes were bright and slightly bulging. His bared teeth flashed. His nose was long and straight now; it had lost its early fleshiness.

'Ah-woah!' hollered Paul, joining in with the stomping dance as if he was a member of some primitive tribe.

When they'd finished, the two boys leant back together and laughed.

The Italians began to applaud.

I looked at Kathryn. She was smiling at them both. 'They're really very good at that, Howard.'

The first waxwork I remember was Sleeping Beauty. You suddenly noticed, after long minutes of admiring her, that her chest rose and fell, rose and fell. It was oddly reassuring to realise that she was really only asleep.

But it was the Chamber of Horrors the boys loved – particularly the alley of famous murderers. Robert insisted on reading out highlights of information about each terrible scene, mouthing the worst of the words exaggeratedly to Paul.

'He AXED his wife to death... filled the bath full of ACID... DISSECTED his victims with a Stanley knife... STUFFED the bodies inside the wall cavities ... '

It went on and on, the both of them laughing as Robert widened his eyes at the horrors.

I didn't find the waxworks lifelike in the least. Their hair was too thick, too low on the forehead, or else their noses were too large, or their hands bent at slightly odd angles. It was the settings that disturbed me: how these murders seemed to happen on ordinary streets, in living rooms like ours. The cosy wallpaper that covered up the cracks where the bodies were stuffed; the bath full of acid with the rusty taps and blackened overflow. I was sure we had the same bath mat as Christie.

'Which one's your favourite, Dad?' Robert asked.

'Sleeping Beauty,' I replied.

part two

Joanna

one

Summer, 1984

Dad starts it off with me and Shane.

I know he feels sorry for him, after the accident. Everyone in Calcot knows about it. Everyone knows Shane's Dad, Derrick, can't have looked. Was probably drunk. Everyone knows about the lorry that pushed them onto the verge of the Darvington Road, crushing the side where Shane sat. He was unconscious for days. Every day Mum would say, 'Poor Sheila. Poor Sheila.' And Dad would say, 'It could happen to anyone.'

It didn't stop Shane's dad driving, but he left soon after that. Now Shane and his mum never go anywhere. Poor buggers.

'Why don't you go and see that boy down the road, Joanna?' Dad asks. He knows Shane's older than me, bigger than me, but that doesn't seem to bother him. 'Why don't you go and cheer him up a bit? He's been through a lot.'

'He's bloody backward, that Shane Pearce, Dan,' says Mum. 'Don't go on at her.'

'He's not backward,' says Dad. 'I know he's not.'

Then there's an argument about what backward means, with Mum saying you can't trust Shane, everyone knows what he gets up to. Nicking stuff from Old Buggery's shop, hanging about late at night down the pools, scaring other kids. 'Someone saw him with a flick knife,' says Mum.

'I've never seen the boy leave the house,' says Dad.

All summer Dad encourages Shane to come over. Shane doesn't actually come in the door. He always stays outside. Dad pays him to help clean our car or paint the gate or clip the hedge. They work in silence, and from the living room window I watch Shane's arms move as he throws buckets of water over the Cortina. Every week his skin's browner.

Shane doesn't talk to me. If I walk out there, he looks at the ground. His black curly hair hangs over his face. His fat lower lip moves as if he's chewing the cud.

On a wet Saturday morning in mid-July, Dad announces he's going to Heaton's Scrap. Mum says, 'Are you taking Shane too?'

'Why not?' asks Dad.

Shane sits himself in the car before me and Dad have even got our shoes on. 'I'll stay here,' says Mum. 'But you go.' She's probably itching to get to Old Buggery's place. As if I don't know that they have a thing. She's always popping up his shop for a sliced white, full make-up and earrings. She's gone hours. And Dad knows about it. 'Your mother's a trollop, Joanna,' he said to me one day when we were sitting on the front step in the sun. He likes to have his tea on the front step if the sun's out. He always takes his shirt off, too, and fingers his hairy nipples. 'Your mother's a trollop.' Slurp of tea. Finger of nipple. 'Don't you be like that, will you?'

Heaton's Scrap is full of puddles with bits of car and gate and fireplace sticking out of them. The scrap's everywhere.

Skeletons of machines and odd wheels and bike handle-bars and bits of engine lie about. And there are loads of men, calling to each other. 'Nice bit of stuff here'; 'How much for an exchange?'; 'Look at the rust on that. Completely buggered.' Stuff like that.

'Don't touch anything,' says Dad. 'Hold her hand, Shane. Make sure she doesn't hurt herself.'

'Dad!' I protest. But Shane gets to my fingers before I can put them in my pocket. And Dad just laughs.

Shane's hand is big and heavy, and I keep running my finger over a wart on his thumb. I want to pick it but I don't. I just rub the edge of my nail over it, scratching at the ridged skin.

We walk through puddles and round bits of machinery. Shane's silent. He holds my hand tight. He's got holes in his grey plimsolls. His feet must be getting wet but he doesn't say anything about it.

'Look, Shane.' Dad points to the remains of a motorbike on the other side of a puddle. 'That's a Norton frame.' He jumps over the water. 'Beautiful, isn't it?'

Shane nods.

'Want to touch it?' Dad runs his hand over the rusted metal.

Shane looks at me, then he steps into the puddle and reaches out to pat the frame. He keeps one hand holding tightly on to mine, so I have to lean over the puddle with him. My feet teeter on the edge of the muddy water. My fingers are crushed in his grip.

Dad smiles. 'You'll have to let go of her eventually,' he says.

August is so hot that the underneath bit of my hair keeps sticking to my neck. I lift it up and fan it around, trying to get air on my skin. Mum says I should put it up, but I've always hated ponytails – who wants to look like a horse? And besides, elastic bands give me a headache. I like to feel my hair there, around my face. Except today it's like an itchy blanket, it's so hot.

We've brought Shane to Shotton Hill for a picnic. Mum has a big tin with a whole chicken inside. Grease seeps through its kitchen-towel wrapping. Chocolate slides off the Penguin biscuits.

The heat seems to slow everything down. Usually it's green everywhere you look up here. But today the grass is yellow and trodden-on. Even the leaves on the trees look tired. There's just this hot wind, blowing dust up from the patches of dirt where the grass has given up.

Shane walks behind Dad. He's wearing cut-off denim shorts and new black slip-on plimsolls, like the ones I've got for PE.

We sit beneath a tree and eat the chicken. The knobbly dirt sticks into our bums. Mum passes round warm orange squash in plastic cups. Shane watches me as I lick chicken grease off my fingers.

'Look at that. It must be a bird of prey,' Dad points into the sky.

Every other bird is a bird of prey, according to Dad.

'What do you think, Shane?'

Shane doesn't reply. His legs are long and tanned, covered in shiny black hairs right down to his ankles.

'Let's play a game,' says Dad.

'It's too hot for games, Dan,' says Mum, lying back so her head's in the darkest bit of shade. 'My head's thumping.'

Dad looks at us. 'You're not too hot for a game, are you?'

'What are we playing?' I ask.

He thinks. 'I'll tell you what. We'll play find the clue.'

'What's that?'

'You go and find something unusual in the woods, an unusual object. And then you bring it out to me.'

'What kind of unusual object?'

Mum smirks. 'I've never heard of this game, Dan.'

'That's because it's a new game. You bring me anything that you wouldn't expect to find in the woods. I decide whose is the most unusual, and the winner gets... a Penguin biscuit.'

'They'll be melted by then,' I say. But I get up anyway. The sun bears down on my shoulders. I'm wearing a strapless dress with an elasticated top, red with white stripes running from my armpits to my knees. The elastic sticks to my ribs. I like the tightness, the feeling of it holding me in.

'Go on then,' Dad lies back in the grass. 'Shane's already got a head start.'

I look over towards the woods. Shane's nowhere to be seen.

It's a bit cooler in the trees. The sunlight comes down in patches. The leaves make an occasional swish in the occasional breeze. I run until I find a piece of dead trunk, crouch behind it and look around on the ground.

What can I find that's unusual? Everything in the wood is exactly as usual. Trees. Dirt. Twigs. Nothing else. Except the heat.

I sit and wait for Shane. I decide I'll let him win the game.

A line of ants marches across the wood in front of my nose. A spider runs over my sandal, but I don't cry out. Everything smells fresh and warm. My thighs begin to ache from crouching, so I kneel down. Twigs dig into my knees, and I know they'll leave a mark, like the sheet does when you've been so deep asleep that you're all twisted round in the bed.

Where is he?

I clutch the trunk with one hand and peer round. Plenty of leaves and twigs and ants. But no Shane.

Then there's a shuffling sound. A twig snaps and the shuffling stops. Then it starts again. I see him in the distance, walking carefully through the trees. He looks like a ballet dancer. Picking his feet up and putting them down, holding his arms perfectly still, his head balanced on his shoulders like a rock.

I duck down behind the trunk. I ball my fingers into fists. I tuck my chin into my chest and try to breathe very slowly through my nose, imagining the hairs in there moving with the air. I close my eyes. Everything has to be as small and tight as possible.

It all goes quiet.

I stay still for the longest time. Breathing in, breathing out.

Eventually I open one eye and peep round the trunk.

A hairy tanned knee is right there, almost touching my nose. I let out an awful squeal, like a little pig. I have to put a hand over my mouth to stop it.

'I can see you,' says Shane.

I try to grip the trunk so I can pull myself up, but a piece of bark comes off in my hand and I fall backwards.

Shane smiles.

'Did you find anything?' I ask from the ground.

He nods.

I stand up, brush myself off. 'What is it?' I step out from behind the trunk. My nose is parallel with his nipples. The sun lies in stripes across his bare chest. His hands are behind his back. He steps closer to me, and I sit back down on the trunk. He's so close, I can smell him. He smells like new grass cuttings on our compost heap.

'Close your eyes and put your hands out,' he says.

'What have you got?' I reach behind his back but he twists away from me.

'Close your eyes and hold out your hands.'

His lower lip hangs down like a soft pink slug.

'What have you got, Shane?'

'Close your eyes.'

So I close my eyes. Let my hands go limp in my lap. 'Go on then,' I say. 'Show me your unusual thing.'

I wait.

'Show me,' I say again.

And Shane puts his hand on my head. It's heavy and warm. He just lets it rest there, not moving.

Then he starts to move his fingers. Very slowly, and right across my scalp. And it's like I can suddenly feel everything: the dampness in his fingertips, the roughness of the trunk against my legs. He keeps swirling my hair round, digging his nails into my scalp, pushing his fingers up my neck and round my ears. The hoop of my earring catches on his nail, giving the flesh of my earlobe a tug.

I open my eyes but don't move. I can see all the dark hairs on Shane's thigh. The trees above us rustle. The earth smells ripe. My elasticated top feels tighter than ever.

In the car on the way back we have all the windows open. Mum keeps saying she'll die of heat exhaustion, she'll surely die. Dad says nothing. Hot wind blasts round the car, battering our heads. It's like a hairdryer has been let loose on the back seat. Shane lets his knee rest against mine. Every time we go round a corner I feel its pressure. A drip of sweat crawls past his dark eyebrow and into the hollow of his cheek. My hair blows everywhere, strands of

it brushing against Shane's shoulder. I keep laughing and
hooking it back with my hand, but he doesn't look at me,
he just keeps his knee there, sweating against mine.

two

Spring, 1985

Shane's doorbell plays 'God Save the Queen' all the way through before his mum answers it.

'Just a minute, love.' She calls back over her shoulder, 'Three eggs, Shane! Only three!'

She turns back to me. 'We're making a cake! A Victoria sponge!'

It's the first time I've been to Shane's house. It's the Easter holidays. Things are bad at our place. And it's not Mum's *thing* with Buggery this time. It's more than that. She hasn't moved from her place on the sofa for two days. There's wet tissues all over the cushions, like strands of melting snow. Dad's face has fallen into a grey heap. He tells me to get out of the house while he sorts her out.

A huge jet-black bun sits on top of Shane's mum's head like a dollop of chocolate. She's wearing green plastic earrings. Her matching metallic eyeshadow has fallen into the creases around her eyes. Shane's mum also has creases around her wide mouth, and all up her neck.

'You're Dan's girl.'

'I'm Joanna.'

'Joanna!' She opens the door wider, reaches out, touches my cheek with papery fingers. Then she stands and stares at me so hard that there's nowhere to look but the ground.

'Sorry, love! It's just – it's so good to see you! Come in, Joanna, come in!'

She pulls me inside and begins taking my coat off. 'Let's chuck that over there,' she says, 'you'll be far too warm in that.' Yanking my arm out of my sleeve, she drags me down the hall, talking all the time.

'Shane will be so pleased to see you!' She stops. Takes a handful of my cheek. Squeezes and releases several times. Then adds, 'As am I, Joanna!'

While walking and talking, neither her chocolate-hair nor her earrings move an inch. 'Dan has always been a good man. Your Dad, that is.' She grips my arm. 'Did he tell you he came to see us in the hospital, after the accident?'

He didn't tell me that.

Shane's house smells of pee. But there's another, musty smell, which must be the oven, because when we get to the kitchen it's much stronger. Steam runs down the windows, making the net curtains stick to the glass in patches. The kitchen cupboards are green, like Shane's Mum's earrings. Packets of cereal stand on the draining board. They've got everything. Sugar Puffs. Shreddies. Frosties. Ricicles. There's a heap of dirty laundry between the bin and the back door. A washed-out flesh-coloured bra straddles the top of the pile.

Radio One plays softly. Shane's sitting at the kitchen table. He sees me come in and he cracks an egg on the side of a glass bowl.

'Shane! You've got a visitor, love!'

She gives me a little shove forward. 'Don't be shy! You can help us bake. We need all the help we can get, don't we Shane?'

There's a smudge of flour on Shane's forehead. He's holding his hands above the glass bowl, half an eggshell in each fist. A patch of red spreads up his throat.

'It's Joanna, Shane.'

A glaze comes over his eyes. He looks down into the bowl.

'Dan Denton's girl.'

Shane crunches the eggshells in his hands. Flakes fall and scatter over the table. Smiling up at me, his mum prizes the remaining shell from his fingers. 'Sit down, love. You can grease the tins.'

Simon Bates announces 'Our Tune'.

I sit opposite Shane and brush a few bits of eggshell from the plastic-coated tablecloth.

'Hi,' I say.

He puts his hands beneath the table.

'Get it in all the corners,' says Shane's mum, plonking two cake tins and a piece of butter paper in front of me. 'Don't stint on the grease.'

I smear the butter on. Black flecks of toast stick all round the tins.

Shane's mum stands behind him and strokes his hair. 'Ooh!' she says. '"Hey Jude".' She reaches over, turns the radio up. Then she sings over Shane's head.

'The lah-lah you need is on your – lah-lah. Nah nah nah nah nah – I love "Our Tune", don't you, Joanna? So moving. I love anything like that. Real life stories.' She sighs. 'Me and Shane have got a few of our own, haven't we, love?' She kisses Shane's curly hair.

'You done with those? Right. What's next. Oh yes. The eggs. Do you want to whip the eggs up, Shane, love? Or shall I do it?'

She leans over him and whips the eggs with a fork.

'Baby Jane' comes on.

'Poor Rod. Not as good as he used to be.' She swishes the volume down and continues to whip. Her mound of hair is completely still. But her tits shake inside her green blouse.

'Tell Shane about school, Joanna.'

'Not much to tell.'

'There must be something.' A drip of egg splashes over the side of the bowl. 'Shane never tells me anything. Sometimes I wonder if he ever goes to that school. He's in the same year as you, isn't that right?'

'He's a year above,' I say. 'I'm a fourth year.'

'You look older than that.' She stops whipping and looks up. 'But then, you're like your mother, I expect.'

She begins to add the eggs to her bowl.

'The secret is to do it slowly, then they don't curdle. Hold out this sieve for me. Now give it a good bang as I put the flour in.'

Shane's eyes follow my fingers. My rings clank against the side of the metal sieve.

'I've heard Shane's pretty popular in his class, Joanna. That's right, isn't it?'

'Is it?'

She winks. 'He should be, don't you think? Handsome fella like him. Takes after his father. I bet a lot of the girls have a crush on him.'

I think about laughing, but then I glance at Shane. The glaze has cleared from his eyes. His mum's tits bounce against his shoulders as she reaches over him to fold the flour into the eggs. 'Oh yes,' she sighs. 'I bet a lot of the girls have a little crush on Shane.'

Mrs Pearce insists I stay until the cake's done, 'then we can all have a big piece together. Shane loves cake, don't you, Shane?'

But Shane has disappeared through the back door.

When I try to say that I have to get going, Mrs Pearce just waves her green-fingernailed hand in front of my face. 'Silly! I'll let Dan know you're here. Why don't you go out in the garden with Shane?' She points a fingernail towards the door.

I look around the garden. The lilac bush at the end of the path belches out blossom. There's a sweet smell a million miles from Mum's lilac bath cubes. I love those bath cubes. You open the gold paper wrapper and hold the cube of salt in your fist over the steamy water. Apply pressure and – bam! – it explodes into the bath and fizzes away like sherbet's supposed to but never does. I always expect a milky-silky bath after that, like the woman in *Carry on Cleo* (Dad loves that one). But you get in the bath and all you feel are grains of salt scratching away at your arse. And the water's fizz just turns to a layer of scum.

I stand there smelling sweet bits of breeze. Then I hear music: Madonna singing about being touched for the first time.

Nobody's about. The windows of the house are all closed. The only place it could be coming from is the shed.

It's a tiny wooden shed, half hidden by the lilac bush. The window in front is framed by a pair of ruched net curtains. A frill like a fancy pair of knickers runs all along the bottom.

I walk towards the music, keeping time with my footsteps.

I stand outside the door and listen. My fingers are so deep in my jeans pockets, I can feel the top crease of my thighs.

I call his name and wait for him to come.

three

Spring, 1985

The shed door opens easy.

I step over the wooden threshold and into the darkness. Blink. Shapes become clear. A tape player. A small table with a can of shandy on it. A dartboard. And underneath the target, Shane, sitting in a high-backed armchair.

He can't have heard me call his name, because he doesn't move from his position in the armchair. He just sits there, toes splayed, head back, eyes closed.

By now, Prince's 'Little Red Corvette' is blasting out.

His body fills the chair, his hands dangling over the stuffed arms, his shoulders squeezed between the velveteen wings of the headrest, his thighs spilling over the seat. His jeans are too short. The knobbles of his ankles stick out.

I can still escape. I can turn around and walk up the path away from the lilac bush and the music and back into the house.

Light struggles through the frilly nets. I stand for a while, chew on a strand of hair, tasting the Elnett. I wait for Shane to see me.

At the end of the song, he opens his eyes. He looks at every part of me, as if he's never seen me before. It's like that every time he looks at me. He examines me with his eyes, starting with the top of my head and ending with my feet. Taking in each hair, each bone, each vein, each blood vessel. I think about the diagrams we have to draw in biology. Close-ups of skin and blood, examined and dissected. Labels like *corpuscle* and *epidermis*. Shane looks at me and there's this light in his eyes. It's almost like a lamp that helps him see. Like the light the optician uses to go right into your eye. *Look up, look down. And look into my light.* But you can't see them, because they've turned the ceiling light off and they're so close to you in the dark, breathing on your nose, making it wet.

'I like that song,' I say.

He continues his penetrating stare.

I step forward. 'You don't mind if I come in.'

He shrugs.

I look up at the net curtain. 'You've got this place looking – ' I pause, let him watch me try to think of the right word. 'Nice.'

He shrugs.

I lick my lips and shrug back. 'Play me something else, then.'

'Take your shoes off.'

'What?'

'You come in, you take off your shoes.'

I begin to laugh, but Shane just stares.

'What if I don't want to?' I say.

'Take off your shoes.'

'These are new shoes.' I try to think of some other reason, something that will melt his stare. 'From Dolcis. Don't you like them?'

'Off.'

'Why?'

'My shed,' he says. 'My rules.'

Leaning back in his armchair, he stares at my bare toes. I wiggle them a bit to unstick them.

He presses play.

We stay together in the shed for the rest of the afternoon. We don't speak much. I sit on the rug and Shane plays his tapes. Sometimes he forward-winds through the ones he doesn't like, but still I just sit there and listen to the spooling tape. Grandmaster Flash sings, *don't do it!* Shane wiggles his toes in time to the music. It starts to rain outside, and as the wind gets up, small gusts of lilac-scent come in under the door.

Then Shane's mum brings the cake out. She knocks on the shed door once. Later I learn this is to signal she's left it outside. Shane cuts into it with a flick knife he keeps in his back pocket. Each slice is even. He hands me a perfect triangle of cake, balanced on his blade. I bite into it. It's light and sweet and full of smooth cream. After three slices, I begin to feel sick. But I eat more, because Shane keeps offering up slices on his shiny knife. Brushing the crumbs from his chest. Licking the cream from the corners of his mouth. Swallowing huge bites of buttery sponge. Looking at me.

I spend all summer with Shane in his shed.

From then on, my toenails are always perfect. Every Sunday night I remove the week's colour and apply a new one. *Hard Cherry. Frostbite Pink. Orange Daze.* Each nail is totally covered, and absolutely even. Sometimes it takes me an hour, locked in the bathroom, Mum knocking at the door as I stroke the brush over, blow, and wait.

I also buy a pink pencil skirt.

Mum calls it a 'hobble skirt'. So tight you can't walk, only hobble.

I buy it in the new Top Shop in Oxford. Mum pushes a twenty into my hand while we're in C&A. 'If you hate everything I pick, just get something yourself.'

I run straight out of C&A and I'm in Top Shop before she can breathe out.

The skirt's *cerise*. The assistant tells me that means bright, shocking pink. 'Cerise has been our biggest seller,' she says, and I know I'll have it.

I cradle it into the changing room. Older girls stand about in their pants and bras, looking at themselves like they're something. I'm glad I'm wearing my pink knickers with the spaghetti straps at the sides. I like running my finger along the crease the side strap leaves indented on my hip.

The skirt is lined with shiny stuff. It sticks to my thighs in the heat of the changing room spotlights. A little pleat at the back kicks out as my legs move, flashing a slice of white calf. There's a big pink button on each of the front pockets. I flick them against my hipbones, smile at myself in the mirror.

'You haven't got the arse to fill that,' Mum says when I show her. 'And I bet you can't bloody wash it.'

I love it.

I arrive at Shane's wearing the pencil skirt. A choking smell of creosote comes up from the warm wood of the shed. I think of Shane's dad painting the walls with it, black treacly stuff dripping down his arms and onto the concrete path. Shane hasn't seen his dad since the accident, five years ago. Derrick left before Sheila could chuck him out,

Mum says. Who could bear to have him in the house after what he did? No one believes he wasn't drunk.

Shane looks at the skirt. He looks at me in the skirt. I run my hands over the creases where the material's tight around my thighs. He swallows and wriggles his toes.

'It's new,' I say.

He nods, still staring at the skirt. Taking in every stitch. Every corpuscle of material.

'Shall I turn around?'

He catches my eye for a moment, then ducks his head.

I turn to face the door. Spend a few moments studying a knot in the wood. Then turn back to face Shane.

He licks his big lips, says nothing.

'Do you like it?' I ask.

He keeps his eyes on the hem of the skirt. I wonder if he's labelling each part in his head. Drawing a straight line and using neat capitals, like we do in Biology. HIPS. LEFT THIGH. RIGHT THIGH. NICE ARSE.

He still doesn't look up, so I sit at his feet. The skirt's so tight I have to twist my legs beneath me, like a posh woman riding a horse side saddle in an old film.

I rest my head against his knee.

'Shall we listen to the new Prince?' I twist round to face him. He catches my wrist and squeezes, hard.

'Will you wear it every time you come?' His voice is low. He's not looking at my face, even now.

'Yes,' I say, 'if you want.'

He lets go. I rub my wrist, but he takes no notice.

After I while I say, 'Perhaps you should think about what you could do for me.'

He keeps staring right over my head.

four

August, 1985

I come home from Shane's shed and Dad's on the front porch, waiting for me. He's wearing Mum's pinny.

'I'm making Irish stew.'

'Why aren't you at work?'

'I told you. I'm making Irish stew.'

'Where's Mum?'

'I used to make it for your mother. Before we were married.'

There's been arguments for the last week, but there always are. Usually it goes on for a few nights, then there's a reunion. 'No one can resist a grin that wins,' Dad will say, patting Mum on the bum. 'Your mum tried to resist my winning grin, Joanna. But no one can resist a grin that wins.'

But this time there's been no winning grin.

I've never known Dad to cook anything. When he's in the kitchen he's either eating or reading the paper. Or washing up, tea towel thrown over one shoulder, whistling an Elvis number. And that's only on Sundays.

But now here he is with Mum's pinny around his waist, rustling through a pile of Tesco's bags.

'Where's Mum?'

'Your mother didn't have any food in the house. Real food, I mean. Not that frozen stuff. So I had to go out.'

I reach into one of the plastic bags. My fingers meet something that feels like blancmange. I let out a yelp.

Dad stretches across me, drags the meat out of the bag, whacks it on the table. 'Look at that. Real shoulder of lamb. Bone in.' The dark red flesh is squashed against the cellophane. Blood gathers in the dimples of the Styrofoam tray beneath. 'That's where the flavour is, Joanna.'

He rips the cellophane from the meat and turns the flesh under the tap. The water runs pink.

'You can scrape the spuds,' says Dad. He holds the blade of Mum's biggest knife up to his nose, flips it from side to side. 'You need it sharp.' He speaks slowly, like he's dragging out each word. 'The blunt ones are the most dangerous.'

'When's Mum coming back?'

He has no answer. Instead, he positions himself at the counter, legs apart, and cuts into an onion. Beneath the pinny, he's wearing a pair of very short yellow shorts. The meat of his thighs flattens out against the cupboard doors. Every now and then he scrunches up his eyes and sniffs. 'Big slices for Irish stew,' he says, scooping up the dry layers of skin and aiming for the bin.

When Dad finally heaves the stew into the oven, there are bits of potato peel and onion skin on the floor, dribbles of gravy down the cupboards, splashes of fat on the wall. The sink is stained with blood and dirt.

Dad wipes his brow with his forearm. 'Dumplings,' he says, emptying the fruit bowl all over the table. He waves the plastic dish in the air. 'This will do. Now. Flour.'

He instructs me in a loud voice. 'Use your fingers to

bring it together,' he says, rolling a ball of dough around the fruit bowl.

'How do you know all this?'

Holding a dumpling in the air, he frowns. 'It was the only thing,' he says, 'the only thing my dad taught me. He used to make it whenever Mum was out of the house.' He drops the dumpling into the bowl and wipes his hands down his T-shirt. Grey lumps of dough stick to the terry-towelling. His bare legs are streaked with flour dust where the pinny doesn't reach. His T-shirt is splattered with blood.

Dad puts *Tomorrow's World* on and we sit in silence while the presenters argue about whether nuclear fuel is safe or not.

He stares at the television screen, hardly blinking. Occasionally he rubs at the flour streaks on his knees and sighs.

I sit there and watch him watching the television.

When Dad finally says that the stew's ready, it's nine thirty. The whole house smells unfamiliar, and I know Mum won't come back tonight.

five

August, 1985

'We're going on an outing.'

The morning after the Irish stew, Dad's sitting on the edge of my bed. His grey-blond hair looks like a frayed brillo pad. His eyes are red. He's wearing his only suit.

I sit up. 'Is Mum coming?'

He rubs at a shaving nick on his throat. 'Get your best togs on.' Whistling 'Heartbreak Hotel', he pats the bottom of the duvet and leaves the room.

A road sign reads 'Heathrow'.

'Is it a day trip to Ibiza?'

'Something like that.'

'Are these shoes OK?'

I wriggle my feet in the footwell. Without glancing at my new cerise pink kitten heels, Dad says, 'They're fine, love.'

When we reach the multi-storey car park, I wind down my window so I can hear everything echoing. Brakes screeching round corners then screeching again. Doors slamming four times. Shouts going on forever.

Dad parks the car.

'A day trip to Oxford?' I ask.

He pulls the handbrake up, turns to me. 'Somewhere in Oxford you haven't been before,' he says.

The streets smell of old fat and melted ice cream.

'Are you getting on all right with Shane?'

Dad's hand is hot between my bare shoulder blades as he guides me down the High Street. I'm wearing a jade green strappy top with a peek-a-boo eyelet in the front.

'Because he needs looking after, you know?'

I don't say anything about anything.

The shops thin out. A sign in a doorway says, 'Queen's College. Visitors welcome.' Behind it there's a patch of bright green grass.

'Where are we going?'

'You'll see.'

As we wait at the zebra crossing, a bus stops right by my legs and pumps hot exhaust fumes round my ankles. My shoes clamp tight to my toes.

'How much further?'

'Nearly there.'

We pass a café with the word 'Tiffin' written on the window. I ask Dad what that means. He says he thinks it's another name for tea.

Crossing the bridge, Dad tries to take my hand. I let him hold it lightly for a minute, but when we reach the other side I slip my fingers away.

'Here we are,' he announces.

He points at a huge dirty building with a tower and windows like you get in churches. We step through the doorway into a dark, silent passageway.

'Is this the University?' I whisper.

'This is it,' says Dad. 'This is the University.'

We walk through the passageway and out into a big

garden at the back. Willow trees swish along the grass in the breeze. All round us, people are shielding their eyes and looking up. A lot of them are clutching guidebooks.

'Where are the students?' I ask.

'Term hasn't started yet.'

'Lazy buggers.'

Dad smiles and we stand for a minute, looking up, like everyone else, at the blank squares of glass that make up the college windows. I imagine the students sitting in there, reading, their un-hairsprayed heads bent over their desks.

I look around at the other people on the lawn. Apart from the people with guidebooks, every girl seems to be wearing a longer skirt than me. And their hair isn't flicked up or brushed out. It just hangs.

I wait for Dad to say something.

'Shall we sit over there?' He points at a tree whose branches are so big and low they look like giant's hands.

'All this time living here, and we never came.' Dad lays down beneath the branches. 'Why didn't we come here before?'

I concentrate on sitting on the grass without showing Dad too much thigh.

After a while he sits up. 'I'm not making a very good job of this, am I?'

I pick a handful of grass and throw it over his knee.

'Do you like it here, Joanna?'

I consider the willow trees with their long fingers, the girls with their long skirts, the blank, black windows. I don't know the answer.

'You could come here,' says Dad, leaning close to me, 'if you work hard.'

I throw some more grass over his legs.

'Mind the suit,' he says, brushing it off. He scratches at

his brillo-pad hair. 'I mean it.' His eyes are big and red. 'I know you've got the brains, even if you don't always use them. You can come here. It's possible.'

I pick up a shard of old bark, dig it under my nail to clean out the dirt.

'No one told me things are possible. I mean, not everything you think is impossible is impossible.'

'What are you on about?'

He sighs. 'I don't know.'

'Shall we go then?' I stand up.

A bell begins to clang.

'Wait. Sit down.'

He grabs my hand and pulls me into his lap. 'My girl,' he whispers, crushing me against him and hiding his face in my hair.

'Dad – ' My legs are twisted under me. My skirt's ridden up too far.

Then he begins to rock slightly, and his breath goes funny, shaky. Hot air from his mouth makes my cheek wet. Above us, the branches make a slight creaking sound, like ships in films.

'Dad – '

'Sorry, love.'

But he's still clinging on. I wonder what I can do to make his job easier. I know he's leaving. I've heard them arguing for weeks. I've heard Dad say that he'd rather chew off his own hand than stay in her trap. Like an animal.

Shoulders heaving, his fingers dig into my spine.

We cling to each other under the tree. 'It's OK,' is all I can think to say.

Eventually, his hands release me. When he looks me in the eye his face is crumpled and red, like a bruise. 'You'll come and see me?'

I nod.

'And you'll look after Shane?'

After a pause, I nod again.

Then he says, 'Your mother's not all bad.'

Then he says, 'I meant what I said, about working hard.'

Then he says, 'I'll drop you off at home, but then I'll go.'

'Where?'

'Not far. I'll phone.'

'Can I come with you?' As soon as I say it, I wish I hadn't.

He reaches out and strokes my hair. 'Not now, love. Maybe later.'

As we walk back up the High Street, past the colleges with their bright green squares of light and back to the multi-storey, I let him hold my hand.

six

August, 1985

In the shed, I sit on the floor at Shane's feet and lean back against his shins.

We're both silent.

Shane always closes the door and he never opens the window, but I'm used to the smell of the warm creosoted wood now. It smells like stewed tea. Cake crumbs are scattered over the floor, already drying in the heat. Spots of chocolate buttercream are smeared into the boards. I swallow the last of our chocolate layer cake and lick each finger clean.

Shane dangles a pair of pink plastic hoops in front of my eyes. I try to turn to look at him, but he catches my face in his hands, tilts my head backwards and clamps his knees hard around my scalp. Taking each earlobe between his finger and thumb, he makes a dip and a pull with the earrings, hooking me up like a fish. Then he runs a finger along my bottom lip, hard. 'Messy,' he says, showing me the chocolate on his finger.

'Mind my lipstick.'

He laughs. Shane's laugh is low and quiet, like it's half-hidden, a long huh-huh. 'Are you my girlfriend?' he asks.

I twist free of his knees and turn round. His T-shirt's too

small. What looks like a waistband of flesh bulges beneath it, and I can see his belly button sticking out. I haven't seen that before. It looks like Shane has a hole that someone's stuck a screw into. A flesh-coloured screw.

'What?'

'Are you my girlfriend?' He keeps his eyes focused on the space above me. 'I gave you the earrings,' he says.

'I know.'

'So you're my girlfriend.'

'My dad left.'

He puts his hand in my hair, the way he did in the woods at Shotton Hill. Working his fingers around my scalp, he says, 'It's all right.'

'No, it isn't,' I say, pulling away from his hand. 'My dad left.'

'My dad crashed the car. My dad never came back.'

I sit there, earrings dangling. Shane stares into the air above me. The line of his chin is strong. The dipping curve of his open lips is still. He doesn't allow his face to twitch as I watch him.

'Do you miss him?' I ask.

He doesn't allow one blink, even though his hair hangs over the side of his face like a strange eyepatch.

'My dad was the only sane one in our house,' I say.

Shane gives a nod.

'What was yours like?'

'Dunno.'

'Don't you remember?'

'No.'

There's a long silence before he says, 'There's no point missing them.'

'What do you mean?'

'Everything's their fault. And when they go it's still their fault. It's all his fault.'

'What is?'

'Anything you bloody well like.'

I start to laugh, but Shane's not smiling. He's biting his lip, hard.

I wiggle my bare toes, but he doesn't look at them. I blink at him and smile, but he keeps staring at the space above my head.

'Shall we have some music?'

'If you like.'

'What do you fancy?'

He has no answer.

It's hot in the shed. My palms are sweating. When I bring a hand up to sweep the hair from my face, I see a small patch of damp on the wooden floor.

'Do you fancy anything, Shane?'

Again, no answer.

So I stand up. 'I could take off my skirt. Shall I take off my skirt?'

I start to wonder if he's heard me. 'Do you want me to – '

'OK.'

Staring at the wooden slats behind me, eyes half closed, he repeats, 'OK,' and not a muscle on him moves as he waits for me to remove my denim mini.

'Shall we lock the door?' I ask.

'Why?'

'In case.'

'No.' He pauses, nods his head. 'Go on, then.'

Beneath my bare feet, the floorboards of the shed are warm. A cake crumb squishes between my toes. I shove my fingers down into my waistband. Shane keeps his eyes below my waist. His big lower lip hangs down so low I can see the spit on his teeth.

I tug the skirt down over my hips. I look at the net curtain behind Shane. I think about how white that curtain is. How clean.

I push the skirt over my thighs. I think about Shane's mum washing the net every week, pegging the rough wet fabric to the whirligig. I think about the whipping sound it might make as it kicks out in the wind.

There's a clunk as the rivets of the skirt hit the floor.

I flick a look at Shane, who seems focused on my knees. He breathes slowly, deliberately, taking a breath in, letting it go.

I cough out a giggle. Shane doesn't move.

Fixing my eyes back on the curtain, I grab the side-strings of my knickers and pull them to my knees. I never wear the wrong knickers to Shane's. I always choose the small black pair with the lace trim. I have to bend down a bit to get them off my feet.

The warm air licks around me. Every bit of me suddenly has a pulse. I slip my hands into the curve above my hips, run my tongue along my top lip, taste chocolate, and wait.

But he makes no sound, no movement, no nothing.

I look at him. His eyes seem to be closed. But then I realise he's looking down at my toes. I'm standing here with just a T-shirt brushing the tops of my hips and he's sitting, staring at my toes. Taking in each red painted toenail.

So I turn round, slowly, like I did in the pink pencil skirt. But this time he can take in each bit of leg, thigh, arse. I pause and concentrate. Perhaps I'll feel his breath on my skin. Perhaps it will be wet. Perhaps he'll put a big hand on me. Perhaps he'll move for me, reach out and pull me over, pull me to him.

But when I've turned all the way round, his hands are clasped on his knees, and they're white and dead looking. His curls fall over his eyes as his head drops lower.

I pick up my knickers, pull up my skirt. Shane doesn't move from his chair.

'I'm not your girlfriend,' I say. And I open the shed door.

seven

September, 1985

He stays over a couple of times before he moves in. I never hear them at it because I go right down under the covers, put my fingers in my ears and breathe through my mouth so all I get is the air moving in my head like a big sea. The door goes, their laughter creeps up the stairs, and I go under.

His name's Simon. In the morning, he's there at our breakfast table, beaming behind his packet of Alpen. Mum goes out and buys that for him because he says he can't eat bacon and eggs. 'Pinch an inch!' he says, digging a tiny roll of flesh out of his waistband. 'Roughage. That's what you need in the morning, Jan.' She nods as if she knows what he means.

I've done something about this in Home Economics, so I speak up. 'Fibre, that's what they call it now.'

He lets go of his bit of stomach. 'Is it now? Same difference, though. New word, same difference. Like *spastic* and *person with cerebral palsy*. See?' He winks at Mum. 'She's a feisty one, Jan!' He puts one hand on my arm and leans towards me. 'Don't let anyone change that, Joanna. Good for you.' He looks at Mum. 'Good for you.'

She gives him her little smile. Her dressing gown's

unzipped too far, showing the yellow-looking dip between her tits. Usually she does the zip right up, because there's no heating in the kitchen. And she isn't wearing her normal slippers, the ones with the cream fur trim. She's wearing the ones with curved heels and fluffy fronts. Dad bought her those one Christmas. 'Whenever am I going to wear those, Dan?' she'd asked him then.

'Muesli, Jan, it's the only way forward for the great British breakfast.'

I twist myself free of Simon's hand. Mum sits down next to him, crosses her legs. Lets a slipper dangle from her foot.

'Wouldn't you say, Joanna?' The glass of his big watch winks at me. His watch is gold coloured. There's loads of dials on the face, and at least four buttons on the side. I wonder what they all do, how many buttons and hands and dials you need to tell the time, and why he doesn't have a digital, like everyone else.

That night Mum's jumpy all through tea, picking at her cardigan, twirling a bit of hair around her finger, getting up to look out the window. She doesn't even put any food out for herself. She keeps dishing the beefburgers onto my plate, getting up and sliding another from under the grill as soon as I've finished one.

She picks at a bit of bread without bothering to spread any marg on it.

'Joanna.'

I can tell she's going to say something she thinks is important, because she starts off with my name.

'I've got some news.'

I chew on burger. I imagine how many cows it takes to stock the new Tesco's with burgers. There's cows in the fields beyond our village, but I've never looked at one up close. In the butcher's round the corner sometimes you see half a cow hung up in the window. A side of beef. Two fat legs and bloody meat on the ribs. I've watched mince turn brown in the pan when Mum cooks it for mince and mash. Dad's favourite. One minute it's pink and soft, the next it's brown and hard.

'What news?'

Before she can answer, his Volvo pulls up and she's out the door, running down the path like he's come home from the war. I go to the living room window and look out. Her flat brown hair flies out behind her as she runs to him. He gets out of the car and puts an arm round her. After he's patted her on the arse, I hear him say, 'Have you told her?'

Mum looks back at the house, so I duck down from the window and get back to my burger. I pick up a blackened chip and bite into it. It's hard and sour.

There's a lot of banging as he brings his suitcases into the hallway. They feel the need to whisper as he does this. Bang, crash, whisper, whisper. Bags scrape along the wallpaper. We've got the bobbly stuff you paint over. Dad was good at that sort of thing, anything with ladders and brushes and screwdrivers. In the summer holidays he'd let me help, and when we sat down for our tea we'd both have paint in our hair. Once we painted my room all different colours: one wall blue, one red, the other white. It was Jubilee year.

'Joanna. Simon's here.' Mum stands in the kitchen doorway, all pink up her neck. You can tell when she's lying or embarrassed, because a pink blotch spreads right up her neck, and she puts her hand there to try to cover it up. But I can still see it. It runs up to her ears and over her jaw and onto both cheeks, like a spilled pot of blusher.

I put down a cold chip and look at her. She wraps her

cardigan around her middle. For a second I wonder if I should cry. Whether that would stop him.

'Hi, Joanna. Remember me?' He's still wearing his raincoat, sticking one hand out towards me. That watch pokes through his cuff.

'Of course I remember you. You were here this morning. At breakfast.'

'That's right! I'm the muesli king! How could you forget?'

He looks at Mum, who nods. He takes a step closer and glances at my plate, still holding out a hand. 'Shake?'

I pick up the remains of my cold beefburger, dip it in the blob of tomato sauce, put it in my mouth, and chew.

Mum touches his shoulder. 'Simon. Why don't you take the stuff upstairs?'

He just stands there, though, arm extended and bobbing.

'Joanna,' he says, 'Joanna, I'd like it if we could get off on the right foot.' He pauses, flicks his fringe. 'I'd really like that, Joanna.' He smiles then, showing his small teeth, and I touch his outstretched fingers, just lightly.

eight

September, 1985

When I get back from school, I don't go in the kitchen. Mum's in there, recipe book propped up on the Special Thing Simon's bought to keep recipe books open (she never had a recipe book before, let alone a Special Thing), wooden spoon in hand, chopping board at the ready, probably weeping over the onions.

'I'm cooking lasagne,' she calls. I swing my bag across the living room floor. 'It's Italian,' she continues. 'Minced beef and big sheets of spaghetti. Nothing you won't like.'

She always cooks fancy things because she thinks he likes them, then tries to sell them to me with these descriptions. But I've seen him slide something greasy off his plate into the bin when she's turned her back to pour him another glass of white wine. 'I hope it's dry, Jan,' he'll say. 'Dry white's the only wine worth a hangover.'

I sit down on the sofa.

'Did you hear me?' she asks.

'I'm going out tonight. Don't bother with food.' I open a copy of the *Guardian*, because it's all there is to hand. He brought that into the house. I flick the pages. We never used to have a newspaper. Dad liked to watch ITN; Julia Somerville's his favourite. 'I'll just catch the headlines,' he'd say. Then it would be flicked over.

Mum walks into the living room and stands behind the sofa. I can picture the shape of her lips exactly: stuck out as if she's got a satsuma in her mouth. Biting on the pith. Probably one eye half closes as she says, 'Fine,' in a voice she'd like to think of as crisp. 'Simon's got a treat for you tonight though.' She lets this one out as she walks back into the kitchen. But I don't move from my spot on the sofa.

'I think you'll like it,' she calls over a clattering of pans. She's got these massive pans now. They went into Oxford and bought them together. When they came back they were cradling and rocking their Habitat bags as if they were newborns.

I don't reply.

'I think you'll like it, Joanna.' She comes into the living room and sits on my newspaper.

'I'm trying to read.'

'I know you don't read that.' She lowers her voice. 'And I don't bloody blame you.' She sticks a long finger into my forearm and wiggles it. 'Women's Page. Hasn't even got any make-up on it.'

She smells of perming lotion. She had it done a few days ago. It makes her face look like a tiny dot in a mass of scribble, like something one of the first years would do in Art. Simon didn't say anything when she showed him, twirling round, patting it with her flattened palm, making a light crunching sound.

'What's the treat, then?' I ask, not looking up.

'You'll see,' she says, wiggling her finger in my forearm again.

When he comes in he's grinning. He's wearing a big raincoat. He thinks it's sexy, this brown mac with a belt.

You can tell by the way he never just hangs it on the peg in the hall. Instead he shakes it out with a huge flap, smoothes it over one arm and takes it upstairs to hang it on a wooden coat hanger.

He stands there with his big grin and big rainmac, making a big thing about keeping one arm behind his back.

'Hi honey, I'm home!' he shouts, like he always does, in a fake American accent, and she laughs, like she always does, floating into the living room in her Delia Smith pinny. 'What's for tea?' he says. 'I like a little woman in the kitchen.' He gives me a wink. 'And any other room of her choice.'

'Lasagne tonight, darling.' She plonks a big kiss on his mouth.

'My favourite. Apart from you, that is.'

They snog.

'Joanna!' he calls, swooping over. 'I have something which I think may lead you to abandon your sulk, if only for a few moments.' I can smell his aftershave as he leans over the back of the sofa. It's one of those expensive ones that still smells cheap. He sticks out his lower lip and breathes over me. 'Don't you want to know what I've bought for you?'

Mum stands there, arms folded across her pinny.

'I hope you like it.' And he brings his arm round in front of him and places a Walkman in my lap.

'I've taken the liberty of including one of my favourite recordings. Vivaldi's *Four Seasons*.'

'You are wonderful, Simon,' says Mum, hugging him. 'Isn't he? Isn't he just wonderful, Joanna?'

But she's not even looking at me as she asks this question.

part three

one

Howard
September, 1985

Robert and Paul were friends for quite a few years, and, looking back on it, it seems strange that I didn't take action before I did. By the time they were fifteen, the two of them were wearing the same outfits, singing the same songs, smelling of the same shower gel and deodorant.

After the London trip, we didn't invite Paul on any more birthday outings. I managed to avoid seeing him very often, as Robert would go round to Paul's house after school on most days, leaving us looking at the clock, waiting for our son's return.

Then one day Kathryn suggested that Paul should come for Sunday lunch.

On the Saturday afternoon after work, she went to Hughes's and bought a whole chicken. Usually we had pieces, as Kathryn doesn't like the bones, but on that Saturday she came home from the library with a carrier bag full of bird dangling from her handlebars. I didn't say anything as she rinsed it under the tap and stored it in the fridge, a bloody piece of kitchen towel beneath, ready for his arrival.

As always, I spent Sunday morning in the garden. The metal of the secateurs was cool on my knuckles as I cut back the chrysanthemums. It no longer pained me to cut things back fiercely. When I'd started gardening, I'd worried that I would go in too hard, overdo it, cut off my chances entirely with those stubby blades. But I was wiser now; things always came back, and they came back all the better for being cut down.

'Hello, Mr Hall.'

Paul stood above me, shielding his eyes from the watery sun. His jacket was bright blue; his training shoes were bright white. Both looked as though they had been pumped full of air.

Robert wasn't far behind. 'Let's go inside,' I heard him say to Paul.

But Paul ignored him. 'Doing some gardening?'

'Pruning.' I clipped off another stalk.

Paul stroked a pimple on his chin and waited for more.

'Dad's always gardening,' said Robert. He touched the gold chain he'd taken to wearing around his neck and looked at Paul. They were about the same height, but now Robert was the more solid-looking. His arms and legs no longer seemed stretched; it was as if they had always been that size. They were settled into their pattern of striding and swinging, swinging and striding.

'My mum says you've got the best garden in the street, Mr Hall,' said Paul.

'Let's go inside,' Robert said again.

'She says you must be obsessed with gardening.' Paul grinned down at me.

'Robert liked gardening, when he was younger,' I said.

Paul let out a hoot of laughter. For a minute I wished I hadn't said anything, but to my surprise Robert didn't flinch; he just stared at Paul until his outbreak of mirth passed.

Eventually Paul looked down at the grass.

'He was very good at it, too,' I said.

'Dad,' said Robert, with a small smile, 'Paul's not interested in that.'

I straightened up. 'Well. You boys should wash your hands. I expect dinner's nearly ready.'

As she took the tray of sizzling potatoes from the oven, Kathryn's face was flushed and damp. Through the oven door, I could see the bird cooking in its juices.

'Lay the table for me?' she said, turning the potatoes in the hot fat.

I arranged the table as I usually did, but when she saw it she frowned. 'No placemats?'

We only have placemats at Christmas and birthdays. We do have a full set – a wedding present; the transfers depict birds of the British Isles.

I spent a moment wondering whether to give Paul a blue tit or a magpie. I eventually decided on a magpie.

Kathryn came in and eyed my work approvingly. 'Won't be long,' she said, 'I'll just make the gravy.' I knew that today she wouldn't be pouring boiling water on granules.

'Anyone would think the queen was coming,' I said in a voice I thought she might not hear, but she stopped in the doorway.

'It's important to him.'

As we stood looking at each other, Robert poked his head over his mother's shoulder.

'Have we got time to go out?' he asked.

'You stay here,' I said. I looked back at Kathryn. 'Why don't we have some wine, then?'

She raised her eyebrows. 'Why not?'

'Why not?' Robert chimed in.

It was a new thing for us, having wine in the house. I

liked the brown bottles of Riesling with their elegant, tapered necks and gold writing on the labels. That writing always reminded me of the lettering on the flyleaf of Mum's old Bible. I used to read Genesis sometimes, thinking that if I could read the whole book it would make me a better person. We were never religious, but Mum kept the Bible on her bedside table, along with a framed photo of Dad and me in the river at Darvington, a porcelain ballerina, and her teeth in a cup. Whenever I opened that book I smelled the mustiness of good words written on feather-thin pages, but I could never read much beyond the first few chapters.

Robert tilted his glass towards me. I half-filled it. Paul also tilted his glass, and he got the same amount.

I stood at the head of the table. The crisped roast potatoes had their own warmed dish; the peas and carrots steamed under a sliding knob of butter. The gravy sat in its jug, next to a jar of cranberry sauce, unopened since Christmas. A ring of chipolatas surrounded the bird; each was pink on one side, deep brown on the other.

'Want to carve, Howard?' Kathryn handed me the knife and three faces looked up, waiting for their meat.

I knew my knife was too blunt for the job. I remembered that somewhere in the cutlery drawer there was a sharpening stick, unused. Paul's father probably knew how to sharpen a knife on such an implement, wiping it back and forth along the granite at just the right angle, flicking his wrist like a painter. He'd know how to plunge the knife into the bird, puncturing the crisped skin with the tip of his blade and slicing through so that slivers of clean, gleaming meat folded down like yards of silk on a dressmaker's table.

'Leg or breast, Paul?' asked Kathryn.

'I'm easy, Mrs Hall.'

The two boys exchanged a smirk.

I sawed through the string that held the legs tight to the bird. It pinged back under the carcass, splattering my hand with pink juice. I stripped off clumps of breast meat and heaped them on the plates. Occasionally my blade hit a bone and there was a cracking noise.

I served myself last: two wings and a stringy piece of breast.

Robert picked up his fork, but before he could start to eat I raised my glass and cleared my throat. 'We should make a toast.'

Robert held up his glass, and Paul followed.

'What to?' Robert asked.

I thought for a moment. The two boys leaned together, their elbows almost touching. I noticed that they both wore matching leather straps around their wrists.

'To friendship.'

We all drank.

Afterwards, Robert and Paul washed up. Kathryn said we should leave them to it, so I poured myself another glass of Riesling and sat with the papers.

I tried to concentrate on the print in front of me, but I kept getting halfway down a column and then realising I hadn't taken in a single word. Their laughter was interrupting me.

When I heard a squeal, I looked over at Kathryn, but she didn't take her eyes off her book.

On the third squeal, I stood up. My head felt slightly woolly from the wine.

'Leave them,' said Kathryn.

'They might have broken something.'

'I didn't hear anything.'

I sat back in the chair and folded the paper on my knees. Then I unfolded it.

There was another squeal, and a splash.

'I think I should go and look.'

'They're fine, Howard.'

'But I think I should check.'

I wasn't sure if I wanted them to hear me open the door, or what I expected to find behind it, but when I stepped into the kitchen the two boys didn't seem to see me at all. Both of them had wet hair; Robert's was covered in soap suds. The kitchen floor tiles were streaked with foam.

I opened my mouth to speak, but before I could, Paul let out a loud hoot of delight as Robert grabbed him by the arm and whipped his behind with a wet rolled-up tea towel. Robert's eyes were shining, and his forehead was damp with perspiration.

Then my son noticed me. Our eyes met, and I thought I saw something like shame in his face. A blush spread across his cheeks. He let the tea towel drop to the floor.

I closed the door and went back to the living room.

'Do you think it's – normal?'

We were in bed; Kathryn was trying to read.

'What?'

'The two of them.'

She closed her book and rubbed her eyes. 'Haven't we been through this before? And didn't we agree that it's good for Robert to have friends?'

'But it isn't friends, is it? It's just Paul. And has been for years.'

She put her book on the bedside table and reached over for the light. 'I think we should sleep now, Howard.'

Turning off the lamp, she lay down on her side. But I remained sitting, staring into the darkness.

After a while I said, 'I think we should separate them.'

She didn't respond.

'He's fifteen. He should be doing other things. Moving on. It's time.'

She rolled onto her back. 'We've been through all this.'

'We could get him in at the other school. A fresh start.'

'It wouldn't make any difference.'

'So you do think there's a problem?'

'I don't know,' she sighed. Then she added, 'They're friends. That can't be bad, can it?'

We were both still. I wanted to put the light on again, but Kathryn turned on her side and curled her legs up towards her chest, as if she was about to sleep.

I let a minute pass, and then I reached over and stroked her hair. 'Are you awake?'

'Yes.'

'A new school would be the best thing for him, I think.'

'We can talk about it tomorrow.'

'I'll ask about the other school. We can get him in there before he takes his exams. We should do it now before the term really gets going.'

'It would unsettle him.'

'No reason to be unsettled. He's a confident boy. He'll make new friends.'

She said nothing.

I pulled the sheets up around me. Robert had a duvet now, but we preferred sheets and blankets. I liked to feel their weight on me.

'I'll make enquiries in the morning. I'm sure they'll be able to squeeze him in,' I said.

He was studying for O level Art. The new school, we were told by the headmaster when we met him to discuss the change, had a reputation for the arts.

'All our departments do well, of course, but the arts are a particular pride for us.' He leaned forward and smiled at my wife. He was younger than I'd expected, and wore round steel-rimmed glasses. On his desk was a framed photograph of a collie dog, and a colourful paperweight in the shape of a snail.

'That was made by one of our fourth years. Pottery class. Lovely thing, isn't it?'

'Lovely,' Kathryn agreed.

'Unusual,' I said.

'Some parents don't seem to hold the arts in much esteem, but we think it's very important to nurture the children's creative sides.'

'Robert's always been keen on art,' Kathryn said. Beneath the table, she took hold of my hand and held it.

'Excellent.'

'And we both think it's very important.'

'Even better.'

Kathryn gave my fingers a squeeze.

'Oh yes. Our son's very good,' I said, 'very good. On the artistic side of things.'

'Splendid. I'll put him down for Monday week, then. Best to start as soon as possible.'

In the car on the way home, Kathryn patted my knee. 'Maybe it will be the best thing for him,' she said.

I tried to think of a way I could soften the blow. What could I do that would help my son to adjust to the new school? I knew that whatever I said wouldn't make it any easier for him, so I decided on a gift.

I bought him a professional-looking art set: a tin of graphite drawing pencils arranged by grade, 9B to 2H (as the man in the shop explained to me), a thick sketchbook with a hard cover, and a set of thirty-six Winsor and Newton watercolours, mixing palette and paintbrush included.

'Thanks,' he said. He ran the tip of the new paintbrush along his top lip. 'They're really soft when they're new.'

We were standing together in the kitchen. It was Saturday afternoon. Kathryn was pouring out some tea. We hadn't told him about the change of schools. Not yet.

'Why don't you do your mother and me?' I asked.

'Draw you?'

'With your new pencils.'

Kathryn put the pot down. 'Howard, I'm not sure – '

'Why not? We can be models.'

Kathryn and Robert exchanged looks.

Then Robert let out a short laugh. 'Really?' he said.

'I'd like it if you would.'

'I don't know…'

'Please.'

His face softened. 'All right,' he said. 'All right. I'll draw you.'

We sat on the bench at the bottom of the garden for the picture, framed on either side by sprays of purple asters. I put my arm around Kathryn's shoulder and held her close.

'You don't have to smile,' said Robert. 'But you do have to stay still.'

We sat for what must have been an hour while Robert, balanced on a stool, squinted at us. It was the first time I'd seen him concentrate for so long; he shifted his gaze back and forth, his eyes darting from the page up to us, then down to his sketchbook. His eyes moved constantly, but his face stayed very still. Occasionally he rubbed at the page with an eraser and frowned.

The bench became cold and I felt my bottom going to sleep, but when I shifted, Kathryn nudged me. 'Can't wait to see how it turns out,' she whispered, giving me a sideways glance.

'Stop moving,' said Robert.

He didn't do that thing you see artists on the television doing – holding up the pencil to measure the perspective. He just sketched, and his touch was light, but deliberate. As he drew, I saw his determination to get it right, to see it properly: his frown was just like it had been on the day we'd watched the peacocks together at Brownsea.

At last, Robert held the sketchbook at arm's length and screwed up his eyes. 'That'll do,' he said.

Kathryn was the first to stand. 'Let's have a look then.'

Before he could protest, she had his sketchbook in her hand.

She stared at the page. 'Look at this, Howard.' She waved the book at me, as she'd done with his spelling book all those years before. 'It's just like us. He's really got it.'

Robert bit his lip and looked away, but I saw his smile.

I stood next to Kathryn and we held the book together. There we were, in grey and white lines and smudges: a middle-aged couple sitting on a bench, surrounded by flowers. My hand looked big on her shoulder, and Kathryn's nose was slightly too small, I noticed, but he had captured something. Perhaps it was her hopeful look, my questioning stare. Whatever it was, we were there, on his page.

two

Joanna
October, 1985

A boy called Robert arrives at school.

When he comes into the classroom, he looks straight ahead as he walks. Not at the ground, or at anyone else (not even at me), but straight ahead, eyes front, like he's in the army. Swinging his arms a bit, but with too much swagger to be military.

His grey school jumper is smooth and straight. A black velvet tick swoops across his chest. No one else has one like it. No one else has trainers like Robert, either, fat and round at the ends and dazzling white. His laces are so white and soft-looking they make me think of the snow-drift we sometimes get at the bottom of the garden.

After registration, I catch his eye. 'You're new,' I say. 'I'm Joanna.' I give him a big beam, noticing the lack of whiteheads on his chin.

He nods. Then he looks me up and down, batting his long eyelashes. He doesn't fix me like Shane does. His eyes don't go that far. It's more like he's summing me up, or taking a snap. Flash. Caught on camera.

'Rob,' he says, not smiling.

'Miss said your name was Robert.'

'It's Rob,' he says, cranking up those eyelashes again.

'My name's Rob.'

All morning I watch him. His thick brown hair sticks up on the top of his head, making him look even taller. He's tried to arrange the front of it in a greased curl, like my Dad's in old pictures. A dry bit pokes out the wrong way, but it still looks good. He's got flawless skin. A few faded freckles on his long, straight nose. A thin gold chain is draped around his neck. He plays with it a lot, twisting it round and round while he looks out the window.

Last lesson that day is History.

I slide in opposite Rob. We're doing Enclosures, which is all about how the countryside was divided up so it looks like a patchwork quilt. I thought the hedges had always been there. I didn't know they were planted to carve up the fields, for money.

Rob twirls a pencil. It's one of those ones with a big rubber on the end. He lets it slide through his fingers, catches it and twirls it again. He's good at that.

Halfway through the lesson, he leans over. 'What have you got for question six?'

'I'm still on two,' I say.

He grins. His cheeks dimple. 'Good pen,' he says, gesturing towards my pink plastic fountain pen. I look down at it.

'I've got one like it,' he continues, rummaging in his sleek metal pencil tin. He brings out a purple one, just the same. Then he says, 'You should have it. It goes with yours.'

I laugh. 'No thanks.'

'Go on. Look. I've got loads more.' He tips his case towards me. Shiny multicoloured pens are all lined up. 'You should have it.'

'I don't think so.'

'Really. Take it.'

I wonder what he wants.

'It's yours. If you want it.'

I reach out for the pen. He smiles like he's given me the crown bloody jewels.

All month, I have Rob in my sights.

One drama lesson I pick him as a partner. The theme of the lesson is 'trust'. I don't usually notice stuff like that, themes of lessons, but today I know I have to make the most of it, so I listen to what the flowery-scarfed teacher says.

'Pick a partner and ask them to do something that you'd only ask someone you trust.'

Skinny Luke McNeill moves towards Rob so I cut in, quick as I can. 'Carry me, slowly,' I say, touching the smooth sleeve of Rob's jumper. I don't know what makes me say it. It comes out before I've even thought.

Luke flicks back his wispy blond fringe and attempts to stick out his little chin. He's the only boy in the class who gets away with wearing a polo neck, and it makes his face seem even longer, his cheekbones even higher. 'Rob's with me, Joanna.'

Rob bats his eyes, first at Luke, then at me. Those lashes make him look like someone in the centre of *Smash Hits*. For a minute I imagine him with staples in his flawless cheeks.

'I'm with Joanna,' he says, not looking at Luke but at me. I put my hands on my hips. I'm wearing a white plastic belt. Mum says that's a fifties siren look, your waist all pulled in and a tight sweater.

Flowery-scarf comes over. 'Good, Joanna, well done for working with someone new,' she says, guiding Luke off by the shoulders.

Rob stands there staring after Luke. 'Come on then,' I say. 'Carry me.'

I'm surprised when he actually lunges forward, hooks his arms underneath mine and lifts me. My armpits are sweaty, but I'm wearing plenty of *Impulse*. My tits squash against his chest and our noses almost meet. I can feel the heat of his face on my cheek.

'Are you going to kiss me, then?' I whisper.

He pretends not to hear, lets go, and drops me right on his toe.

'Joanna will never trust you if you drop her like that,' calls Flowery-scarf. I swear she winks at me as she says it.

Luke McNeill looks at us from the corner of the room, pulling the sleeves of his polo neck down over his fists.

I start to work Saturdays at Buggery Stores. I sit behind the counter and read magazines, take the money for fags and milk. *Just Seventeen* is usually spread on my lap. Old Mr Buggery would like to be there instead, of course. You should see him when I reach up to the top shelf for a packet of Dunhill. You'd need a trough to catch the drool. You can smell it too, something down there in his nylon trousers, giving off this nasty niff. I reach out one hand for the Dunhill and feel my polka-dot shirt riding up over my belly. Balancing on one leg, I stick an arse cheek in his direction, knowing he can see the bit where my tights go thin over my thighs.

'Joanna, do you want a hand, dear?' he asks, all innocent.

I bet he's really thinking of Mum without much on, though. She probably wore that sheer teddy she stuffs in her bottom drawer especially for him when they had their thing. She's got a whole load more like that since she met Simon.

One Saturday, Rob comes in.

'Have you got *Melody Maker*?' he asks, leaning a grey leather elbow on the counter, flashing his gold chain. 'It's a music magazine.'

'I know what it is,' I say, half-closing my eyelids in a Bet Lynch style. I don't read magazines like that. They're for boys who've got no girlfriends.

Rob says nothing. There's something about his mouth, the way his upper lip bows, that I like. So I open my eyes wider. 'Is it good, then? *Melody Maker*?'

He looks over my shoulder at the cigarettes on the shelf and considers, then licks his curving upper lip. 'Yes.' He starts a little smile. 'You'd like it.'

Outside it's raining. Water's streaking down the shop windows, leaking onto the lino whenever anyone comes in. Pools of mud begin to creep around the doormat. It won't be long before Buggery's handing me the mop.

Then Shane comes in the door.

It's the first time he's been in since I started working here. The first time I've seen him for months.

He stands by the magazines, staring at me. His parka's dripping wet. He looks like a big shining bulk of green. I think of the Green Cross Code Man. The Jolly Green Giant. The Incredible Hulk.

Rob leans on the counter. 'I think you'd really like it,' he says.

But all I can do is look at Shane. He's had his hair cut but it still hangs in his eyes. His face is framed by patches of new half-fluffy, half-spiky stubble. It makes his lips seem fuller, his eyes darker.

He gives Rob a quick glance, then turns towards the chiller cabinet.

I take a breath. 'Do you want me to order it in for you, this *Melody Maker*?' I brush Rob's elbow aside to make room for the order pad. I chew on the end of one of those chubby pens. It's got glitter inside, and I imagine chewing a hole in it so the glitter falls out all over my mouth and down my chest.

By now Rob's noticed the presence of Shane and we're both looking over at his back. Water dribbles down his parka and onto the floor. He sniffs a huge sniff, runs the back of his hand under his nose.

'That's disgusting.' Rob is speaking to me but his voice is loud enough for Shane to hear.

Shane doesn't turn around. Instead he picks up a Wall's sausage roll and flips it over a few times. Then he wipes his nose again with the same hand.

Rob says, 'Should he be doing that?'

'Do you want to order this Melody whatsit?'

'Shouldn't he buy that first?'

Shane is unwrapping the sausage roll. He holds it in both hands as he rips a corner of the cellophane wrapping with his teeth. Then he pokes his tongue inside the wrapper and dabs it against the pastry before taking a big bite. His black curly hair is still wet from the rain, and a droplet of water hangs on the edge of his fringe.

'Shouldn't you do something?'

I reach out and grab Rob's collar. It feels cold and rubbery, not what I expected. I expected soft cowhide, smooth beneath my fingers. I lean over the counter and whisper in his ear, inhaling the sweet smell of his hair gel. 'Do you want to see me tonight?'

I let go of his collar and he blinks. I smile and nod at him. 'Tonight,' I say in a loud voice, 'eight o'clock.'

I dart a quick look over at Shane, who stops eating the sausage roll.

'Down the pools. OK?'

Rob's mouth goes slack.

'OK? Eight o'clock. The pools.' I say again.

Rob steals another peek at Shane.

'OK, Rob?'

When Rob's closed his mouth and finished looking first at me, then at Shane, he nods once, says nothing, and walks out. He walks quickly, his hands jammed in his pockets. And I let Shane follow him, sausage roll unpaid for.

A dousing of hairspray, a flick of lipstick, and I'm done. I decide on a pastel green mini-skirt and matching cap-sleeved T-shirt for my date with Rob. It'll be cold, so he'll get the odd glimpse of nipple if I leave my denim jacket undone.

Walkman on. I should find a new tape to play, but Frankie will do. Walking through Calcot is the same every time, even to the beat of 'Relax'. Wherever you are, you can see the outline of the power station above the trees. Great big things, those towers. So wide I can't imagine how many people you could fit in one of them. More than there are in this village, or our school. Much more than that. I went there once, for the Open Day. Me and Mum had hot dog after hot dog while Dad drank beer on the grass. There were rides and games, but what I remember most is the smell. Thick and metallic. I won a cuddly banana, bright yellow. 'I ask you,' Dad said. 'What would anyone want with a cuddly banana?'

But I shouldn't think of Dad, because he said he'd phone and he hasn't.

I can only just see the outline of the power station tonight. It's dark already. Orangey plumes of steam wind up into the sky.

Passing Buggery's window, I catch my reflection. My

face looks strange, superimposed on all the advertising postcards people have stuck up there. *Rabbits for Sale. Earn extra cash for Christmas* (big writing across my forehead), *come turkey plucking* (small writing across my nose).

I stop to practise. Eyes wide, looking up from under, mouth just open, ready. I wet my lips and blink. He'll like that.

Then I remember standing with my hands on my naked hips for Shane, the way he just stared at my feet, and I close my mouth.

I wonder if he'll come.

There are no lights down the lane that leads to the pools; the bushes hang right over. I turn the Walkman off and listen to the sound of my own footsteps.

You can't get close to the pits where they're still digging. Massive fences are all around them. But the old ones are full up with water, which is why people call them the pools. Also, it sounds better, which attracts people who like walking around on Sundays. Not that they ever go anywhere. They just walk round and round, without a destination.

I step off the gravel path, push through some skinny trees, and reach the biggest pool. It's dark as death itself, as Mum would say. I get as close to the water as I can. There are bushes and weeds all along the edge. Big spiky branches stick up in the air like spears. But there are gaps where the plants thin out. Gaps where you could slide through, if you were to slip on a muddy patch. I lean over. The water smells slightly acidic. Cold.

I can just see the outline of one of the warning signs. They're everywhere down here. I know them off by heart.

'DANGER – Deep Water!'

'Keep Away From Edge!'

'Deep Soft Mud Leading to Possible ENTRAPMENT!'

And a skull and crossbones beneath each one.

Deep Soft Mud. It sounds inviting. Like a mud bath in a beauty salon, or like drowning in a face pack. It would be cold at first, but then it would get warm, and its smoothness would creep over you. It would hold you there, suspended in the warm mass of mud. It would get in all your cracks. You'd suck it up your nose, like chocolate milkshake through a straw, until your lungs would be full of mud. Fit to burst.

I back away from the pool and sit down on a bench to wait for Rob. The bench is there for people who like to watch birds. Twitchers.

In the summer the pools look like big beautiful baths. When Dad was around we used to come here if it was really hot. He found a safe place where we could edge down to the water. He pushed through the weeds, holding them back for me, then stretched out his hand. *Come on. Don't be afraid.* We walked sideways down the mud, inching our toes closer to the water. The murky pool gradually found its way up our feet, our ankles, knees. Dad lifted me, his hands gripping my upper arms. He bent his knees so he was submerged to his neck. Then he lowered me down.

As the water took me in, my skin fizzed with cold. The sun was warm on my hair, but the rest of my body was freezing. We bobbed together in the icy water. I looked down and all I could see was black. I couldn't even see my feet, wrapped around Dad's waist as he held me in the water.

And then Dad went under. Everything went quiet. I looked out over the unbroken surface of the pool, and although Dad's hands were still around my waist, holding me up, I was sure he'd gone. I was ready to scream out, when he came to the surface, whooping and flicking his hair away from his eyes. Laughing.

I'm thinking about him again.

*

I wait for Rob. There's a faint whirr from the power station. I look towards the church. The branches move in the breeze. There's a sliver of light from the one streetlamp at the end of the lane, but there's no silhouette, no Rob.

There's nobody at all.

The seat's damp. A shiver makes my skin bump and I wrap my arms across my chest, clutch my own flesh.

Then there's a rattle and rustle from the lane and Rob swerves his bike out of the trees and towards me. He doesn't sit on his saddle as he pedals; it's up, down, up, down, little arse bobbing away.

He stops and stands in front of me, bike between his legs, breathing hard. There's a gleam on his jacket from the moon. His hair's gelled, I can smell it. L'Oreal, I'll bet.

'Hi,' he says, loudly, like he's in some American soap. He glances all round as if he's missing somebody. 'Look. Can we go somewhere else?'

'I like it here.'

'It's bloody weird.'

I stand up and wipe my hands on my skirt. Then I grab his handlebars in my fist. I get a lungful of L'Oreal as I lean forward. 'What's wrong with it?'

'It's just weird.'

I put my hand on his shoulder and give that cold rubbery stuff a squeeze. It's definitely not the real thing, whatever it is.

'Let's just go, OK?' he says, a bit louder.

'I want to stay here.' I stretch my fingers out and stroke them up his neck. I catch his gold chain, flick it up and let it fall back against his skin. He pulls away a bit, but I keep my hand on his neck. It feels as smooth as my own. 'We can go anywhere you like,' I say, 'in a minute.' I take a look down the lane, but there's no sign of movement.

Rob smells very clean. He must wash every day. There's probably a shower cubicle in his bathroom. Maybe even a power shower. He'll have L'Oreal shower stuff to go with his hair gel.

We stand there together, watching the lane.

Then he tries again. 'We could go to Luke's. His parents are never in.'

I look up at his *Smash Hits* profile. Dropping my hand from his neck, I ask, 'Why does he follow you everywhere?'

'What?'

'He's always with you.'

He doesn't reply.

'Is he why you don't want to be here, with me?'

He perches back on the saddle. 'Look. I'm going,' he says. 'You can come if you want.' He pushes off.

I don't move until he stops and looks back. 'Come on then,' he calls.

We head towards the lane. Rob's staring ahead, balancing on his saddle and using his feet to push his bike along, not speaking. I keep one hand on his handlebars as I walk beside him.

Then I hear the hiss of a Walkman.

I thought he'd never come.

I see the bulk of him walking towards us, his long legs taking big strides through the grass. His hands are in his pockets. He's stepping in time to the music. As he comes closer I recognise the hiss: Frankie's 'Two Tribes'.

Rob stops and grabs my hand. 'It's OK,' he whispers.

But I can't look at him now. I can't take my eyes off the figure coming towards us.

'It's OK,' Rob says again, his fingers sweating over mine.

The hissing gets louder. Rob keeps a tight hold of my

hand, making my rings dig into my skin. But I don't say anything. I stand there, not saying anything, until Shane notices us. He stops, but he lets Frankie play on.

Even though it's dark, dark as death itself, I can tell he's not quite looking at us. His eyes will be on the ground, moving across the grass, maybe flicking up my legs occasionally. But he won't be looking at my face.

Rob's not-real leather jacket creaks as he takes a big breath in.

Shane goes to move, to step past Rob's bike, but Rob twists the handlebars so his wheel catches Shane's shin.

Shane looks up at me. His dark eyes are soft.

Then he pushes past, knocking Rob from his saddle.

Rob yanks his fingers free from my hand and twists round. 'Spacky,' he shouts. But he doesn't go after Shane. He just stands there, straddling the crossbar, coat creaking, feet planted in the wet grass. Repeating that word to Shane's disappearing back.

three

Howard
November, 1985

In the end, it was Kathryn who announced the change. She took Robert to Mr Badger's tearoom in Darvington and told him, gently, that we thought his school wasn't providing the best guidance. There was another school, a better one, one that could nurture his artistic side. Wouldn't he rather go there and develop his talent?

No one mentioned the Paul issue.

And, to give Robert his credit, there hadn't been any nonsense. It had been a swift, seamless change to the new school. He hadn't actually said much about it at all. He'd just gone very, very quiet. And Kathryn had trailed after him, trying to get a word, a smile.

One Saturday evening, not long after the change, Kathryn suggested we make a blancmange, ready for Sunday lunch. 'It might make him laugh,' she said. We'd made a rabbit-shaped blancmange on green jelly grass for almost every birthday until he was eight. After that, I felt he was too old for such things.

I remember the first time we made one. Kathryn had

bought a silver mould in the shape of a rabbit in preparation for his third birthday party. That first time we tried, the custard wasn't thick enough, and when Kathryn turned it out, the rabbit's features were indistinct, its ears no more than bulges, its tail a mere ridge on its behind. 'Whatever is it, Howard?' Mum asked, as Robert pointed at the pink blob and laughed.

'It's a blancmange rabbit on jelly grass,' I said, looking over at Kathryn.

'Silly me,' Mum smiled, enclosing Robert's pointing finger in her hand. 'What else could it be?'

But over the years, together, we mastered it. It was my job to tear up cubes of green jelly, pour on boiling water, pop out to the kitchen every now and then to check on the state of the setting. It was difficult, at first, to get it just right – too soft and it would be watery, too hard and it would be rubbery. When Kathryn had turned the blancmange out onto our largest serving dish, the one with the blue rim and blue dots in the middle, I'd be there, waiting with the knife, ready to chop and shred the grass. My blade would cut through the shining green jelly, and I'd scatter the glassy fragments on the plate around the wobbling rabbit.

So it was Saturday night, and we'd made the blancmange – even though he was too old, even though we knew that if he did laugh it would be only to indulge us – and we'd gone up to bed. Robert had been out all day. He'd said he was studying at a friend's house, and there wasn't much I could say to stop him; he was fifteen, after all, and since the change of school and the silence that had followed, I'd felt I shouldn't question him too much. He knew, though, that he was to be in by eleven.

I remember Kathryn wore pyjamas that night. Stripy pyjamas, with a tassled cord around the waist to keep the trousers up. They were exactly like a man's pyjamas. She hadn't announced the fact that she intended to make this switch; she just turned up in a pair that night, tassle dangling over one striped thigh, slipped between the sheets, and opened her novel.

'Is that pyjamas you're wearing?'

She nodded, not looking up from her book.

'They're new, then.'

'They're warm, Howard. And they don't ride up.'

I switched off the light on my side of the bed, lay my head on the pillow, and watched her read for a few moments. She balanced her novel in one hand, her index finger tucked between the creased paperback cover and the first page.

I wondered if the pyjamas had a slit in the front, like mine. 'You could have worn mine, if you'd asked.'

She turned a page. 'I've got my own now.'

When I woke, I was sweating, and my hands ached. Kathryn was sleeping, so I knew that Robert must have come in. I flexed my fingers beneath the covers, feeling the tightness in the joints. Probably I had been clenching them in my sleep again. It started around that time, this waking up with my hands feeling stiff, my fingers aching and useless.

I shifted on the mattress, brushing Kathryn's foot with mine. I'd forgotten about the pyjamas, and was surprised by the feel of the thick hem around her ankle.

Then I heard the tinkling sound that must have woken me.

I raised my head a fraction off the pillow and looked

towards the light coming through the crack in the door. There it was again, a faint scraping sound, like metal on metal. I waited, blinking into the darkness. There was a juddering noise. It sounded like a drawer closing.

I swung my legs out of the bed and pushed my feet into the nests of my slippers. I looked back to check Kathryn was still sleeping. All I could see of her was a mess of thick hair on the pillow, unmoving. I pulled on my dressing gown and opened the bedroom door.

As I made my way across the hallway, down the stairs and along the corridor to the kitchen, I flicked on every light switch I could, not wanting to step into any dark spaces, any unlit corners.

I stood in front of the kitchen door for a few moments, listening. There was another scraping sound, then a giggle. *Give me some more*, someone said.

A strange boy was in our kitchen.

My hands ached again. I flexed them in my pockets before pushing the door open.

They were standing close together, both leaning their hips on the counter by the draining board. The other boy was fair haired, and very slight. He wore a black cap on the back of his head. Even his head seemed slim, his cheeks bony, his nose thin and slightly hooked. His eyes were fixed on Robert, who held a spoon overflowing with pink blancmange up to the boy's waiting lips.

The boy took a mouthful and swallowed before they twisted round to face me. A pink blob of pudding shone on the blond boy's chin. They were both smiling, puffing their cheeks out slightly to keep their laughter in. Through the gap between them, I could see the rabbit's head had been sliced in half, and bits of green jelly lay scattered over the counter.

I wished I'd put some proper clothes on, so I wouldn't

be facing them like this, in my dressing gown and slippers.

'Hello Dad,' said Robert. 'This is Luke.'

'What on earth are you boys doing?'

Neither boy replied. Robert dug his spoon back into the flesh-like surface of the blancmange. There was a sucking, squelching noise as he scooped out a dollop of pink pudding and held the spoon up to Luke.

I looked over at the clock. A quarter past one.

'Do you know what time it is?'

Silence.

'Robert? What's your mother going to say when she sees this mess?'

But he wouldn't look at me. His eyes were on Luke's, and they remained there as he moved the spoon towards the boy's lips.

'Put that spoon down, please,' I said.

Neither boy moved. Robert had stopped smiling now. His mouth was fixed in a straight line.

'Robert. Please put the spoon down.'

Luke took a step back, but Robert's hand kept moving towards him.

'Put the spoon down, Robert.' I tried not to shout; I didn't want to wake Kathryn.

Robert tipped the spoon against Luke's tight lips. 'Open up,' he said, in a stagy whisper. 'You said you wanted more.'

Luke glanced over at me. My hands were clenched, aching inside my pockets. I tried to say my son's name again, but found no sound would come out.

Then Luke put his hand over the spoon. 'I've had enough, Rob,' he said, 'thanks.' He guided Robert's hand down to the counter before turning to me. 'I think I should be going.' He wiped the pink blob from his chin.

'I'll ring you tomorrow,' Robert called after him.

After Luke had closed the back door, we stood in silence for a long time. Robert gazed at the floor. Then he started to pat the top of the destroyed blancmange with his spoon, sending droplets of quivering pudding over the worktop.

I walked across the room, meaning to take the spoon from his hand. But before I could, I saw the ring in his ear. A bright gold loop, right through.

'Whatever is that?'

'What?'

I thought I might pull him towards me by his ear, but I stopped just short and flexed my hands. 'You look like a damn gypsy,' I said. I knew my voice was too loud.

He touched the gold ring and smiled.

'Where did you get it?'

'In the library,' he said, rolling his eyes.

'Now is not the time to be clever, Robert.'

He looked straight at me and continued to stroke the bright hoop.

I swallowed. 'Where did you get the money?'

'Mum gave it to me.'

'What?'

He let his spoon drop into the blancmange. 'Mum gave me the money and I went and had it done today. We both had one. Luke and me.'

I picked up the plate of pink pudding and stood with it in my aching hands, staring at him. This time he did not look back at me. Instead, he ducked as I raised the plate to my shoulder and heaved it at the back door.

We both stood and watched as the blancmange crawled down the paintwork, leaving a long trail of pink slime.

four

Joanna
November, 1985

I stand behind Rob in the dinner queue. The dinner hall's damp and greasy; oily smells lurk in corners even in the afternoons, when the serving hatches are locked up. Rob stands with his weight on one leg, arse cheek jutting out towards me. Luke McNeill stands next to him. But his arse cheek doesn't jut out. Luke's so skinny he hasn't got an arse. They've both had their ears pierced. Their matching gold rings shine in the food counter lights.

Rob looks over the steaming steel counter to where today's choices are chalked up. Pizza. Sausage Roll. Chips. Beans. Curry. I can't stand curry. At primary school a boy called Patrick bent his dark head over his plate of curry trimmed with rice and puked. Since then, the two smells are the same for me.

The dinner lady with square hair and coral lipstick looks at Rob. 'What's it to be, handsome?'

He hesitates. He's still scanning the list.

I pray it won't be curry.

'Just a sausage roll.'

'Just a sausage roll?'

Rob nods and Luke watches. He's tried to comb his blond wisp up, like Rob's. He's dolloped a load of gel on the top of his head and stuck up a few tufts.

'No chips?'

'No chips.'

The dinner lady holds up her trowel of grease. 'You're sure?'

'I'm sure.' He flashes her his smile, cheeks dimpling. Then he moves towards the till.

The dinner lady waves her trowel at Luke. 'What about you, love?'

'Just a sausage roll. No chips.'

I take my plate of pizza and chips and follow them to the corner table. I ease into the seat next to Luke, so I can look at Rob opposite. They both have an apple and a carton of blackcurrant juice lined up by their plates.

'Mind if I sit here?' I say.

Luke looks at Rob and Rob says, 'I don't mind.'

Rob takes a bite of his sausage roll. A flake of pastry sticks to his bottom lip. He wipes it off with his sleeve and sucks his carton of blackcurrant. His Adam's apple bobs. Next to me, Luke drinks noisily from his carton of juice.

'God, you're a slurper.'

Luke's cheeks go pink. Rob fixes me with his green eyes and continues to suck up his juice.

I push my plate over to Rob. 'Chip?'

'No, thanks.' His lips are stained black on the inside.

I bite at my pizza. A string of greasy cheese lands on my chin. I stick out my tongue to lick it off.

When I'm done, I hold out a fat, shiny chip. The end bends towards Rob's nose. 'You should have one. In return for the pen.'

'Rob doesn't eat chips.'

I swivel in my seat to face Luke. Rob's eyes are still on me. 'Do you want it, then?'

Luke shakes his head.

'Sure?' I dangle the chip by his mouth.

'He doesn't want it, Joanna,' says Rob. 'Thanks anyway.'

I tip my chair onto its back legs and throw my head back. My hair trails down so it almost touches the floor. I look at the cracked ceiling tiles. 'I've never heard of boys on diets,' I say in a loud voice.

I think of Shane and me, eating cake. The way the icing sugar nearly chokes me if I breathe in too hard. The vanilla softness of the buttercream in our mouths.

I let my chair fall back to the floor and sit upright with a jolt. My hair swings around my shoulders.

Rob picks up his juice carton and sucks it dry, cheeks hollowing with the effort. Then he smiles at me. It's a big, glamorous smile. 'See you,' he says.

They leave together, taking their identical empty trays with them.

Mum puts her hand on my shoulder as we're watching TV. 'Simon's got something to ask you.'

The last time he had something to ask me it was whether I smoked. Mum had to leave the room when I said 'no', because she knows different. I used to go down Buggery's for her Silk Cut. She never said anything when I came back with two packets, one opened and already half-smoked. She's been trying to give up since she met Simon. 'Like kissing an ashtray, Jan. A very beautiful ashtray, but an ashtray nevertheless,' he says whenever she sneaks out the back for a fag. Then she'll shout that he doesn't understand, maybe throw something at him (nothing hard, a cushion, a tea towel), and in the end he'll say, 'It's the craving, my love, for the evil nicotine,' which only makes her worse, so he'll go out and buy her some chocolate, and they'll disappear upstairs to make up. At that point, I'll go outside for a fag.

'I'll leave you to it, then,' says Mum.

Finally Simon finds the button on the remote and *Coronation Street* fades to black.

'I was watching that.'

He raises his eyebrows and touches the edge of his red-rimmed glasses. These are new. I wonder if he even needs glasses.

'It was getting to a good bit.'

'Joanna,' he begins. 'I could help you understand what a "good bit" – a crucial point in the plot – might really be. At your age you should be reading something that will stretch your mind more than TV soap.'

'I read.'

'What do you read?'

I try to remember what we're doing in English. 'Shelley,' I say.

He touches his specs. 'Percy Shelley?'

'*Frankenstein*. We're doing it at school.'

A smile flickers across his lips. 'Interesting. That's good. Anything else?'

'Can I have *Coronation Street* back on?'

'Do you like *Frankenstein*?'

I think about the monster *bounding over the crevices at superhuman speed*. For some reason, that bit stays in my head. 'No,' I say. 'It's crap.'

'You could try something else. Another classic.'

'Like what?'

He breaks into a smile. Rubs his thigh. 'Like *Wuthering Heights*.'

'Is it good?'

'Oh, it's more than good.'

'Any sex in it?'

'Plenty. Of a sort.' He touches his specs again. 'But

that's not the point.'

'Can I put the TV back on?'

'The point is,' he says, ignoring me, 'the point is that… you're a bright girl, and yet your mother tells me you don't apply yourself at school.'

'I do all right.'

'I know what it's like. All those old schoolteacher types droning on from on high. School's bloody dull for a girl of your spirit.' He flashes his little teeth at me.

'It's all right.'

'Joanna,' he says, 'I'm giving you a chance.'

I look him in the eye and I'm surprised when he looks right back at me.

'You can get out of – all this,' he says, gesturing towards the television. 'You can escape, like I did.'

'If you escaped, how come you're here with me and – ' I gesture towards the television, 'all this?'

He takes his glasses off and leans towards me. 'Look. I'm offering you tuition.' He rubs his specs on his burgundy trouser leg. 'I have got a degree. I know that doesn't mean much to you, but it does count for something.'

I can smell the Nescafé on his breath.

'Just an hour every week. Just us. Just going through your homework.' He pats me on the knee. 'And anything else that happens to crop up.'

There's a pause before he slips his specs back on and attempts to look over the top of those red rims. But his glasses are so big he can't quite pull it off. 'It will be fun, you'll see.'

I notice that the skin above his top lip is moist.

'What's in it for me?' I ask, reaching for the remote.

He closes his hand over the remote before I can get to it. 'If your marks improve, some suitable reward.'

'I get to choose?'

'Yes.'

I tug the remote from him. 'Maybe.'

All Saturday I wonder where Shane is.

Old Buggery reaches across from the till and touches my wrist. 'A penny for your thoughts,' he says.

'You'll have to cough up more than that.'

I lean on the counter and look out the window. I wonder if Dad will call tonight. It's been two months since he left.

But I'm not thinking about him.

Outside, cars drag through the rain.

In the back room, Buggery shouts at a match on *Grandstand*.

I stamp my feet on the floor. You can't wear socks with slip-on flats, and Buggery's so tight he won't let me put the Calor gas on until December. *In consequence*, as Simon would say, *in consequence*, I can't feel my feet.

My body is so frozen with cold and boredom that when Shane shoves open the shop door, it takes a minute for me to blink.

I keep turning the pages of *Just Seventeen*. Shane moves over to the magazines, picks up a copy of *Classic Bike*. He spends a few seconds flicking through before slamming it back on the shelf. Then he moves towards me. His black curls dance. Without looking up, he digs in his parka pocket and places a can of Elnett on the counter, nods, then pushes it in my direction.

We both stand there, staring at the can. 'What's that?' I ask.

'For you,' says Shane.

I take a good look at him. His parka's straining over his

shoulders. He'd be tall enough to reach the porn mags on the top shelf.

'Are you my girlfriend?' he asks.

I smile.

Buggery roars in the back room. Goal.

Shane grins back, a half smile that shows his uneven teeth.

'I'll see you, then,' he says.

And before I can think of a reply (where? when?), he turns and walks out the door, leaving the bell clanging.

I wrap my fingers round the can; it's still warm from Shane's pocket.

I meet Simon in Mr Badger's tearoom, a café that does tea in a china pot and has lace everywhere: all over the tables, on the walls, in the loo.

When I come in he's sitting there, wiping his glasses on the tablecloth and peering at the menu. A pot of tea steams in front of him.

He jumps up. 'You're late, young lady.'

'I was discussing crucial plot moments with a teacher.'

He touches his specs and grins. 'Touché. I've ordered you a coke.'

'No ice?'

'No ice, exactly as you like it.'

I take off my denim jacket and sit down.

I see him give my pink scoop-neck T-shirt a good once-over.

'Where's your school blouse?'

'I changed in the toilets before I left.'

A girl wearing an apron covered in toilet-roll-dolly frills puts down my coke. It's in a half-pint glass, resting on a doily, resting on a china saucer.

Simon stops looking at my T-shirt and rummages in his rucksack. 'Here we are. You're doing *Frankenstein* at school, aren't you?' He slaps a paperback down on the tablecloth.

I take a sip of coke and nod.

'What can you tell me about Mary Shelley?'

'She wrote a book that was made into a lot of films,' I say.

'That's true. Have you seen any?'

'I've seen that cartoon with Frankenstein in it. And *The Munsters.*'

Simon raises a finger. 'Can you tell me the mistake you made there?'

'What?'

'Think about *identity*. Who precisely is the monster – and who isn't?' He puts both elbows on the table and leans across with his gob open in a half-smile. This is one of the first things we covered in class, but I don't mention that. Instead, I stretch my legs out under the table and feel for his ankle with the point of my shoe. 'What are you on about?'

Looking triumphant, he shifts his ankle out of my shoe-line. 'Doctor Frankenstein is the scientist; the quote-unquote *monster* is not, in fact, Frankenstein at all. But you could say that what the doctor does is quote-unquote *monstrous*.' He beams.

'Quote-unquote monstrous? What's that supposed to mean?'

'I'm placing monster within quotation marks, denoting a certain... so-called-ness about the term. Like, you might say, people think that Joanna is a quote-unquote *monster*, but in fact she's just a mixed-up girl.'

'Who says I'm a quote-unquote monster?'

He laughs. 'No one. No one.' He pours himself some

more tea, lifting the teapot so high that the stream of water sounds like a stream of piss.

He takes a slurp, looks out the window and starts again. 'It's so good that you're reading a book by a woman. When I was at school it was strictly for the boys – you know, Trollope, Dickens, Sir Walter Scott... God, he was terrible,' he smiles. 'Anyway. I'm sure you can identify more easily with Mary Shelley. As a – young woman.'

'Why?'

He swallows. 'Well.' He looks round the room, flicks his fringe. 'Well. For example. Shelley could be said to be writing about her own miscarriages when she calls the monster *my hideous progeny*. Quote-unquote.'

'I haven't had a miscarriage.'

He takes off his glasses and pinches the top of his nose as if his eyes hurt. 'Do you want another coke?'

'I'm not even pregnant.'

'I didn't say you were, Joanna.'

I try to find his ankle again with my foot. 'Mind you, I could be.'

He clears his throat. 'What do you mean?'

I hook his trouser leg round the point of my shoe. 'I'm old enough. Mum had me when she was seventeen.'

'You're fifteen.'

'What's two years?'

He reaches down to disconnect his trouser from the end of my shoe. After waiting a bit, he asks, 'Did your mother really have you when she was – *seventeen*?'

'Didn't you know that?'

'Was she married to your dad then?'

'No. But she was soon after.'

Simon puts his glasses back on. His lenses are smeared. He nods slowly. Then he tries to pour more tea, but there's only a dribble.

'Are you and Mum getting married?' I ask.

He puts the pot down. 'I honestly don't know, Joanna.'

I can't see his eyes properly behind the smears.

'Then why are you living in our house?'

'This is supposed to be a tutorial, not an interrogation,' he says, his hand pressing down on the teapot lid.

I finish my coke and crash the glass back on the saucer. 'Isn't it time we went home? I'm starving.'

As I get up to go, he clasps a clammy hand round my wrist and nearly pulls me back into my seat. 'Joanna, it means a lot to me, that you've agreed to these... sessions.'

His top lip is sweating again.

'I mean, I want to help your mother – although sometimes I wish she would help herself a bit more – and I want to help you, and I really think that, you know, together we can do something... something good.'

The girl in the frilly apron comes back over and drops the bill on his plate. While he's looking at it, I take the opportunity to slip my wrist out of his fist.

five

Howard
November, 1985

I rested my forehead on the wood of Robert's bedroom door and listened. Some music tape he'd bought recently was playing, its beat relentless, the singer's voice high and beseeching, even though it was a man's.

Robert, I whispered into the gloss. A glass of coke, my pretext for knocking on his door, was cold and slippery in my fingers.

There was a clunk as the tape finished.

I pushed the handle down and stepped in to find him right there in front of me. We stood for a moment, face to face. He wore the same expression he'd been wearing ever since Kathryn had told him about the change of schools: an unblinking blankness, cheeks smooth, lips straight. It was as if he was utterly bored by everything he saw. Everything in this house, everything I said, everything his mother and I did.

'I thought you might want a drink,' I began.

'I'm going out.'

'Oh.' I looked past his shoulder and into his room. It was a shock to realise that I hadn't been in there for months.

'I wanted to talk to you,' I said, brushing by him, still holding the coke.

He shrugged, as teenagers are supposed to, and closed the door behind us.

There was a smell in there, a spicy, sweet smell; it was something like marigolds.

I looked around the room. We'd painted it for him a few years ago; everything had to be blue and plain, he was very clear on that particular rule. No patterns. Plain curtains, plain duvet cover. It made his room look a little like the whole thing was underwater, as if he was sleeping in a sea of blue.

Robert remained standing in the doorway, staring at me. His chin was lifted a little, and I recognised the gesture as his mother's.

I tried not to look at the ring in his ear, but found my eyes fixed on the glinting gold loop. The word *gypsy* came into my mind again. Whenever she saw a woman in the street with gold hoops through her ears, Mum would nudge me and say, 'Where's her crystal ball, then?' and laugh. Mum never wore earrings. Kathryn has a few pairs, small coloured gems that screw on to her lobes; they've always appeared to me to be devices for torture.

I looked away from the earring. In the corner, Robert's old Midland Bank school bag lay in a crumpled heap.

I pointed to the bag. 'Is the strap broken?'

He gave another shrug.

'I could mend it, if you like.'

'But it's not broken.'

I put the coke down and flexed my cold hands. On the table beneath his wall mirror (I'd put that table there, with a chair, for his homework), bottles and tubes were lined up, along with two hairbrushes. I wondered why anyone would need more than one hairbrush.

'So how's the new school?'

'Fine.'

'You always get on well.'

He twisted his gold chain around with one finger.

'We're very proud of you. It's good we made that change. Now you can concentrate on your exams. And your art, of course.' I went over to the window and looked out on the back garden. Condensation had gathered in a little pool on the corner of the sill. I tried to wipe it off, but ended up spreading it across the glossed wood. Outside, the garden was asleep, covered by a dusting of frost. A few browned chrysanthemum leaves were holding on, limp with chill.

'Look at that,' I said. 'Isn't it incredible? Everything's still. But nothing's dead. It'll all come up next year.'

Robert sighed.

'Come and look,' I said.

He came over to the window and looked out in silence.

'Do you remember your garden?' I asked.

'It wasn't a garden.'

'It was a patch of garden. That's much more than some people ever have.'

He traced a line in the water on the windowsill.

'Those sunflowers were good that year,' I said. 'In the end.'

'They were OK.'

'You did a good job.'

He laughed then. 'You did it, Dad.'

'We did it together. It was our patch. Wasn't it?'

As I turned to him, I was slightly surprised, as I always was, that his green eyes were level with mine.

'Where did you get that pullover?'

He was wearing a white sweatshirt with a collar. Embroidered on his chest was the word 'Champion'.

He looked down.

'It's Luke's.'

'It's too small for you.'

'It's not,' he said, plucking at the front of it.

'Doesn't Luke want it back?'

'He's lent it to me.'

'He'll want it back, though.'

'Eventually.'

I stared out of the window at the frozen garden, and there was a long silence.

'You see each other a lot,' I said.

'Yes.'

'His parents don't mind?'

'Why should they?'

'Perhaps you should be studying more. You've got your exams in the summer.'

'We study together.'

I caught the reflection of his face in the window. For an awful moment I thought he looked like Jack, his hair high on his head, his shoulders broad, his chin straight.

'Has he given you anything else, this Luke?'

He laughed again and shook his head. 'What are you trying to say, Dad?'

'I think you should give it back to him.'

'I will. When he asks for it.'

I nodded.

'Dad?'

'Yes?'

'Will you stop staring at my earring?'

'Sorry.' I tried a smile. 'Did it hurt?'

He shook his head.

'No. I suppose the girls like it?'

'What?'

'Earrings. On boys.'

'Maybe.'

On the wall above his bed there was a reproduction of a

painting. It showed a naked woman standing on a shell, hair streaming out on both sides.

'That's a famous one, isn't it?'

'Botticelli.'

'Right.' I tried to think of something I could say about it. 'It's very – unusual.'

'I like it.'

'She's very lovely, isn't she?'

'That's because she's supposed to be Venus.'

'Oh.'

'Goddess of love.' He ran a hand through his thick hair.

'Yes. So what have you been sketching lately?'

He gave me a sideways look.

'I don't suppose you'd show me something?'

'Like what?'

'Anything.'

He shrugged and opened a drawer. It was stuffed full with paper and paints. He pulled out a big hard-backed black book which said 'Rob Hall, 5b' on the front. Then he leant back on the drawers and flicked through the pages.

'Most of it's rubbish…'

As he flicked, I caught a glimpse of a watercolour of hills and sky, a line drawing of a girl with long hair sitting on a stool, a pastel study of the leaves of a rubber plant – all detailed, all precise.

'I didn't know you'd done so much.'

'Here's one,' he said, and he held out a painting of my dahlias. I recognised them immediately: perfect 'Holland Festivals', deep orange petals tipped with white. He'd painted the wall of our house as background. He'd caught them at their peak; they looked like perfect orbs of flame.

'When did you do this?'

'Ages ago.'

'Look at that. It's very good.' I reached out and ran a

finger along the bumpy paint.

He gave a small smile. 'It's OK.'

He closed the book and put it back in the drawer. Then he looked at his watch. 'I've got to go, Dad. I'm meeting Luke.'

'Oh.' I took a breath. 'So is Luke – courting any girl?'

I saw his face flinch, just a tiny fraction of a flinch, but a flinch nevertheless.

After a moment's pause, he sat down heavily on the bed and put his chin in his hands. 'Why do you want to know?'

'I'm interested.'

He was silent.

I gazed out of the window and tried to make my voice sound unconcerned. 'You must know, you're his best friend.'

'Why is it important?' his voice was too loud.

'It isn't – important. I'd just like to know.'

'Is that what you really wanted to talk to me about?'

'Please don't shout.' I sat down on the other side of the bed.

He gathered the edge of the duvet in his fist and stared at it.

'Robert.'

When he finally looked at me his eyes were bright with anger, but I ploughed on.

'I don't mean to interfere. It's just that – '

'Please don't interfere again.' He almost whispered it, twisting the corner of the duvet around his hand like a mangled bandage.

'I'm only saying this because I don't want you to end up – '

'What?' All colour had gone from his face now. Even the few freckles left on his nose were pale, like washed-out stains.

' – unhappy.'

He released the duvet and let out a long breath.

'Don't do it again, Dad.'

'Robert,' I said. 'I just want what's best.'

'What's best,' he repeated.

'What's best for you.'

Then he stood up. 'I'm going out now,' he said, heading for the door. 'Luke hates it when I'm late.'

six

Joanna
November, 1985

On Saturday Simon drives Mum and me to Wootton. 'You should see the palace,' he says. 'We can call it a history lesson.' Big wink. His leather gloves make a swooshing noise as he feeds the steering wheel round.

But when we get there, Mum wants to go round the shops. 'I can't stand all that history,' she says. 'Dead things in cases.' She would never have admitted this a few months ago, when he first moved in with his leather-bound Reader's Digest *Complete History of the World* collection.

Simon opens his mouth, but before he can start, I say, 'We can still go. I like palaces and stuff.'

So he drops Mum off in the High Street, where I know she won't buy anything because it's all too expensive, and we roar off down the palace drive.

The sky's bright blue and the house is surrounded by hills that Simon tells me are man-made, put there especially to show off the building. 'That's the wrong way round,' I point out.

It's so cold my lipstick goes hard and cracked within a minute of getting out of the car.

'Are you going to buy me a souvenir?'

'We haven't even been round the grounds yet,' says

Simon. He's wearing a new checked woolly scarf that Mum bought him. I can tell he doesn't like it because he's tucked it right inside his mac.

'We could skip it. Go straight to the gift shop. You should at least buy me some chocolate, now we're here.'

He flicks his stiffened fringe, gives me a look. Every morning I hear the long squirt of his hairspray. The laundry-fresh stench is still in the bathroom when I go to flannel my face. When he moved in, he promised us a shower. Shiny taps. Blasts of hot on demand. I was looking forward to soaping myself all over in the steam, arse pressed up against the wet glass. But no shower has ever appeared.

'What's your favourite?' he asks. 'For future reference.'

'Bourneville.'

For some reason, he looks pleased. 'The dark one. Good choice.'

We walk on in silence. Sheep shit is everywhere; dry balls and wet clumps of it splattered over the path and the grass. Some of it's shaped like it's been piped on a cake.

'Want to know what mine is?'

'What?'

'Favourite.'

'Let me guess,' I say. 'Yorkie?'

'No. Too big.'

'Turkish Delight?'

'Too soft.'

In the distance, the big lake in front of the house reflects the white clouds and the sand-coloured house.

'This place is like a chocolate box,' I say. 'I like it.'

'I'm glad. But you haven't guessed yet.'

'Bounty.'

He considers. 'The taste of paradise. Nice. But not my favourite.'

I look at him and laugh, and then I step in a rounded knob of sheep shit. 'Look what you made me do.'

'You should stop dreaming about chocolate and watch where you're going.'

I lift my foot and flick the shit at Simon's trouser leg.

'Oi!' He hops to the side.

I let out a yelp and start running towards the lake, but not so fast that he can't chase me.

'What are you doing with that boy?' he asks when he's caught up with me on the bridge. His face is flushed and shiny from running. I can see every pore on his chin. He pushes his specs back up his nose. Then he undoes his mac and rests his thumbs in his belt loops.

'What boy?' I lick the sweat from my upper lip and get the margarine taste of lipstick.

'The one your mum says is backward.'

I lean against the wall of the bridge and puff out into the frozen air. My breath hangs there.

'Joanna?'

'What?'

'Are you going to answer me?'

I turn away from him and look out over the lake. The clouds are going grey and stringy.

'Joanna?'

'Do you think he's backward?'

'I was asking you a question, but since you've asked, I'll tell you. I think he's – different. Damaged, certainly. Remedial, maybe. In need of professional help.'

I turn round. Behind Simon, the big house is glowing, its iron gates twisted, too high to climb over.

'Everyone says that. But I don't think they know what it means.'

He gives a little 'huh', like a TV journalist who thinks the answer's all too obvious. 'You know what it means, Joanna.'

'I don't.'

'It means not all there. Not quite the ticket. Not the full quid. No one's blaming him, but the boy's not right, is he? Wasn't he in some car accident? A bump on the head could have done it. Brain damage. They didn't look into that sort of thing when he was young. Not properly.'

'A bump on the head?' I start to laugh. 'It sounds like a cartoon.'

He shakes his head and sighs. 'To be honest, I think it's a shame,' he says, in a quieter voice.

'What is?'

The sun's going down and his face is partly in shadow.

'What is?' I repeat.

'I think it's a shame that he's like that. I think the whole thing's a shame. It's a shame for you.'

Then he grabs me by the elbow and yanks me over to him. He clamps both his arms around me and holds me so close that I see all the fine lines on his cheeks. 'Poor Joanna,' he whispers. I don't pull away but I hold my back stiff, keep my arms by my sides. 'Have you heard anything from your dad?' he asks.

I pull away from him and walk to the other side of the bridge. If Dad was here, we'd be in the gift shop. If Dad was here, we wouldn't be here at all.

After a while Simon comes over and coughs in a fake way. 'We're supposed to be talking about history. Did you know that guy was just given this house? For winning a battle?'

'Winning a battle's a big thing.'

'Not for his type. His type win battles by leading poorer men to their deaths. Stepping on people's heads to get what they want. They're bullies. Taking advantage of people like you, Joanna.'

'And people like Shane.'

'Isn't Shane the bully?'

I laugh at that, but Simon looks serious. 'You should be careful, Joanna. If your father was here, he'd tell you.'

'What do you know about my dad?'

He stares at me.

'Dad likes Shane, anyway.'

Before I can back away, he's got an arm round my shoulder. The metal of my earring clicks against his watch. 'Anyway,' he whispers. 'Don't worry. I'll look after you. If you'll let me.' His cold fingers are on my neck.

I snort. But I let his fingers work their way up into my hair.

'What will I do if you're not here?'

'Then you'll have to look after yourself.'

'I can look after myself already.'

'Can you?' His breath is on my scalp.

'Mum will be wondering where we are.' I shrug his arm off my shoulder and walk back across the bridge. My legs are shaky, but each step I take is deliberate, and I don't get any shit on my shoes.

seven

Howard
November, 1985

The sky was almost black, and from the way the wind whirled the remains of leaves around on the front lawn – first one way, then the other, each time a little more frantic – I knew there was a storm coming.

I didn't try to stop Robert going out, not that time. We'd had our chat and I told myself I should be willing to give him another chance.

When he'd gone, I found Kathryn standing at the bottom of the stairs, waiting for me.

'What did you say to him?'

I didn't respond.

'He was out of here like a thunderbolt, whatever it was.'

She followed me down the hall. 'What did you say to him, Howard?'

'Nothing.'

'Did you ask him about that new boy?' She blew up into her fringe and waited for my answer.

'Howard?'

'All I wanted was to help him,' I said, picking up my coat.

'Kathryn not with you?' Mum asked as she opened the door. She was still wearing her flowered tabard.

I shook my head and stepped into the familiar smell of cooked meat and furniture polish. 'That'll need doing again soon,' I said, tapping the hallway wallpaper she'd chosen a few years ago. It was brown and stripy, which we'd thought wouldn't go out of fashion. There was a patch of beige where the sun had shone too fiercely through the glass in the front door.

'You're very busy, though, Howard.'

We went into the kitchen and Mum untied her tabard. She hung it on the back of the door and pressed both sides of her hair, as if to straighten her head. 'Shampoo and set tomorrow,' she said. 'I'm afraid I wasn't expecting you.' She cleared some newspapers from a chair. 'It's not often I have my son all to myself.'

'I'll make some tea,' I said.

I reached for the caddy with the Chinese pattern. I'd loved playing with the empty tea caddy as a child, filling it with dominoes or marbles and wondering at their reflection on the shiny gold insides. That tin always seemed so much more precious than its contents.

'Is Kathryn all right?' Mum asked, spreading her hands out flat on the tablecloth.

'Fine. She's fine.'

'Still working – '

'At the library. Yes.'

'Good. That's good, isn't it?'

'She likes it.'

'It's good for her to be busy. Now that Robert's growing up.'

Steam from the kettle dampened my face. A slick of yellow fat lay on the milk I'd poured in both our cups.

We waited for the tea to brew.

'Is there a reason for this visit, Howard?'

'No reason.'

I could tell Mum was studying my face, so I looked away. A small silence grew.

'Tea,' I said.

Mum watched me pour.

'I was looking at some old photos yesterday,' I began.

'Oh yes?'

'Yes. There was one of me sitting on your garden bench. By the forsythia bush. I must have been about nine. It was funny. I hardly recognised myself.'

'You were all frizzy hair and freckles then.'

I put the pot down. Rain had started to batter at the window, big drops of it running down and settling on the sill. The back door gave a rattle in the wind.

I brought our tea over to the table and sat down. 'But I didn't remember looking so, well, *feminine*,' I said.

'Oh, you weren't girly,' Mum said with a wave of her hand. 'It's just you looked a little different. And you were a bit – gentler than the other boys.' She reached for the sugar and dropped a heaped teaspoon into her cup. 'I remember one day you came home with a girl's belt on! Lord knows where you got it.' She blew on her tea and chuckled. 'You can only have been four. Red it was, with a white buckle. You wouldn't give it up for all the tea in China! I had to hide it from you, in the end.' She shook the tin with the woven handle towards me. 'Biscuit?'

I didn't respond. I'd forgotten the details of the belt, but I did remember Mum taking it away. I'd cried to have it back, and she'd told me that people would think I was like a little girl, if I cried over such a silly thing as a belt. And I remembered that she'd held me by the arm, hard, and shaken me, the belt jiggling up and down in her other hand.

She chewed a digestive, then put her cup down. 'Is something wrong, son?'

'Then he is like me.'

'Who is?'

'Robert.'

'How do you mean?'

'He's like me.'

'Of course he is! He's your son all right.'

'He's a sissy, like his dad.'

'What?' Mum looked into my face. 'What are you talking about?'

I fiddled with the handle of my teacup. 'I was feminine.'

She let out a loud hoot. 'But it wasn't anything – anything *serious* – that thing with the girl's belt. Of course not.' She smiled for a moment. 'I knew I didn't have anything to worry about, with you.' She pressed a hand, still warm from her teacup, onto mine. The skin on her knuckles was lumpy and white, as if it had been moulded in plasticine.

Her cuckoo clock chimed five. I realised my hands were aching again.

She stood up and began to rinse her cup in the sink, her thumb squeaking on the side of the china. 'You haven't touched your drink, Howard.'

I flexed my fingers. They were long and thin, hairless, freckled. Despite years of gardening, I'd never let myself have dirty fingernails. I wondered what was wrong with me.

'It's bucketing down,' Mum said, staring out of the window. 'Perhaps you'd better stay. We can have our tea together. Do you want to phone Kathryn?'

When I didn't reply, she came away from the window. 'Howard?' The plastic cushion on the kitchen chair gave out a puff of air as she sat down. She sighed. 'Look,' she said. 'I'll tell you something. After your father died, people thought I might not be able to carry on. But I had you, and in a few years, if I'm honest, I barely missed him.' She caught hold of my chin and looked me in the eye. 'I hardly missed him, Howard, because you were my little man. No one could ever say you aren't man enough. Not in my book.'

She put a hand on my shoulder and rubbed. A sob built in my chest, and I knew that if she embraced me my tears would fall. But she just let her hand rest on my shoulder.

'Robert will be fine. You'll see.'

I watched the rain hammer on the glass of the back door, and I pictured my beds turning to mud.

Later that week, I came home from work to the noise of a drill. The sound of a whirling blade biting into wood or plaster has always set my teeth on edge.

I followed the noise upstairs to Robert's bedroom. I put my briefcase down and tapped Kathryn on the shoulder, but she didn't stop drilling into his doorframe. Her cheeks were warm, her eyes bright with concentration. I was reminded of the look she'd had the day she leant out of our back bedroom window and let the poppy seeds fall to the ground.

I tapped her on the shoulder again. She stopped the drill but didn't look at me. Instead, she stooped down to pick up a bronze bolt lock from the top of my toolbox, which was by her feet.

'You could have just screwed that in,' I said.

She shrugged and rummaged in my toolbox for screws. I thought of how her fingers would smell metallic when she was finished.

'You're early,' she said. 'I wasn't expecting you.'

'What's going on?'

'I would have thought that was obvious,' she said. 'I'm fixing Robert a lock on his door.'

I didn't want to respond irrationally, so I took a few moments to remove my coat and hang it over the stair banister. 'Why didn't you ask me to do that?' I said, loosening my tie.

'Because you would have said no.' She held a screw against the hole in the bolt and squinted.

'That won't do it,' I said. 'And you know there's no need for him to have a lock.' Getting angry, I told myself, would not help this situation. It would not help this situation at all. 'When did he ask for a lock?'

Kathryn turned the screw. 'It was my idea.'

'What?'

'He needs some privacy.'

'He's fifteen!'

'Exactly.' She wiggled the bolt over in its carriage. 'It's a bit stiff. Is there anything I can do about that?'

I stared at her and she raised her eyebrows back at me. 'Well?'

'Where is he, anyway?' I demanded.

'He's gone to see about a job on the farm. Plucking turkeys. Christmas money. I said he could.'

'With Luke?'

'All the boys do it, Howard.'

I flexed my hands in my pockets and breathed out. And in again.

I took the screwdriver from her. 'Let me do that,' I said. I leant into it with all my weight and twisted the screw tight to.

Kathryn watched me in silence.

'I'll just test it.' I stepped into his room, giving Kathryn a gentle push out into the hallway, and closed the door on her.

I slid the bolt over into its hole and stared at it. Kathryn had chipped the paint on the doorframe but hadn't done a bad job, overall.

'Is it working OK?' I heard her call through the door.

I didn't answer. I rested my forehead on the cool wood of his door. With one hand I gripped the bolt and pulled it out of its home, then pushed it back.

'Is it sticking?'

I was aware of the marigold smell of his room again. The blank blueness of the walls and bedclothes. The brightly coloured bottles and tubes containing God knows what. The jewellery box for his earring on his chest of drawers.

'Howard? Are you coming out?' Kathryn rattled the door handle.

'In a minute.'

Was he with Luke right now?

'Howard?'

Champion emblazoned across his chest.

'What are you doing in there?'

Sweater too tight.

'Are you coming out?'

She had given them her blessing.

'I've got to go to work,' Kathryn called. It was Thursday. Late opening at the library. 'I've got to go, Howard.'

'Yes.'

'Are you all right?'

'Yes.'

She waited for a moment, then said, 'I'll see you later, then. There's a casserole in the oven. It should be ready about seven. Save me some.'

I listened to her footsteps on the stairs, and, after a minute, the front door slammed.

Where would I find a trace of him? I wondered. In the

drawers of the table we'd bought from MFI for his homework? Underneath his denim-like valance sheet? In the wardrobe I'd once pasted with cut-out pictures of Sooty and Sweep? Then I noticed that, on his bedside table, he still had the model *Somua* tank I'd bought for him at the museum, years ago. I picked it up. Its wheels and gun were furred with dust. I weighed it in my hand, studying the blank face of the soldier sitting in the armoured turret. I decided to take it with me. I would have to keep it safe for him.

I unbolted the door.

eight

Joanna
November, 1985

Simon strides ahead, binoculars swinging from his shoulder. He's wearing his new Barbour jacket. The tartan inside flashes at me as he walks. I let him go on, so I can swagger by Shane's house slowly enough to see if he's at the window.

There's a twitch in his curtains as I pass. I let out a damp breath, flick my newly Elnetted hair, walk on with a slow swing, hoping he'll follow.

Simon waits at the lane by the church. His watch slides up his wrist as he reaches for me. I stop far away enough for him not to be able to touch. 'Come on, then,' he says, 'if you're coming.'

He's suggested we have an outside tutorial, despite the freezing damp. We can look for birds down at the pools, he says; the fresh air will do us good. But I know he wants to escape Sunday afternoon in our house. Who wouldn't want to avoid Mum in her pink weekend jogging outfit (which has never been outdoors), the *Antiques Roadshow* and the Sunday supplements?

Down the pools, a line of wetness forms around my white slip-ons. Cold moisture oozes up from the ground, catching the bare twigs, making them sag.

A dog-walker stands and waits, looking off towards the cooling towers as if nothing's happening while his pooch bends its hind legs and lets its behind tremble.

'Here's the look-out,' says Simon, pointing at a wooden building that looks like a shed with a slit around it. Inside, the walls are covered with information sheets, telling you what kinds of birds you can expect. Each sheet has the power station's logo in the corner.

I've seen the twitchers down here before. They have all the gear. Huge binoculars, and cameras with lenses like the fashion magazine photographers have, for snapping models. Zoom in, focus, snap. They sit there watching, waiting for their birds, lenses pointing. Primed and ready.

'What are we doing here?' I ask.

'Observing the wonders of nature.'

I sit on the bench and look through the slit at the greyness outside.

'And you can tell me what you're doing in history, while we're at it,' Simon adds.

Everything's going dark. The water looks like Simon's mac: thick and heavy. The branches hang over it like they can't wait to fall in.

'We're doing cholera.'

Simon raises an eyebrow. 'Tell me about cholera, then.'

'You get it from dirty water. You vomit, and you shit yourself at the same time. Then you die.'

'I see. And what's this got to do with history?'

'I was hoping you could tell me.'

He looks blank. 'Perhaps we'll come back to it,' he says. Then he thrusts *The Pocket Guide to Birdwatching* into my lap. Green cover. Pencil drawings. 'We'll do some ornithology instead.' He taps the side of his glasses and looks pleased with himself. 'Have a peek in there. You'll be amazed at the variety.'

I keep looking for Shane through the slit in the wall. But all I see is grey branches and white steam from the cooling towers.

'I'll test you,' I say, opening the bird-watching book.

'Go on, then.' He sits down on the bench and nudges me with a waxed elbow. 'Do your worst.'

Keeping my thumb over the name, I show him a picture of a bird and read out the description. 'Active, inquisitive and quarrelsome. Distinctive "tsink-tsink" call.'

Simon wraps his mac tightly around him and shivers as he thinks. 'It's a tit,' he says. 'I know that much.'

I don't say anything. He pinches his thin lower lip and closes his eyes. 'A yellow tit. No, wait. A coal tit.' He beams. 'It's a coal tit.'

'Wrong.' I remove my thumb from the name. 'Great tit.'

Simon shuffles up to me so he can see the book over my shoulder. 'Close enough,' he says, his breath damp on my neck.

I close the book and shift along the bench, away from him. After a moment, he goes back to his binoculars, twiddling with knobs and dials. Squinting. Dad used to do the same sort of thing with his record player.

I click my Walkman on.

Just as the chorus of 'Into the Groove' is about to start, I see something move in the trees, so I turn the tape off. 'Let's borrow those a minute.'

'I thought you weren't interested in bird-watching.'

'I changed my mind.'

Simon flicks his fringe and hands over the binoculars. They're greasy from his hands. I wipe them on my jacket before bringing them up to my eyes. Peering through them, everything goes tiny. Tiny pool, tiny trees, tiny twigs. I look out at a shrunken world.

'You're looking through them the wrong way,' says

Simon. He grabs the binoculars and turns them round. I get a big whiff of his expensive-cheap aftershave.

'Silly girl,' he says, holding out the binoculars to me. 'For all that front, I think you're a bit silly.' His smile lengthens. 'In a rather charming way.'

I let him pinch my knee with a cold hand.

'Do you think Mum's silly, too?'

He lets go of my knee, snatches back the binoculars. 'Even sillier than you,' he says.

Then I hear something weird. Something like *ah-ah-ah*.

I wonder if he saw me from his window, walking down the road with Simon. I wonder if he noticed I'm wearing the pink pencil skirt, even though it's freezing bloody cold. I wonder if he noticed I walked behind Simon, so I didn't have to look at his face, so he couldn't look at me. I wonder if he followed us, his long legs carefully stepping in the places my slip-ons had been, ducking behind walls and hedges in case I looked back (although I never did).

'I'm going for a walk.'

Simon lets out a breathy *ha*. 'I don't think you should go anywhere. It'll be dark soon.'

I touch him then. I let my fingers fall over his hand, and it's smoother than I expect. 'I won't be long.'

He lowers his binoculars, blinks at my hand on his wrist. 'OK. But I'll be watching you, silly girl.'

I pick my way through tangled brambles and spiky holly leaves. Mud gathers around my shoes as I stand on the edge of the pool, looking out over the water. I toss my hair back and open my eyes wide. I hang on to a branch and lean over the water, looking for him. He might be hiding behind a trunk, or crouching behind some brambles. He might be watching me, like he did that day on Shotton Hill.

My hand, in its white fingerless glove, starts to freeze on the branch.

Then I hear that sound again. A high-pitched *ah-ah-ah*. I look all around for a flash of his green parka. Nothing. Smoke from the power station chimneys looks like snow clouds above me.

Perhaps it's a bird.

But it gets louder, and seems human.

I let go of the branch. I have to grab a bramble to stop myself sliding down the bank and into the pool. Tiny thorns stick through my fingerless glove and into my skin. And then I remember coming here years before, slipping on the mud, grabbing a bramble to steady myself and tearing my palm on the thorns. A line of blood, edged by a flap of limp skin, pumped to the surface. Dad was already in the pool. I stepped forward into the water, and as I went deeper, the slime squeezed up between my toes. I went down. The cold water lapped underneath me – that was a shock, but a good one, I remember. The water licked me right along the place where I pee. I forgot the pain of my torn hand as the pool took me in. When Dad swam over and lifted me I felt like he could balance me on one outstretched palm.

If he was here, he'd tell me to look after myself. To take care. But those aren't things you can do by yourself. You need someone else to do those things.

Ah-ah-ah.

Then I see someone.

Ah-ah-ah.

But it's not Shane. It's Rob.

I look again. There's another boy. Their jackets move together on the other side of the pool. Rob's going *ah-ah-ah*. Half singing, half sighing. I pick my way through a tangle of twigs and holly leaves so I can get a closer look.

Then I crouch down and watch, still as a twitcher. I watch. I wait.

Rob is leaning on a trunk right by the water's edge, and Luke is standing in front of him, very close. They're staring into each other's faces as if they're going to fight. They're focused, wide-eyed, squaring up to one another, chests puffed out, feet planted on the floor.

I think Rob must be about to make his move, because he twitches his arm. But he moves it so slowly towards Luke I know he's not going to make any impact. Not at that speed. Then Rob stretches out his hand and slips all his fingers into the front pocket of Luke's jeans. He slips them in, easy, like I slipped into the pool when I'd torn my palm. Luke doesn't flinch. He leans back against the trunk, as if he's relieved, and I see them kiss.

When we get back, Mum says, 'That boy came round for you.'

He's never done that before.

'He stood on the step and just gawped at me. There's no light on in there, is there? No one's home.'

'Who's this?' asks Simon, shaking out his Barbour jacket with a clacking noise. Mum raises her voice. 'That boy. The backward one. You know.'

'Oh,' says Simon, with a look at me. 'Him.'

'I told him you were out with your boyfriend,' Mum says. She lets out a tinkly laugh and flings her arms around Simon's waist, beaming up at his glasses. She's probably inspecting her reflection in them. Her perm's dropped out now, but she's wearing a new shoulder-padded cardigan and full eye make-up. Simon clamps her round the middle and she gives a squeal. 'Ripe for the plucking,' he says, winking at me.

nine

Howard
November, 1985

I hadn't been in the library for years, but nothing had changed. The heavy door still kept the outside world out, and sealed the silence in. The boiled wool doormat was a little thinner than before, the returns counter a little more scuffed, but the thick lettering of the signs, 'Issues', 'Reference', 'Quiet please', remained.

When I walked in, I was met by a blast of warm air from the overhead heater, and I remembered sweating beneath such a blast when I'd asked Kathryn on our first night out. That she'd said yes had felt like a miracle back then.

There was the familiar smell of sweaty hands on old books, of unwashed men with beards and overcoats, dozing by the radiators beneath the windows. I didn't see the man with the carrier bags, which surprised me.

And she was there, of course, my wife, Kathryn, behind the counter, on the phone. She didn't see me come in, so I stood and watched her for a while. I wouldn't say that I hid behind the shelf, but I was sure that she couldn't see me where I stood, holding a book on *Tractors and Other Farm Vehicles* before me. I took a good look at her. She was wearing a green polo neck jumper, I hadn't noticed that during the afternoon, and her hair, slightly grey in her fringe but otherwise still a good colour, looked odd because one side was tucked into the woollen roll around her neck. I wanted to go and straighten it for her, but I remained standing with the book open in front of me. She leant on the counter and laughed at something one of the borrowers said, and I watched the wave of hair that was tucked into her jumper bend back and forth as she moved.

I reflected that I hadn't seen her behind the library counter for about fifteen years, and that now I had secret knowledge of her. Now I could watch her and know that she was wearing a slip with a rose pattern in black lace. Now I knew that it was thin and worn at her side, and that one strap was frayed on her shoulder. No one else in the library had that information. Secret information.

As I approached the counter, I found myself smiling. I kept one hand in my pocket, and I ran a finger over the gun of the model *Somua* tank that I'd taken from Robert's bedroom.

'Howard, what are you doing here?'

I kept smiling, feeling my teeth going dry in the hot air of the library.

'Are you all right?' asked Kathryn. 'I was a bit worried about you when I left.'

'Kathryn,' I said. 'I'm going to take that lock off Robert's door.'

Kathryn glanced around the library. 'Can we talk about this later on?'

Behind her, one of the librarians had stopped filling in whatever form she was apparently concentrating on.

Kathryn leant over the counter and touched my sleeve. 'Why don't we talk about this later?'

I was still smiling. 'He's my son and I'm going to remove that lock. I just came to tell you that. There's nothing to discuss.'

Kathryn let go of my sleeve. 'If you do that, I'll replace it.'

'I won't have locks on doors in my house.'

A woman with a little girl in a bobble hat on her hip slapped a pile of picture books on the counter. 'I'll take these, please,' she said, stepping close to my side. 'When you're ready.'

Kathryn opened the top book and picked up her stamp.

'It's coming off,' I said. 'There's no discussion.'

The little girl in the bobble hat looked at me and laughed.

Kathryn thumped her stamp onto the white page. 'Due back on the thirtieth,' she said to the woman, sliding the books back over the counter. The woman put them in the bottom of her pram; her little girl waved at me as they walked away.

'Children should not be allowed to have locks on doors.' In my coat pocket, I grasped the long point of the tank's gun.

'I think you should go now.' Kathryn's voice was steady but low.

'It shouldn't be allowed. I didn't have a lock.'

Kathryn slammed the stamp down on the counter. 'Sometimes I wish I had a lock,' she said, sticking out her chin, 'I wish I had a lock. Did you know that, Howard?'

The librarian behind her pretended to sift through a pile of forms, but her head was cocked in our direction.

'Did I ever tell you that? Did I ever tell you that, when we were first married, it drove me absolutely – ' she paused and bit her lip, 'spare, it drove me absolutely spare, the way you watched me all the time, the way I couldn't move without you flinching, without you asking if I was all right, if I needed anything, asking what was I doing, asking where was I going. All the time, asking questions, checking up on me, all the bloody time! It was a relief when Robert was born because at least then you had someone else to keep your beady eye on.'

We stood for a moment, staring at each other. The librarian behind Kathryn had stopped shuffling her papers and was perfectly still.

I let go of the tank's gun and buttoned up my coat. The last hole was so stiff that my fingers slipped as I tried to grip the button and force it through. 'I'm taking the lock off Robert's door. As I said, there's no discussion.'

Kathryn blew up into her fringe. 'Each time you take that lock off, I will replace it.'

'There's no discussion, Kathryn.' I turned to go.

'Howard?'

I looked back.

She gave a little laugh. 'Everyone calls him Rob now.'

ten

Joanna
November, 1985

Shane isn't in his shed, so I ring the front door bell. 'God Save the Queen' plays three times before Mrs Pearce emerges.

'Joanna! I haven't seen you for such a long time.' Her face looks baggy from sleep. The theme music to *That's Life* blares from the living room.

She touches the sleeve of my new black wool coat. Boxy shoulders, square front pockets, stand-up collar. Simon gave me the money for it, folding a fifty, still warm from his wallet, into my palm. He keeps his wallet in the breast pocket of his rainmac. The black leather's so new it creaks when I open it. Inside, there's a photo of a woman – not my mum, not me. A neat blonde bob and flat red lipstick. It must be his ex-wife, the one Mum told me chucked him out because they couldn't have children. I've thought about taking that photo, hiding it in my knicker drawer. Just to see what happens.

'Come in and have a cup of tea, Joanna, love.'

'Is Shane in?'

She cranes her neck around the doorframe, as if she can spot him from there. 'He's in the shed, where he always is. Isn't he?'

'No.'

Her mouth makes a round 'O' shape and she blinks a few times and yawns. Then she grabs at my sleeve again and holds on. 'Come in and have a cup of tea.'

'I can't.'

'There's cake. *The Thorn Birds* is on in a minute.'

'But I have to find him.'

My voice must sound urgent, because she nods and lets go of my arm. 'All right, love.' She thinks for a minute. Then she says, 'Oh. I know where he might be. He's got a new job.'

'Where?'

'Down the farm. Plucking turkeys for Christmas.'

As I open the gate, I hear her call out behind me, 'Have you heard from your Dad?' But I know she knows the answer.

The farm is on the other side of Calcot. There's a short cut from the church lane, past the pools and across the fields. Shane won't worry about walking back this way, even though it's really dark now. So dark he won't know where the fields stop and the sky starts. Or where the gap between the bushes down to the water is.

There's still a light on down the lane. I run my hand along the icy graveyard wall. My fingers are stiff with cold. The wind's getting stronger. It blows strands of hair across my face, into my mouth. I hook them out and look into the blackness ahead.

That sign will be above me now. Possible Entrapment.

I step off the path and head through the twiggy trees to the look-out where I was with Simon earlier. I can wait for Shane to walk by there.

The place is totally different in the dark. I have to feel

along the wall for the entrance, and I snag my fingerless glove on a splinter. There's a smell of piss that I didn't notice this afternoon.

The bench shoots cold into my arse cheeks. I sit up very straight. My hands are rammed into my pockets. I listen to every sound. Bare branches click against the wooden roof in the wind. Something plops in the water. There's a long, low creaking noise somewhere that could be a tree.

I think about Rob and Luke. I wonder if they came in here, after we'd gone. I wonder if they lay on the cold bench together. Half singing, half sighing. Kissing. Their hands in each others' pockets.

I wonder if Rob would do that with me.

Then I hear his beat.

I sit. Shiver. Wait.

It gets louder.

I step out of the look-out and push through the branches. I'm right in his path. He doesn't flinch or shout out, even though there's no way he could have known I was there. He just turns off the Walkman, licks his big lips and blinks, like his mum.

'It's me,' I say.

My heart's banging. My hands don't feel cold any more.

He sniffs and looks over my shoulder at the darkness that's the pool behind us. The wind blows the hood of his parka up against his neck. I imagine it getting caught on the patches of stubbly-soft hairs there.

'I came for you,' he says.

'I know.' I hook the hair out of my eyes and smile at him. 'I came to find you.'

He starts laughing then. Not his half-hidden laugh. A loud laugh that sounds like a honking goose. He doubles over with it.

'What's funny?' I ask.

'We're always – '

But he's laughing again.

'What?'

'Looking. Looking for each other,' he says. He honks out some more laughter.

I step closer to him. My hair blows into his face but he doesn't brush it away.

Then I slip my hand in the pocket of his trousers. It's not easy to do, not like it looked for Rob and Luke. I have to step in really close so my nose touches his shoulder and twist my wrist round at the right angle. There's not much room in there.

He stops laughing and swallows. 'I've got a job,' he says. 'Turkey plucking.'

'That's good,' I say, digging around in his warm pocket, breathing into the shiny parka material, until I feel what I'm after. 'That's good, Shane.'

He goes very quiet. His dark eyes look like glass. The fur of his parka hood brushes against my cheek. I stretch my fingers out in his pocket, circling them round and round on his thigh. With my other hand, I shove my fingers beneath his belt until I find the zip. I open his fly. I don't look at his eyes. I look instead at the fur in close-up. Strands of it go wet with my breath, get stuck on my lip. I stroke him, and it feels softer than I expected, but also drier.

Shane stands there and lets me do what I want in the darkness.

I want my fingers caught in his little hairs. My hand rising up and down. I want his hand over my head. His hand over my whole head.

Every night after that, we meet in the look-out, and I open

Shane's fly and dig until I find what I want.

On Shane's hands there's turkey blood from his job at the farm. One night he brings a bird's foot with him. 'Listen,' he says, pulling the tendons back and forth. The claw stretches towards me.

'I can't hear anything.'

'Listen.'

He pulls again and the bones inside the turkey's skin shift and groan. The sound reminds me of the creak of Rob's not-real leather jacket.

'Are they dead?' I ask, 'when you pluck them?'

''Course.'

'Are they whole?'

'Headless,' he says. Then he adds, 'And bleeding.'

I imagine rows of them hanging up, their necks sputtering gore, their feet creaking.

'They're completely dead, though,' I say. 'They're not twitching, or anything.'

'They're still warm,' he says, leading my hand to his pocket.

Sometimes, he brings me back a handful of the prettiest feathers, speckled with brown and yellow, like tiger fur. Not gaudy, though. Fine. On the way home from the pools, I stick them behind my ears, through my buttonholes, in my hair. And at night, in bed, I run them over my belly, my tits, letting the lightness linger on each nipple, and I think of Shane's hands.

eleven

Howard
December, 1985

I came home from work on Friday night and found Kathryn sitting on Robert's bed, talking to him and Luke. The two boys were propped up on pillows, leaning against the headboard, and my wife was curled at the end of the bed, one foot dangling over the side.

'Before I was married, I might have done,' she said, laughing.

Kathryn was the last to see me standing in the doorway. Robert nudged his mother's knee with his foot, and she twisted round. 'Oh,' she said. 'Howard. You're home.'

I loosened my tie. 'Yes. I'm home.'

The three of them watched me in silence as I pulled the tie from around my neck and let the fabric snake over my wrist before wrapping it into a tight ball. Then I turned and walked downstairs.

After tea, I asked her, 'What do you talk to them about?'

'I don't know,' she said, not putting her book down. Then she added, 'Sometimes we talk about how things were when I was their age.'

Kathryn at fifteen. I remembered it well. I remembered once walking past her house and seeing her sitting on her front lawn. Her father was trimming their hedge. She had a big blue flower pattern on her dress. I remembered her knees: how rounded and soft-looking they were, and how they fitted perfectly together – the full bone of one snug in the hollow of the other – as she sat with her legs tucked around the swirl of her skirt. I thought she was admiring her father's skill, but the roar of a motorbike behind made me realise why she was sitting there. Who she was waiting for.

The next morning, after Kathryn had gone to the library, I left the house and got in the car to drive to the new supermarket. I had to scrape the windscreen and wipe the side window to see out. My hedges were bare, but I'd managed to keep the grass out front looking fairly healthy. The garden would survive a hard frost, I thought.

I was halfway down the road when I saw Luke cycle past, hat perched on the back of his head, white scarf hanging loose.

I pulled in and watched him in my rear-view mirror. He cycled up our path and didn't bother dismounting his bike to ring the doorbell. Robert answered, grinned, ducked back inside, and then came out of the side passage, pushing his bike.

I balled my fingers inside my jumper, thinking it would be warmer there.

Luke's bike wasn't, I noticed, quite as good as Robert's. We'd bought Robert's just a year ago – at the time he'd wanted the same model as Paul, but I'd got him a better one, a Raleigh Dynamite. No Minnie Mouse bell this time, either. It had metallic paint that reflected all colours in the sun. The spokes ticked cleanly as he wheeled it down the path.

They pedalled slowly together, rising up and dipping

back down to their saddles. I heard a hoot of laughter. Robert wore a new black woollen jacket which looked like the ones the men in the turbine hall had, except his didn't have C.P.S. stamped on the back in chalky white letters.

I started the engine.

When they'd turned the corner of the road, I gave them a few minutes, then I followed, keeping well back.

Coming into the High Street, I saw their bikes propped up against the window of Burgrey Stores. I was careful to pull in a fair distance down the street. I watched the door of the shop. A man with a dog and a paper rushed out; a woman walked in, shaking her open purse and frowning; and a few minutes later, the two boys emerged together. A girl with long blonde hair followed them. I recognised her as the shop's Saturday girl.

I hadn't planned to be doing this, I reminded myself.

Then something unexpected happened. Before the boys cycled off, the girl held Robert by the elbow for a long moment and looked into his face. Robert smiled at her, and Luke looked the other way.

I sat for a while, watching the two boys pedal down the road, wondering about what had just happened. The girl stood on the pavement and watched them until they turned the corner. I thought she might shout out after them, but she didn't, she just stood there, gazing after my son. Then she swung back into the shop, her hair sweeping behind her.

That afternoon, I visited Burgrey Stores.

I hadn't been using the shop as often as I once did. The supermarket now met all our weekly shopping needs, and I liked strolling along the wide bright aisles, considering which brands offered the best value, surprising myself with the occasional impulse buy.

Burgrey Stores consisted of two narrow aisles, a chiller cabinet and a magazine rack. Packets of hair grips, combs and tights hung in the window. The shelves were heavy with dusty tins – peaches, pies, peas. Magazines and newspapers were piled on the floor as well as on the rack. The sound of a televised football match floated in from the back room.

The girl was leaning on the counter, reading a magazine. The sleeves of her jumper were pushed up past her elbows. The skin on her arms was blotchy; the pattern of vein and skin made me think of pith on an orange. Both her elbows were smeared with a patch of ink. As her arms moved over the pile of newspapers on the counter, I wondered how she managed to scrub off all that ink every evening. Did it turn the sink grey as she stood in the bathroom, up to her elbows in soapy water? Perhaps she didn't bother washing at all, but just let the ink rub off on her sheets as she turned in her sleep.

I asked her for a packet of cigarettes, pointing to a gold box. It was all I could think of. I've never smoked, and I've always hated to see women's mouths, particularly, pulling on the tips of those things, sucking them dry.

I could see why a boy would choose her as a girlfriend. She had lots of shiny blonde hair that fell like a scarf around her shoulders, smooth cheeks, a pink little mouth, ready to open, and eyelashes painted with blue. Her curves were a bit like Kathryn's used to be, only more so.

'Is that it?' Her earrings winked at me as she spoke.

'And a box of matches. Please.'

She turned and reached for the matches. Her skirt lifted a little and she seemed to pause for a moment. I looked away.

Her bangles clattered as she slammed the matches on the counter. 'One ninety.' She held out her hand and looked directly at me, and I was struck by how grown-up she seemed. She was like a woman in a painting, standing there in relief against all those multi-coloured cigarette packets, a patchwork of government health warnings and gold seals behind her.

I cleared my throat. 'You know my son, I think.'

'Yeah?'

'Robert. Robert Hall.' I tried to smile.

She didn't smile back. Her mouth was open, rimmed with lipstick, waiting. 'Anything else?'

What had I come here for? Whatever plan I had, it seemed ridiculous now.

'No. Thanks.' I put the money in her palm and turned to leave.

'Rob's nice.'

I stopped.

'Rob's a really nice boy,' she said.

I turned round. She gave me a quick smile, and as she did so, the lipstick on her bottom lip cracked.

'Yes,' I said. 'He is.'

She tossed her bright hair over one shoulder. 'Don't think he likes me much, though.'

I approached the counter again. 'What makes you say that?'

She laughed. Then she half-closed her eyes and said, in a drawn-out voice, 'I cannot imagine.'

'What does that mean?'

'You know,' she said, and shrugged.

'I don't think I do.'

She looked up at me with big eyes. She didn't blink as she curled her lips into a long, slow smile. Her pink jumper was tight on her shoulders and her chest as she leant over the counter, her bare elbows smudging the newsprint beneath. 'You know,' she said again.

twelve

Joanna
December, 1985

It's Saturday and I wake up with a nose full of snot. I lie in bed, blinking at the light. My eyes feel like they're sweating.

The phone goes. I think about leaving it but know Mum and Simon won't get up. He makes her breakfast in bed on Saturdays. I usually hear him imitating the noise of a coffee machine, like on that advert. Then she moans that he gets muesli in the sheets.

RING. RING. RING. RING. The phone keeps going and my head feels like it might roll off my body, it's so heavy when I get up.

'Joanna?'

Dad. He's in a phone box. His money's clanking.

Then I think. He's probably called every Saturday. Probably he's called every Saturday and I haven't known because I've been at the shop. Probably he's called every Saturday and no one bothered to tell me.

'Joanna?'

Or perhaps this is the first time he's called. He could have called me at Buggery's. He could have found out the number.

'Is that you, love?'

I could refuse to speak. I could slam the receiver down like Joan Collins in *Dynasty*.

'You've a right to be angry. I'm sorry I haven't called before. I've been working nights. It's been a bit – difficult.'

My just-woken-up breath stinks in the receiver.

'Are you all right?'

I sniff.

'Have you got a cold?'

I sniff again.

'Listen,' he says. Lowers his voice. 'Why don't you come and see me? Would you? I'd really like it if you would.'

'Where are you?'

'Darvington. Didn't your mum tell you? You can get the bus.'

'Can't you come and pick me up?'

'Your mother's got the car, Joanna.'

'I've got a cold.'

'Please come,' the pips start to go. 'It's Two Saxton Close.'

The line dies.

I don't bother calling Buggery to tell him I won't be in.

I wear the coat Simon bought me. I want Dad to ask me about it, but I'm not sure what I'll say when he does.

The sky's blue and the freezing air makes my eyes feel less burny. The pavements shimmer with frost, like shop displays at Christmas.

The heater on the bus blasts my ankles but nothing else feels hot. Everyone who gets on comments on the weather, claps their hands together and breathes into them, stamps their feet, then sits there steaming. By the time we're halfway to Darvington, the bus smells like wet dog. I get my compact out to re-dust my nose. The powder's started to crack around my crusty nostrils. My lips are tight. If I stretch the lower one the wrong way it'll split and bleed. I do it, taste blood, then slick lipstick over the top.

Dad's flat is on an estate just like ours. There's a pushchair, an old TV, a pile of wet newspapers and a black bin liner full of empties in the hallway. I climb the concrete stairs and stop outside the door. His number two sticker is peeling off around the edges.

Before I can knock, Dad's opened up. 'I thought I heard your shoes,' he says.

He looks neat. Blond hair brushed to the side. Clean-shaven. *Blue Stratos*. I bought him that last Christmas. He's never worn it before.

He holds the door open and I walk in.

'I wanted to get the place straight, before you came. That's another reason I didn't phone before. Not that it matters now.'

And it is neat, just like him. But it's like he's piled all his stuff around the sides of the room. Everything's arranged around a small rug in the centre of the floor. Record player. Stacks of albums. A couple of dumb-bells (new). A pile of paperbacks. Two chairs that look like they belong in a pub. A portable TV in the corner.

'Well,' he says, looking round. 'It's coming on. Tea?' And he disappears into the kitchen.

I hear the tap choking, the water gushing out, Dad saying 'shit'.

There's a photo of me, aged about six, in a frilly frame on top of the portable TV. I'm wearing a green zip-up cardigan and wellies, and I'm grinning. Dad bought me the wellies. Mum asked him why he bothered. 'It's not like we go anywhere there's mud,' she said. 'Sensible people stick to the pavement.' But I loved jumping in puddles, splashing dirt up my cream tights. I'd pick it off later, leaving balls of fluffy mud on my bedroom carpet.

'You can take your coat off.' Dad turns in a circle on the rug, looking for somewhere to put the mugs down.

It's too cold in here to take anything off, but I unbutton. Dad watches me. 'That's new,' he says. 'It's nice.'

'Simon bought it.'

Dad nods quickly then looks away. He gestures towards a chair, spills a bit of tea, rubs it into the rug with his toe.

I throw the coat into a corner.

We sit on the pub-like chairs. Dad hands me my tea and puts his down on the floor. Then he presses his palm to my forehead. 'You're hot,' he says. 'I'll get some aspirin.' He's up and out into the kitchen again. I hear him rummaging in drawers, opening cupboards. 'There's some here somewhere,' he calls. 'Just a matter of finding the buggers.'

After a minute, Dad comes back. 'Can't find them. Sorry.' He shows me his empty palms. 'Useless.'

I smile and my lip splits again.

Dad stands there for a bit longer, empty hands hanging at his sides. 'Sorry,' he says.

I sniff and swallow.

'I have got tissues.' And he's off. Cupboards and drawers opening, doors banging.

He hands me a battered box. 'Mansize,' he announces.

I take one and blow.

He puts a palm on my forehead again. This time he presses so hard that my head touches the wall behind.

'Do you want to lie down?'

'No.'

Dad nods at my coat on the floor. 'It's nice, that. Must have set him back a bit.'

There's a silence while Dad chews his bottom lip and twists his watch round on his wrist. He's lost weight.

'Do you get on, then? With him?'

'He's a dickhead.'

Dad looks surprised for a second. Then he slaps the top of the portable, throws his head back and laughs. We both laugh. I laugh until I start to cough. I taste the blood from my lip. Then we laugh some more.

Afterwards, Dad says, 'Shall we go out? Do you think you'll be OK? I was thinking we could go out. Pub lunch. A treat. Would you like to? We could, if you want.'

When I stand up he stops gabbling and stares. Then he covers his mouth with one hand and screws up his eyes and looks like he might burst. He puts his free arm round my shoulder. Brings me in close. His chest heaves. I smell him beneath the *Blue Stratos*. A smell like fresh mud. A Dad smell.

Phlegm rattles in my throat. Dad puts both arms round me.

'Lemonade? Good for colds. Best thing. Vitamin C.'

'Coke,' I say. 'No ice.'

It's warm in the pub. Even with my blocked nose, I can smell the fug. Unwashed carpets, spilled beer, fag ends, old chip fat. I like it.

While Dad's at the bar, I go to the loo. The doors are thick with paint. There's grime around every handle. The window's open and it's freezing. Artificial flowers, grey with dust, shiver in the breeze.

I sit on the bog and the seat's so cold it burns my bum. There's no lock. I get a bit of pee on one hand because I have to keep the other on the door in case anyone comes in.

When I'm done, I stand at the sink and look in the mirror. Someone's scraped 'I LOVE COCK' into the paint beneath. Only too much paint has chipped off and it looks more like 'I LOVE COOK.'

My face is as yellow as my hair. My nose is as red as my *Scarlet Fever* lipstick.

I take the end of my lipstick brush and scrape Shane's name into the paint, underlining it, twice.

Then I fish my can of Elnett out of my bag, spray, and go back to the bar.

Dad's sitting at a corner table, fingering a wilted menu.

'Hi,' he says, as if we didn't arrive together and it's the first time he's seen me today.

'Hi.'

'They do everything in here. Burgers. Sausage. Steak Pie. Chicken Kiev. Scampi.'

'I'm not very hungry.'

'Feed a cold, starve a fever. You should eat something.'

'Maybe I've got a fever.'

A woman with crystal drop earrings and a red mouth puckered like an x is staring at us from the bar. She twiddles an empty glass round in one hand. The slice of lemon inside flops from one side to the other.

Dad sees me looking at her. 'She's a friend,' he says, nodding in her direction. And that's enough to make her walk over, her x mouth unpuckering into a smile.

'Is this your girl, Dan?'

'This is my Joanna.'

The woman studies me. She waves her empty glass towards Dad. 'It's about time love, isn't it?' she says, putting a hand on Dad's shoulder. 'She's a lovely looking girl, Dan.'

'She is.'

She bends towards me and the crystal drops swing forward to her chin. 'Look after your dad, Joanna. He deserves it.' I smell gin.

After she's gone, Dad downs half his pint. 'Joan,' he

says, shaking his head and smiling. 'She means well.' He glances at the bar and she raises her glass to him. 'Looks out for me.'

'Do you know everyone in here?'

'I've come in quite a bit. It was lonely. You know. At first.' He looks into his pint. 'Anyway. You're here now.' He pats my knee.

'I'll have a burger,' I say. 'No onion.'

He goes to the bar, gets another pint.

We sit looking at the door, as if we're waiting for someone else to appear.

'How's your mother?' Dad asks.

'She's fine. The usual.'

Dad nods. 'I don't hear from her.' He sups his pint. Pauses. 'And school. How's school?'

'Usual.'

'Shane?'

I don't say anything for a while. I study the swing doors, imagining him pushing his way in.

'Joanna?'

'He's – usual.'

'Do you see him much?'

'More than usual.' A hotness pulses in my face. I look down at the menu. 'Have they got ice cream?'

'You're looking after each other?'

'Yes.'

Dad puts his elbows on the table and breathes out through his nose. The sleeve of his jumper dips in a puddle of beer. 'He needs looking after, you know. It's not his fault. Any of it.'

My eyes feel hot again. 'What isn't?'

'Being – like he is. It's not his fault.'

I run a finger down the condensation on my glass, tracing the bump near the lip. I think about my hand in

Shane's pocket.

Dad drains his pint. 'It's not been easy for Sheila.'

'No.'

'Or for me.' He looks into his empty glass. 'Want another?'

When Dad comes back from the bar, I've destroyed his beer mat. Shreds of soggy cardboard are scattered across the table. But he manages to clear a little space for his pint.

'How's school?'

'You already asked me that.'

'Oh.' He gulps more beer, wipes his mouth with the back of his hand and belches softly.

'Are you remembering what I told you? About working hard?'

I flick my hair over my shoulder. 'Simon's helping me with my homework.'

Dad's knee jiggles up and down, making the table shake.

Then a red-faced girl arrives, puffing like a bull. 'One burger. One pie. That's it.' She crashes the plates down on the table and swings back round towards the bar. Pieces of beer mat go flying into our laps.

My burger bun has already gone limp. I bite into a chip. Everything tastes of snot today.

Dad picks up his knife and fork and releases the steam from his pie lid. 'He's the brainy type, then.'

'Kind of.'

Dad loads his fork with pie, blows. 'You can do it on your own, anyway. No need for extra help.'

'It keeps him quiet.' I wipe my mouth on a stiff serviette and examine the browned blobs of lipstick I've left behind.

I give it a minute, then I say, 'Why did you leave?'

He swallows. 'I thought you knew.'

'The Power of Love' comes on the jukebox. Jennifer

Rush. I hate that one.

'I tried with your mother, God knows. But in the end – ' he looks off towards the swing doors, searching for something. 'There's not much you can do when you find out you don't want to be together any more.'

I look up to the bar and Joan raises her glass to me.

Dad reaches over the table for my hands. His fingers are damp and hot. 'You're cold,' he says.

'I'm ill.'

'I'm sorry.' His eyes look massive and black. His eyebrows strain in his forehead.

'It's OK,' I say, hoping he won't cry.

'I didn't know what to do.'

His fingers are tight on mine. I think of how I never showed him the rip in my palm that day at the pools.

'Dad.'

'Yes, love?'

'I've got to blow my nose.'

He lets go of my hands and I rummage in my bag for a tissue. They're all reduced to strings. I blow, and taste the saltiness of snot on my upper lip.

It takes Dad five goes to get the gas fire lit. Finally it bangs into life and I kneel in front of the burners, warming my hands in the hissing heat.

Dad comes in with the tea. 'Get that down you.'

We drink. After a bit, he says, 'Is there anything you need?'

'Like what?'

'Anything. I'm still your dad. It's my job to get you whatever you need.' His voice sounds scratchy and worn out.

'I don't need anything.'

'What about Shane? Does he need anything, do you think?'

I look over at him. He's slumped in the chair, eyes closed. His chin looks baggier than it used to. His checked shirt pokes through a small hole in the elbow of his jumper.

He opens his eyes and catches me staring. 'Something the matter, love?'

I shrug and he comes and kneels by me. We sit in silence and breathe in the burning dust.

Then Dad talks again, and he sounds weird, whispery but urgent, like he's been running. 'I should have told you something ages ago.' He coughs and there's a smell of beer. 'I meant to. But it was difficult. I suppose it's all right, now.'

The gas fire's scorching my sleeve. I wonder if it's possible for your clothes to melt while you're wearing them and still not feel warm.

'Thing is.' He pauses, gives me a look.

'What?'

'Perhaps I shouldn't.'

I wait for him to say it.

He does a little cough. 'The thing is. You should know something.'

'What?'

'I think Shane might be – close. To you. To us.'

Could he know about my hand searching in Shane's pocket? About the feathers in my hair? About the way I nearly slipped down the bank into the pool last night when he shoved his fingers past the elastic of my knickers?

'I mean, I think he could be related.'

'What?'

'You know. Family.'

'Family?' I look at Dad then. I see his hopeful, nervous smile.

'I think he might be my son, love.'

The snot in my nose makes my face ache.

'Sheila says not. But I think he might be.' Dad stares into the orange gassy glow. 'I think your mother suspects.'

I fix my eyes on the hole in his jumper.

'It's probably one of the reasons things went wrong for us.'

I think, stop talking. Stop talking.

'I'm not sure. He looks nothing like me, of course…'

Stop talking.

'But I've got this – feeling, you know?'

I can't move.

'I'd like to tell him. But I don't suppose it would do any good.'

Then he puts his hand on my head. It's heavy and hot. He strokes my hair.

'So you two have to look after each other for me.'

Stop talking.

'Understand?'

Each time his hand falls on my head it's like he's pressing me down a bit more. Pressing and holding.

thirteen

Howard

December, 1985

I'd always been better than Kathryn at Christmas. It was the planning, the anticipation, that I enjoyed. The lists of cards to send, food to prepare, presents to buy. Wrapping Robert's gifts, I loved the sound of sellotape ripping off its hoop, the feel of slicing through paper with the sharpest edge of the scissors. Hiding Robert's presents in the bottom of our wardrobe, I felt almost as much excitement as I had as a boy, discovering a child's encyclopedia and a foil-wrapped chocolate Santa beneath Mum's bed.

I even liked the shopping, as long as it wasn't at the weekend. And so, that December, I arranged a day off work in order to take Kathryn Christmas shopping, as I did every year. This time, though, we went to the new complex in Swindon.

There was a pink neon sign above the entrance, framed by matching tinsel. 'The Eastgate Centre' it said, and for a moment the place seemed like a glamorous location.

Inside, the warm air felt very close to my skin. The walls were tiled in reflective grey. The ceilings were mirrored, which I thought was a bad idea, because groups of teenagers tended to gather and point up at themselves, pulling faces and laughing.

A Christmas jingle played, over and over. Every surface shone, and each shop window reflected the two of us back to me: Kathryn walking slightly ahead, her white scarf still wrapped around her neck so it looked slightly like a bandage, me a few paces behind, my heels worn, the collar of my jacket kicking up. The crease in Kathryn's forehead sharpened as we walked further into the centre, and she held on to her patchwork shoulder bag like it was a shield, slung across her body. Her tweed belted coat looked bulky, as if she had been bundled into it.

'When did you buy that coat?' I asked, noticing the way one shoulder was skewed with the weight of her bag. She was walking slightly ahead of me. We hadn't spoken since getting into the car that morning, and my voice sounded unfamiliar in the echoing shopping centre. 'Isn't it time you had a new one?'

'We're supposed to be Christmas shopping,' she said.

'We could get you a new one. For Christmas.'

Kathryn stepped out of the path of a child's buggy. A woman with bags bunched up both arms pushed past me.

Kathryn strode on. 'It's Rob's present I'm worried about,' she called back.

We reached the entrance to Boswell's Department Store. Husbands waited in the doorway while their wives picked at shelves of multicoloured twinkle. There was a strong, almost nauseating, perfume. It took me a few moments to realise this was coming from the soaps that were piled in big baskets along one wall. Each one was shaped like a fruit or a flower, and was wrapped in new plastic. The whole place smelled like a just-cleaned bathroom. It gave me a headache.

We took the escalator to the next floor. As we glided upwards, we were greeted by layer upon layer of hanging snowflakes, each spike precisely cut from silver foil. A voice over the tannoy interrupted 'Jingle Bells' to promise us a *Happy Christmas with Boswell's own pine-scented artificial tree.*

We stepped off the escalator and into the lingerie department. Kathryn had told me how to pronounce that word some months after we were first married. We'd been shopping for her birthday present, I remember, and I'd suggested that she might like to go to the *ling-er-ree* department. She'd laughed at my pronunciation, corrected me, and allowed me to buy her a peach-coloured silk petticoat.

'If you don't want a coat, what *would* you like for Christmas?' I asked. A moulded female torso without arms or legs was perched on a shelf above us, its blank face topped with a red Santa hat. It wore a frilled bra printed with red love hearts. Each heart was round and full, as if it might burst.

'I don't want anything. Really.' Kathryn glanced at the bra.

'Not even that?' I said, trying a smile, pointing at the love hearts.

She shifted her shoulder bag further across her chest. 'Especially not that,' she said.

In the menswear section, my wife ran her hand over a rail of red sweatshirts. I hooked one out. 'Too bright,' Kathryn declared.

I followed her to the next rail, where I selected a padded checked shirt, the kind you'd expect a lumberjack to wear. 'Not smart enough for him,' was her response.

I found a sweater with a single giant snowflake on the front and offered it to her. 'Christmassy,' I ventured.

'A bit babyish.'

'What about this?' It was a white shirt with a button-down collar.

Kathryn stuck out her bottom lip. 'It's like his school shirt.'

'It's smart.'

'I don't think he'll like it.'

'I like it.'

'I was thinking of something more like this.' She displayed a turquoise-coloured T-shirt with a pair of lips, puckered into a kissing shape, printed on the front. The lips were big and black, and they pouted at me.

'Will he like that?'

'I think so,' said Kathryn.

'It's a bit – loud. Isn't it?'

'Luke's got one like it.'

'So that means he'll like it.'

Kathryn slung the T-shirt over one arm and sighed. 'You've got to let him be himself, Howard.'

The pain behind my eyes had reached my jaw. 'I know that.'

She shook her head and laughed softly.

'What?' I asked.

She looked over towards the escalator and bit her lip. For a moment we both stood absolutely still, listening to Judy Garland giving it her all over the tannoy.

I waited for a response.

Then Kathryn stepped closer to me and touched my elbow. 'You've got to let him grow up. In his own way.' She looked me in the eye, and I was surprised to see that her look was soft, almost pleading.

'Do you know what I mean, Howard?'

'Yes.'

'Even if it's not a way you think is – right.'

'Let's not talk about this here.'

'We've got to talk about it somewhere.'

She tried to catch my eye again, but I stared at the sizing chart in front of me, which showed a man's bulky silhouette marked with arrows. Large. Medium. Small.

A sales girl approached. 'Can I help you with anything? We've got a special offer on boys' boxer shorts.'

She can only have been sixteen. Her curly hair was arranged on top of her head and fell around her shoulders like a cascade of bubbles. On her low-cut blouse she wore a large badge in the shape of a reindeer head. Its nose flashed red. On. Off. On. Off.

'He wants to leave.' Kathryn's voice was very quiet. 'He told me. He wants to go as soon as he can.'

The sales girl looked at Kathryn, then at me. 'I'll leave you to it, then,' she said, and trotted back to her till, reindeer badge still flashing.

Kathryn held the T-shirt tight to her middle. The black lips rolled over her fist. 'Howard. He wants to leave us.'

'I heard you.'

We looked at each other. I took a breath. 'What do you mean, leave us?'

'Not right away. But as soon as he's finished at school.'

'What about his A levels?'

'He wants to go to London. In the summer. He told me.'

'London?'

'I wasn't supposed to tell you.'

The bright department store lights revealed the creases around Kathryn's mouth and eyes. I noticed that the line around her full lips was not as definite as it once was. It was as if someone had smudged the edges of her mouth with a damp finger. But to me, her face was still soft, still curvy, like the rest of her.

'He means it, Howard.' There was a slight tremble in

her chin. We were both breathing hard.

I reached out and put a hand on my wife's shoulder. She didn't flinch or move away. Instead, she said in a quiet voice, 'I don't know what I'll do if he goes,' and when she looked at me her eyes were wet.

I drew her towards me then, and held her. I put my arms around her and dug my fingers into the scratchiness of her tweed coat. She let herself go limp against me, and I felt the heat of her breath on my neck. Her shoulders sagged, and I held her tighter.

'He won't leave.' I spoke into her hair, and she gripped my waist and nodded her head. I knew she was crying now.

'He won't leave.'

As we swayed together beneath the glare of the shop's spotlights, I remembered the orange light that had surrounded us on the day she'd told me she was expecting Robert. I remembered how my whole body had felt suddenly warm.

Kathryn's hair brushed my lips as I whispered to her. 'He won't leave. I promise.'

Kathryn was sobbing too much to speak, but I felt her tighten her grip. There was nothing to do, then, but hold on to each other.

fourteen

Joanna
December, 1985

It's art and we're doing portraits. We have to turn round and draw whoever's next to us. I'm glad I'm sitting next to Rob. Rob's good at art, everyone says so. He has a set of professional pencils: soft ones for shading, hard ones for fine lines. Each one is sharpened to an evil little point, and none of the ends are chewed. On the sides there's gold lettering: HB, B, 2B.

'Posh pencils,' I say. 'New?'

'Not really.'

'Expensive.'

Rob selects a pencil from the tin and examines it. 'They were a present.' He digs the point into his finger, like he's testing it. 'From my dad.'

'What for?'

He looks to the ceiling. 'I don't know.'

'Your dad buys you presents for nothing?'

He reaches for his sketchbook. 'I should be drawing you.'

It's always hot in the art room. There's plants and sky-lights and sweaty boys and it's a bit like a greenhouse. I take my jumper off and arrange my silk-touch blouse over my tits, glad that Luke McNeill is on the other side of the room, having his sketchbook marked by the teacher.

Rob rolls up his shirt sleeves. I watch his knobbly wrists move as he starts to sketch me in.

'Wish my dad would buy me stuff,' I say.

Rob doesn't respond. He's frowning at his page. Then he frowns straight at me and I wonder if I should look away. But his eyes go back to the paper before I can blink.

'You must get some presents,' he says eventually.

I notice the way his gold chain snakes around the base of his long neck.

'My mum's boyfriend tries to buy me things.' I give my hair a shake.

'Keep still.'

'He'd probably get me anything I wanted, actually.'

'Like what?'

'Like anything.' I try to think of something. Simon still hasn't given me my reward for our tutorials. 'He gave me the money for my coat.'

Rob's eyes settle on mine. 'That's different.'

'How?'

'Just giving you money. It's different.'

'I got the coat.'

Rob gives a little smile, like he's sorry for me. 'But he wouldn't know what to get you unless you told him, would he?'

'Maybe.' I lick my lips, lean forward. 'But did you really want those posh pencils?'

'Not exactly...'

'So your dad might as well have given you the cash.'

He shrugs. 'He wouldn't do that.'

'They never know what you want,' I say. 'Money's better.'

Rob drops his pencil back in the tin and picks up another. Again, he digs the end into the tip of his finger and stares at it. I can see the skin there going white. 'They never ask what you want,' he says in a quiet voice.

'Aren't you drawing me?' Luke sits down with a loud huff.

'He's doing me,' I say.

Luke gawps over Rob's shoulder. He's got his blond fringe to stick up and stay in place now. He follows Rob's eyes as they flick up at me, appraise, flick down.

'Are you going to be an artist, then?' I ask Rob.

'Of course he is,' says Luke. 'He's good enough.'

'I bet that's what your dad wants. That'll be why he bought you those pencils.'

Rob gives a 'huh', but doesn't stop sketching. His hands move across the page like they're on wires.

'I hope you're not doing my nose too big.'

'Keep still.'

I get sort of mesmerised by the whispery noise his pencil makes on the paper and I don't say anything for a while.

'What about you?' he asks. 'What are you going to be?'

'Astronaut.'

He glances at me. Then he starts drawing again. 'You could be an actress.'

I spit out a laugh.

'You could,' he says, not laughing. He looks at me with that photographing gaze. Snap. 'If you could be bothered.'

Behind him, Luke sniggers.

'Haven't you finished that yet?' I snatch the pad, turn it round, and see a careful line drawing, just like the portraits they sell in Oxford. The girl in it has massive eyes, pouty lips and a mane of hair.

'Is that me?'

Luke looks over. 'You've overdone her a bit.'

'Perfect likeness,' I announce.

Rob lines his pencil back up in his shiny metal box.

'Are you coming down the farm tonight?' Luke asks him.

'The farm?' I say, rearranging my silk-touch blouse.

'Turkey plucking,' says Rob. 'I need the money.'

'Your dad won't give it to you?' I have to smirk.

'I can't ask him for it.' He looks straight at me. 'I need it to get out. I'm leaving here. As soon as I can.'

'Rob wants to go to London,' says Luke.

'We're both going,' says Rob. 'To make our fortunes.' He gives a short laugh.

'Really?'

'That's the plan. Anywhere's better than here, right?'

I flick my hair over my shoulder and nod slowly. 'Definitely. In fact, I'm going, too.'

'Yeah?' says Luke, screwing up his eyes. Even his lashes are blond. His skin's so pale it's like you can see through it, right into the veins and muscle and bone beneath.

'You're going to London?' asks Rob.

'Of course. I'm not staying in this dump.'

'Have you got the money?'

I look at Rob's green eyes. There's not a speck of brown in them. They're clear green, like marbles. One of my primary school teachers liked to go on about people with pure green eyes. Saying they're rare. Different. I told Dad about it once, and he said, 'Irish, more like.'

'Almost,' I say. 'I'm working on it.'

'She should come and pluck a few birds,' says Luke. 'Sometimes their insides haven't been cleaned out properly and they dribble blood and guts all down your hands.'

Rob gives him a look. 'I wouldn't,' he says to me, 'unless you really have to.'

'I can do that,' I say. 'I already know someone who works there anyway.'

'The spacky,' says Luke.

'Shane.' Before I can stop myself, I add, 'And he's not really a spacky.'

'How come he was in the Sin Bin, then?'

I think of the precision of Shane's fingers in my hair. The way he knows all the words to every song he plays me on his cassette player. The way he knows exactly what to buy me. Or rather, steal for me. He was in the Sin Bin because the normal teachers couldn't handle him, is what I think.

'I can pluck a turkey.'

'And the blood?' asks Luke.

Rob rolls his eyes.

'Blood's fine,' I say. 'I can handle blood.'

That night after school, I'm the only girl in the turkey shed.

The corrugated iron door screeches as I pull it open with both hands. It scrapes my fingernails and sends a cringe right down my back. Inside, dead birds hang in two rows. Next to each bird, there's a boy, plucking. White feathers fall all around like spiky, blinding snow. In the background, there's a constant turkey racket from the birds who so far haven't had their throats cut. It's a weird gurgling noise that comes in waves, like Buggery's stomach at the end of the day. And the place stinks like an old sanitary pad.

My skin flicks up its hairs in the cold air. I'm wearing my denim mini with red wool tights, red hoop earrings and red fingerless gloves.

I walk in and see Shane first. He's standing with one hand round a pink turkey neck. His other hand goes in and out, in and out, in a blizzard of feathers. He's doing it faster than I've ever seen him do anything. In front of him there's a basket which looks like it should be full of washing. But instead it's full of bald headless birds, all collapsed on top of one another.

No one's talking to Shane. There's more space around him and his bird than any of the other boys.

He turns to look at me. His big bottom lip hangs as he watches me walk over to Rob. He opens his mouth wider, as if he might say something.

Don't look at him again, I think. Don't look at him.

'Hi.' Rob flashes me a white grin and leads me to a man in a sheepskin coat. As I walk along the rest of the row, each boy stops plucking and looks. Their turkeys swing as I go by, claws groaning gently on the bar. The sanitary pad smell wafts over me.

'This is the girl I said about,' Rob announces. The man in the sheepskin nods, looks me over. 'Next time, wear trousers. And boots. Don't want you slipping on turkey gizzards.' He huffs out a not-funny laugh.

The birds are much bigger than they look under cellophane. Some of them hang down almost to my knees. Their feet are tied to a hook and their claws stick up like killer fingernails. Their heads are missing, and their necks are still bloody. I'm glad their heads are gone. I wouldn't want to see their beady eyes.

Sheepskin Coat hands me a turkey on a hook. 'Secure your bird on the rail,' he says, hanging it up. 'Don't want him flying away.' He smiles. He's missing a tooth. 'Best way is to pluck quickly, but carefully. Don't go grabbing great handfuls.' He plucks the feathers out – one, two, three – and lets them drop to the floor. 'See?'

All the time, Shane's staring at me and the bird.

'Shouldn't look too hard, son. You'll wear her out.' As he walks away, he taps Shane on the head with his clipboard.

My turkey sways in front of me. Its wings are spread out like the bird in our school logo. Its white feathers are flecked with dirt. I tap it, lightly, and it swings some more. I dig my fingers into the greasy feathers and grab hold of a few. My fingertips meet warm flesh.

I let go, leap back.

'You get used to it,' says Rob.

'I thought it would be cold.'

'They haven't been dead long.' Rob looks serious, as if he's apologising.

I try again. I wrap my fingers round a single feather. It's hard and spiky. When I tug, there's a tearing sound. It doesn't come easy.

Then Shane comes over. He doesn't speak. He just grabs my bird in one hand and starts ripping feathers out with the other.

Rob steps back and looks round to see if Sheepskin Coat's noticed Shane's doing something he shouldn't.

Shane's arm is going in and out, in and out. Grab, pull, rip. Grab, pull, rip. Grab, pull, rip. He chucks feathers over me like confetti.

'Is the spacky helping her?' says Luke. 'Why doesn't he help me?'

A glob of turkey blood hits Shane's parka.

'Don't do that,' I say. I put a hand on his arm. He can't notice, because his elbow keeps moving back and he catches me under the chin, hard. My teeth slam together.

I cry out.

Shane stops plucking. He blinks, slowly. His eyes are black. He puts out a hand to touch my chin.

'Don't, Shane,' I say. I step backward.

Don't look at him. Don't look at him.

'I don't need your help.'

He lets go of the turkey.

'I don't need your help.' I rub my chin and try not to look up.

Then Shane smashes the turkey with his fist like it's a punchbag. White feathers and claws and a bloody neck swing towards my face. I duck. Feathers skate across my hair.

Sheepskin Coat comes over. 'If you're going to distract my workers, blondie, then you can forget it,' he says. His voice is loud but he's giving me a half-smirk. 'Get on with it, now. All of you.'

He walks Shane back to the other side of the shed, leaving my bird swaying on its hook.

Rob leans over. 'What's with him?'

I don't have an answer.

He puts a hand on my shoulder. 'You OK?'

I nod, try a brave smile.

On the other side of the shed, Shane's craning his neck round his turkey, looking for me again.

I plunge my hand into the feathers and start plucking. Soon I'm stripping birds clean in under fifteen minutes.

fifteen

Howard
December, 1985

That evening, I went to find him.

I didn't know what I was going to say. That he mustn't think of leaving. That he couldn't be what his mother said he was. That I loved him. That I couldn't understand what was wrong with him. What was wrong with me.

I had thought he might not go through with the turkey plucking plan, even though Luke was doing it. I'd told him he didn't need to go there; I'd get him a job with me at the power station – cleaning the offices at weekends, perhaps. I couldn't imagine Robert on that farm. He was like me, too neat for dirty work. It wasn't uncommon, I'd heard, for a bird to be still half-conscious when it was plucked. Like the headless chickens you hear about, still running round the yard. That wasn't the sort of thing I had the stomach for.

I put on my wellingtons before I went down there, thinking the turkey shed might be mucky. I didn't consider the fact that all the birds would be dead, and the sawdust would be covered with feathers, soft and light, not mucky at all.

I walked past the church and down the lane towards the pools. There was no wind that night; the sky was clear and scattered with stars. I wore my woollen hat – a present from Mum one Christmas. The fibres scratched the tops of my ears. The ground was frozen, and several times I had to grasp hold of a branch to keep myself from slipping. I began to regret wearing the wellingtons, which didn't have much of a tread.

It had been years since I'd walked down here, and I remembered the day I'd come with Kathryn to photograph her in her yellow dress. I remembered how the yellow contrasted with the dense, dark green of the yew trees in the churchyard. The only dark thing about Kathryn that day was her eyelashes.

Steam from the cooling towers still pumped high into the sky and over the village. The moon lit the whole scene, and I could see that the trees and bushes were much taller and denser than they had been the last time I was here. Without their leaves, all the branches seemed very straight and solid. They criss-crossed the sky and scored the pool.

I didn't look over towards the water, even though I could just see it glinting between the branches. I concentrated on my destination: the farm.

As I got closer, a strange sound became more and more insistent. It was like a radio that hadn't been tuned in properly and was turned up much too loud; there was no release, and no soothing note. There was just the squabbling, squawking noise of turkeys. It seemed to drift one way and then the other, making me feel a little dizzy. I realised that this must be the sound of the remaining birds, the ones who had so far escaped slaughter, as they swept from one side of their pen to the other.

I approached a large shed that was lit up inside. The rusty corrugated iron door was slightly ajar and I could see feathers floating in the air.

I opened the shed door and stepped inside. It was no warmer in there, despite the lights, whose brightness seemed to encourage the mealy smell – an overwhelming mixture of sawdust, blood and turkey flesh. Along each wall, dead, headless birds hung from hooks, in various stages of plucking. Some still had thick plumage on their breasts, others were almost bald, save the odd patch of greasy feathers. Feathers were everywhere, falling to the ground, nestling in the hair and on the coats of the boys who stood in front of the birds. Each boy had a basket for his finished work, and a man with a clipboard stood at the far end, handing out new birds, already attached to hooks so they could be hung from bars on the ceiling.

The strange thing – the thing I hadn't imagined – was that each turkey's wings were spread out on either side. As they were plucked, the birds bobbed in the air, and their wings made a flapping motion, as if they might still fly away.

Robert was standing next to Luke. Their hands worked to the same rhythm as they tugged handfuls of feathers away from the turkeys. I noticed the girl from the shop was standing on the other side of Robert. Her bright hair was littered with feathers, and she was turned slightly towards my son, as if she was listening for his next words. Opposite her, on the other side of the shed, stood the large bulk of Derrick Pearce's son, the boy everyone knew, even then, to be backward. While he ripped the plumage from the headless turkey before him, he stared at the girl.

I took my hat off and felt my forehead prickle in the cold air.

The girl looked over and saw me. She nudged Robert.

Robert looked around. As soon as our eyes met, he flicked his away and turned back to his bird.

The girl nudged Robert again and gestured in my direction, but Robert would not turn around.

Derrick Pearce's boy unhooked his bird. He had a

feather stuck to his big bottom lip. The turkey's bloody neck hung down by his thigh. He threw the limp naked bird into his basket and walked to the end of the shed to get another. As he did so, he trailed one hand along the edge of the girl's short skirt. She stepped away from him.

'Robert,' I called. The sound of chattering turkeys outside was still loud, even with the shed door closed, and I tried to raise my voice. 'Robert.'

The girl smiled at me. Her lipstick was so light, her mouth looked like it was covered in frost.

'Robert,' I called his name again.

The man with the clipboard approached.

'Can I help?' He raised his eyebrows, which were the same colour as his sheepskin coat.

'I'm here to speak to my son, Robert Hall,' I said, nodding in Robert's direction.

The man walked over to Robert and tapped him on the shoulder. 'Rob,' he shouted, 'Your dad's here. Go and see what he wants.'

The other boys near Robert laughed. Derrick Pearce's boy laughed the loudest.

Robert left his half-plucked turkey swinging from its hook and came over to where I stood in the doorway.

'What do you want?'

'Shall we go outside?' I suggested.

'No. What do you want?'

'I think maybe we should talk outside.'

'I'm fine here,' he said, crossing his arms.

I tried to push the word *gypsy* from my mind as I looked at his glinting earring.

'What do you want, Dad? I've got work to do.'

'I wanted to tell you something.'

He breathed out heavily through his nose, shook his head and gave a little laugh. 'Go on, then.'

'Sexy wellingtons, Mr Hall,' the shop girl called over.

Luke laughed first and Derrick Pearce's boy followed. His laugh was so loud it drowned out the gobbling turkeys for a moment.

Robert sniggered. Instinctively he covered his mouth with his hand, but then he changed his mind and took it away. His green eyes were clear when he looked at me and let out a loud hoot.

When he'd finished laughing, he said, 'What did you want to say, Dad?'

'I just wanted to tell you. I wanted to say… ' I stopped. I tried to look him in the face, but my eyes kept straying to his hair. It was stuck up on his head; his plumage was straight and strong now, I noticed. He no longer had that cockatoo touch at his crown.

I began again. 'I wanted to tell you that, that I'm sorry.' I flexed my hands in my pockets. The ache in them was sharp and deep.

'I'm sorry.'

Robert blinked; he said nothing.

'That's all I came to say.'

Robert looked at me for a long time. Then he nodded, just once.

I walked out of the shed and back into the darkness.

sixteen

Joanna
December, 1985

'Lapsang Souchong,' says Simon. 'Not, in any circumstances, to be taken with milk. You have to take it black. You'll understand that, Joanna.'

He lifts the lid off the teapot and wafts the steam with his hand. It smells like a packet of bacon flavour Frazzles.

We're in Mr Badger's tearoom again. Simon promises this will be the last tutorial before Christmas. He says we're making 'progress'. When he says this he rolls up the sleeves of his diamond-patterned jumper, like he's going to do some dirty work. Like he's getting his fists ready for something, or someone.

'Try a cup?' He holds the pot over my side of the table and raises his eyebrows. His hair's a bit off today. The fringe isn't as sculpted as usual. I can see the grooves where he's tried to comb the hairspray through.

In the background, classical music is playing at low volume. Violins and cellos chug along together. That sort of music always sounds like it's straining for something.

'I'm hungry.'

'They do good soup here.' He pours himself a cup of smoke-coloured tea, then gestures to the girl in the frill-on-frill apron. She gives it a minute before unpeeling herself from the kitchen doorway and walking over to our table with her greasy pad, chewing on a plait.

'This young lady would like something to eat.' Simon takes a good look at frill-on-frill. She's got sharp cheekbones, little pig eyes lined with electric blue pencil, thin pink lips.

'Sausage and chips,' I say.

'Don't do chips.' Her plait falls from her mouth. 'We've got sausage in a roll.'

'That'll be fine,' says Simon.

When she's gone, he leans across the table. His watch glints at me. 'Good appetite. I've always liked that about you. Can't ever imagine you being *anorexic.*' He says this with a smirk and a gleam on his small teeth. As if it's a filthy word. Like *cocksucker.*

'Mind you,' he continues, 'I have been worried about you, Joanna. You haven't seemed yourself lately.'

He lets a silence grow. He spends a long time looking over my shoulder, squinting into the air, as if he's considering the swag-tied chintz curtains. He even drums his fingers on the table. He's waiting for me to spill it.

All I can think of is money. How much I'll need to get to London with Rob.

Finally he picks up his copy of *Frankenstein* and fans through the pages. 'I love the smell of books,' he says, sucking a breath in.

'We've finished that.'

'You didn't tell me.'

'We finished it ages ago.'

He puts the book down and folds his fingers together in a tent shape. 'What are you doing now, then?'

'Poetry.'

He waits for more. I look out the window. It's greyer than my school uniform out there. The tea room's lit by a couple of pink corner lamps, which means I can't see Simon's wrinkly cheeks in detail. But he looks grey, too. Grey and wilting.

'What poetry are you doing?'

'John Donne.'

He takes off his glasses and places them on the tablecloth. Then he closes his eyes and starts. '*Mark but this flea, and mark in this, how little that which thou deny'st me is...*'

'It's good.'

'Yes! Isn't it?'

'Having someone who worries about me, I mean. It's good. Nice.'

He pinches his bottom lip between finger and thumb, fixes me with a stare.

I tug on a strand of hair and wrap it round a finger. 'I just wanted to say, you know, thanks.'

'Well. I do worry about you. Your mother says you can look after yourself. But I'm not so sure.'

The violins grind away, quietly. I gaze at the tablecloth, concentrating on a pink embroidered daisy, petals stained with grease. I let a moment pass, then look back at his grey crinkly cheek. 'Tell me more about John Donne,' I say.

'You've changed your tune.'

'I'm interested.'

'Well. Donne is perfect for you, Joanna. Now I think of it, he's absolutely perfect.'

'Yeah?'

'Oh yes. He's a bit bawdy. Bold. Like yourself. Colloquial – that means he uses everyday language. Likes playing games. But doesn't shy away from true feeling, real passion.'

He's gripping his teacup and he hasn't blinked for ages.

'My favourite's always been – ' he pauses, chuckles,

' – "To his mistress going to bed".' He winks, takes a breath, opens his eyes wide. Then starts again. '*License my roving hands, and let them go, before, behind, between, above, below.*'

Simon slaps the table before stretching his arms out on either side like he's won the 100 metres. Olympic Gold. 'Fantastic. And all in the seventeenth century.'

My sausage arrives. A ledge of margarine spills over the roll's crust. I take a bite. Grease leaks out of the bread and onto the rose-patterned plate.

When I've swallowed, I say, 'There is something I'd like to talk to you about.'

He nods and tries to stop himself smiling.

'I need money.'

He stops smiling.

I blink a lot and gaze down at the grease-stained daisy. 'I really need money, and I don't know where to get it.'

'What for?'

'I can't tell you.'

'What for, Joanna?'

'You don't want to know.'

He leans forward. 'If you won't tell me, I can't help you.' He waits. I can see my reflection in his specs. My cheeks with their little blusher-spots of flush. My lips wet and a bit quivery. I wrap another strand of hair around my finger and examine the splitting ends. I think about taking another bite of sausage; decide against it. Eventually, I say, 'I'm in – trouble.'

Simon puts his glasses back on and flicks his stiffened fringe. The violins chug to a stop.

'What kind of trouble?'

I make my voice very, very, very small. 'The usual kind.' I sweep my lashes up and look out from under.

'Joanna – '

'The kind teenage girls get into.'

He huffs out a breath.

'Will you help me?' Under the table, I put a hand on his knee and rub at his rough trouser leg. I even stroke a bit down his shin. 'Please. I need your help.'

He's silent.

'I didn't mean it to happen.'

He's staring into his cup of smoky bacon flavour tea.

'I don't want to waste my life.'

'Whose is it?'

I bite my bottom lip and look towards the window. It's dark outside now. The tearoom's emptied. The music's stopped. There's just the big tick of a grandfather clock in the corner, as regular as an ECG monitor on one of those hospital programmes.

'Joanna. Whose is it?'

My sausage will be cold by now. The roll soggy. The margarine too soaked in.

'Whose is it, Joanna?'

'You don't know him.'

'Oh lord.'

After a minute he says, 'It's not that backward boy, is it?'

I hang my head and wilt my shoulders, like a sunflower that's on its last gasp.

'He didn't – force you, did he?'

Don't say anything.

'Oh my God.' He grasps both my hands in his and pulls them to his thighs. 'It's all right,' he says, pumping my hands up and down.

Tears would be perfect.

'Poor girl. Poor girl. Poor girl.'

After another minute of combined hand squeezing and thigh rubbing, I say, 'I just need the money.' I give a little sniff. 'Then I can, you know, start again.'

He crushes my fingers and stares at me with pop-eyes. 'I've got an idea,' he says. He's breathing like a buffalo. 'It's crazy, but maybe…'

'What?'

His crinkly cheeks get a sudden rush of blood and he looks almost shiny. 'You could get yourself – fixed – and then, then we could go away. Start again, like you said.'

'What?'

'I mean. We could go somewhere. Together.'

'What?'

'You and me. As – friends. I could look after you, Joanna. It would be perfect. You'd escape all this. And I could get a new start. We both could.'

'What about Mum?'

'She'll understand.' His lips settle into a tight line and he looks straight at me. 'We can visit her.'

I can't speak for a moment. He's twisting my fingers now, wringing them like wet washing.

'It will be for the best. We'll be friends, that's all. You need to get away – and so do I…'

I tug my hands loose. They're damp from his grip.

'I can get you the money, Joanna.' His eyes bulge. There's a ridge of sweat on his upper lip. He swallows. 'When do you need it?'

I shrug.

'Well, how far gone are you?'

I stare at Simon's V-neck jumper. The diamond patterns move with his heavy breaths. I can't think of an answer.

A minute ticks by, slowly.

'You are sure, aren't you?'

'I – think so.'

He lowers his voice. 'Have you done a test?'

Frilly apron appears and swipes my plate and glass. She

lets her plait dangle over the liquid left in Simon's cup. 'Closing now,' she says, slamming the bill in his saucer and reclaiming the teapot.

Simon waits until she's gone. Then he takes off his glasses. 'Joanna?'

'We'd better go.'

'Joanna.'

'What?'

'You're sure you're – ' he lowers his voice, 'pregnant?'

I trace a line in the crumbs on the tablecloth. I run my tongue along my bottom lip and give him two blinks. 'I really need the money.'

He sort of throws himself back in his chair. Lets out a big huff. Then a little huff. Then a big one again. He shakes his head.

When he's finished shaking his head, he puts his hand over his mouth and wipes away some invisible crumbs.

'Are you pregnant or not?'

I blink at him some more. 'It's possible.'

'Yes or no, Joanna.'

We stare at each other for a minute. Then I do a big shrug.

'Priceless,' he says. 'Bloody priceless.' There's a lot of huffing and wiping of the mouth again.

Finally he slams his hand down on the tablecloth. The Lapsang Souchong shakes in his cup. He scrapes back his chair and throws *Frankenstein* into his rucksack.

'You're as bad as your mother.' I think he's going to spit. Or use that fist.

But he doesn't. He walks out. He walks out, and then it's just me, the bill, and the ECG monitor clock. Tick. Tick. Tick.

seventeen

Howard
December, 1985

The next night, I was late leaving work and I drove a little too fast on the way home. I listened to Radio 2 in the car. The mystery voice. It had gone on for weeks, that one. A man saying, 'Of course, that was back in my day.' There was a little laugh somewhere in his voice; a slight northern accent. No one could get it. They'd tried everyone from John Noakes to Brian Blessed.

I'd thought it might be a start, the apology. He'd had a day to mull it over, and I'd hoped that when he came back that night, we could all sit down together over dinner and Robert might even smile. He might see that I was willing to make an effort, at least.

But when I arrived home, having completed the journey in five minutes under my usual time, our house was filled with a strange smell. There was a reek of fried onions, and something else I couldn't name.

'What are you making?' I called to Kathryn from the hallway.

'Curry.' Through the open kitchen door, I saw her glance at her recipe book. 'Lamb curry. I thought I'd try it. To warm Robert up when he comes back from the farm.'

We'd never had curry before. As I removed my coat, I

inhaled the other smell, something beneath the fried onion, something rounded and savoury. It's stayed on my clothes ever since. Later that night, when I held my wife's hands up to my face, I could smell it there, as if it was thriving under her nails. Kathryn told me, afterwards, that it was garlic.

I sat down with the news and the weather forecast. Even Michael Fish looked cold as he stuck the temperatures on the map.

'Freezing again tomorrow,' I called to Kathryn. She came in from the kitchen and stood in front of me.

'Rob's not back yet.' She folded back the edge of her cuff and looked at her watch. 'Shouldn't he be back by seven?' She was wearing two jumpers, I remember that. Her green polo neck underneath Robert's grey school V-neck.

'Will the dinner spoil?'

She looked puzzled. 'No,' she said. 'No, the dinner won't spoil, Howard.'

I recognised the catch in her voice. 'We'll give him an hour,' I said. 'I'm sure he won't want to be plucking those birds for any longer than he has to.'

She went back into the kitchen.

'I expect he's hanging about with Luke,' I called.

I sat at the kitchen table and stared at the empty place settings.

'It's not like him to be late,' said Kathryn. She was standing behind me at the stove. She gave the curry another long stir, then rapped the wooden spoon on the side of the pot with some force. I watched as a dollop of brown liquid fell back to join the rest of the sticky gloop. The sweet-savoury smell of it reminded me of the scent of daffodils. That first strong, peppery whiff of spring.

'What did you say to him last night, when you went down there?' she asked, folding her arms across her chest and holding the glistening spoon up by one shoulder.

'I told you. I apologised.'

'How did you apologise?'

'I said I was sorry. That was it.'

'And what did he say?'

'He didn't say anything.' I showed her my palms. 'He didn't have anything to say to me.'

Kathryn blew up into her fringe. 'He's almost two hours late,' she said, looking towards the back door.

'He'll be here soon.'

'Are you sure you didn't upset him again?'

'He didn't seem upset. He just didn't respond.'

Kathryn drove her wooden spoon back into the curry and stirred again.

'I'm not sure when to put the rice on.' She picked up a packet of Uncle Ben's. We had rice sometimes in the power station canteen, but I always avoided it.

'It'll be his own fault if his dinner's spoiled.'

She frowned. 'Where is he, though?' She shook the packet of Uncle Ben's and stared at the man on the front, as if he might give her an answer. 'He must be starving by now.'

Kathryn went to the window and lifted the corner of the blind. She rubbed a spy-hole in the condensation on the window and peered out. 'Perhaps you should go down there, Howard.'

I thought of the rows of turkeys hanging limp and lifeless in the cold air. 'Again?'

'Just to check.'

I stood up and went to join her at the window. 'Why don't we give it another hour?' I patted her hand. 'He'll come when he's hungry.'

Together we looked through the spy-hole in the condensation until it had almost disappeared.

Half an hour later, the phone rang.

Kathryn answered it. From my chair in the kitchen, I heard her say, 'I'll get him for you'.

I never receive phone calls.

She handed over the receiver, but stayed standing next to me in the hallway, tea towel in one hand, tilting her head towards my ear.

'Howard? Kevin McNeill.'

'Sorry?'

'Kevin McNeill. Luke's Dad.'

'Oh. Hello.'

'Listen, I didn't want to worry your wife, so I thought it best to speak to you.'

'What is it?'

Kathryn tilted her head closer to mine.

'Nothing to worry about, I'm sure it's nothing.' He coughed. 'I know it sounds odd, but Luke's just got in and he says he's lost your Rob.'

'Sorry?'

'He says Rob's run off. And he seems a bit – rattled. I don't know if they've had an argument or something. You know what teenage boys are like! But you might want to go and have a look for him, just to be on the safe side.'

'He's not there, then, with Luke?' I looked at Kathryn. The crease in her forehead deepened.

'No. Luke says they were on their way home from the farm, and he looked back and Rob was gone. He'd just left him, or something. I can't fathom it, myself.'

'They were finished there hours ago, though.'

'Like I said. I can't fathom it.'

'It doesn't sound like Robert.'

There was a pause.

'Has he got a girlfriend, your boy?'

'What?'

'A girlfriend – has Rob got one? I bet that's it, he'll have given Luke the slip for some girl.'

'He hasn't got a girlfriend.'

'As far as you know.'

'Robert hasn't got a girlfriend.'

'Look, I'm sure there's a simple explanation, but like I said, you might want to go and have a quick look.'

'Yes.'

'Bound to be a simple explanation. Nine times out of ten, there is.'

'Thank you for letting us know.' I put the phone down.

Kathryn dropped her tea towel and clutched my arm, her wide eyes waiting for an explanation.

'Something about Luke losing him.' I took her hands in mine and she gripped my fingers. 'I'm sure it's nothing. But I'd better go and have a look.'

'Howard – '

'Nothing to worry about. I'll be back in a bit.'

I tugged my hands from hers and opened the front door.

I ran right out into the road, without my coat. The frost on the tarmac crunched beneath my shoes.

He would be still on the farm. There would be a simple explanation. There was no need to run, I told myself. No need at all.

I walked to the junction, past the garage, past Burgrey Stores and up the High Street. I tried to keep my steps brisk, but not panicked.

The church bells were ringing. Thursday is practice day. Each clanging bell seemed to pound in time to my footsteps on the road.

Probably he was home by now. There would be a simple explanation. He'd be asleep on the toilet. And I'd carry him back to bed.

Nine times out of ten.

A simple explanation.

The icy air made my lungs feel raw.

Nine times out of ten.

I kept walking, walking, walking. Not running.

There would be a simple explanation.

Nine times out of ten.

Once I reached the lane by the church, I had to break into a run. I slipped and stumbled along the icy mud, and once I went down on my knees, but I recovered and ran again. I ran across the field to the farm. I have never been a natural runner, and the exertion made my heart thump hard against my ribs.

The steam from the power station clung to the tops of the towers, white against the blue-black sky. I used to think of those clouds of steam as like snow clouds, hanging on mountaintops, just as you see in paintings. But that night they looked exactly like what Mum had always said they were: clouds of smoke, billowing into the atmosphere; dirty, thick, unstoppable.

I couldn't see anyone on the farm; it was all dark, and there was a dog barking, so I hammered on the big corrugated iron doors of the turkey shed and I hollered Robert's name, but there was just the dog barking, louder and louder.

I hammered on the shed doors again. My pulse was pounding in my throat.

'What do you want?' A torch was in my face; a man's breath was wet in the air between us.

'I'm Robert's – Rob's – father. Howard Hall.'

'Yes?'

'He was here, earlier, working for you, he's gone missing, nothing I expect, nothing at all, but I was worried, so – '

'There's no one here.' The man switched off his torch. I could see his round face, his red-rimmed eyes, and I recognised him as the man with the clipboard. 'They all went home hours ago.' He looked at me and I realised my teeth were chattering. 'I'd go home, if I were you.' He put a hand on my shoulder. 'He's probably there by now, eh?'

When I got back to the house Kathryn opened the door before I could knock, and I knew he wasn't home. I pushed past her and strode down the hall and into the kitchen, shouting for him.

'Robert, Robert! I'm getting fed up with this game! Where are you, for Christ's sake?' I opened the back door and stood on the frozen grass and yelled. 'Robert! Robert! Where are you?'

Kathryn was still standing in the front doorway, so I pushed past her again and rushed into the road, calling. I must have been out there for ten minutes, calling like that, with Kathryn standing on the doorstep, watching me in silence. I could see people looking out of their curtains, lights going on in upstairs bedrooms, nets suddenly shuddering, but I carried on shouting my son's name. But it didn't matter how loud I shouted, my voice just disappeared into the night.

Eventually Kathryn came out into the road and put her hand on my arm. 'Call the police,' she said.

★

We didn't go to bed until three. When I took off my clothes, I was surprised to see that my trousers were covered with mud and torn at the knees.

'No point staying up, tiring ourselves.' I spoke to Kathryn in the darkness of our bedroom. 'We've done all we can. At least the police know, now. It's that Luke, I expect. Some trick. He'll be back in a bit, you'll see.' I kept saying these things. I held her frozen fingers, and I smelt the garlic. I knew her feet would be icy, but she kept them away from mine, pointing straight down the bed, her knees together, her head absolutely still on the pillow, looking up at the ceiling, saying nothing. There was just a slight twitch in her left eyebrow as I whispered my promises. *He'll be back in the morning. He'll be back in the morning. He'll be back in the morning.* I said it again and again, until a crack of light slid under the curtains; and then I lay there, staring into the brightness of the day, not wanting to get up and face the cold floor and the silent telephone.

eighteen

Joanna
December, 1985

Simon's tutorial makes me late for turkey plucking, because I have to go home and change first. I choose my suede ankle boots and denim mini with black wool tights. I won't do trousers and wellies for anyone.

I charge down the lane by the church like I'm an American cheerleader in a film with Matt Dillon. Frozen puddles splinter beneath my stamping feet, but I don't care. I swing my arms, stick out my chin, smile.

Then a bramble catches my calf and scrapes off a long line of skin. My flesh smarts in the polar-temperature air. I reach down and feel the gap where my tights have snagged. The skin there is raised and hot.

There's no time to go back and change again, so I walk further down the lane, by the pools. I can see the black water of the biggest pool is half frozen over. I want to go down there and test it with my foot, just to hear the crunch-crackle of ice breaking.

I'm nearly in the field by the farm when Shane steps out of the trees and grabs my wrist. I skate along the icy ground towards him, my joints suddenly turning to sponge. It's easy for him to drag me closer. His warts dig into my fingers. His nose touches my cheek.

'You didn't wait last night,' he says, his voice an edgy whisper. 'I was looking for you.'

The power station whirrs.

'I was looking. Waiting.' Shane flicks a smile and tightens his grip.

'We're late,' I say, looking towards the farm.

He shoves my hand downwards and jams my fingers into his trouser pocket. It's hot in there, especially with Shane's clammy fist over mine. I keep my fingers stiff, refusing to move. But he keeps pushing.

His lips are bunched together. I think it's the first time I've ever seen him with his mouth closed tight.

He keeps pushing. My lungs can't seem to get enough air. It's like every breath takes minutes to thaw in my chest.

He keeps pushing. His brow is scored across his face now.

'Let me go, Shane!' I shout.

And he does. He lets go and I fall against him. His patchy stubble scrapes my forehead, and I get a face full of parka fur.

Then he presses both hands on my head and shoves me down, hard, so I fall to my knees. Gravel drives into my shins. The broken ice of the puddle soaks into my tights.

'Sorry,' he says, and puts his hand on my head, gently. He runs his big fingers through my hair, going up and down and round and round and round so I can't see anything for all the hair he's messed up over my face. As he's groping my scalp, he moves my head gradually towards his groin, until the cool scratchiness of his fly zip is on my lip.

'I'm not your girlfriend.'

He laughs. He keeps messing my hair up with his hands.

'I'm not your girlfriend.'

His hands stop moving. Then he kneels in the puddle

with me so we're face to face, and he blinks his big wet eyes. His hair curls onto my cheek, he's so close.

I look at him. And I see that he's nothing like Dad.

'But,' he whispers. 'But – '

And nothing like me. But I have to end it.

'I'm not your girlfriend, Shane.'

'You are my girlfriend.' He fixes me with the biology-diagram look. He sees all my veins, my blood and tissue. He examines me in close-up.

I shut my eyes and keep my voice even. 'No. I'm not. I'm Rob's girlfriend now.'

There's a minute where I keep my eyes closed and he just breathes over me. Then I look at him and he falls back onto his haunches and bashes both fists into an icy puddle. Smash. Smash. Smash. Smash. Chips of ice fly over my hands and legs.

I get up and try to run to the farm. But I can't. Instead, I keep slipping and yelping, slipping and yelping like a puppy on the ice.

In the turkey shed, I hook up my bird and pluck and pluck and pluck like nothing's happened. My feet are numb with cold and wet, my knees throb from the stones. I keep plucking, plunging my fingers into the greasy feathers and ripping them out until all that's left is a lank carcass of bird.

It's quiet in the shed tonight. There's no squabbling noise from the pen outside. All the turkeys have been slaughtered by now.

Luke and Rob stand close together, plucking.

After a few minutes, Shane comes in and strides over to the end of the shed to fetch his bird. He hangs it up and begins to pluck.

Then it's like we're in competition. Who can pluck the

fastest. Who can strip a bird without stopping. Our hands dip in and out together. We throw feathers in each other's direction. I pile up three naked birds in twenty minutes. They flop over each other in my basket and I just keep going to get more.

'You OK?' Rob leans across. His clean L'Oreal scent wafts over me as he glances down at my ripped muddy tights. 'You're quiet.'

I smile at his flawless cheeks. 'I'm fine.'

Luke puts a hand on Rob's shoulder and shoves his skinny blond head between us. 'Can you hear the spacky grunting?' he asks. 'He sounds like a pregnant pig.'

'He's working hard,' I say.

'Is he – ' Luke puckers his lips and makes a kissing sound, 'your boyfriend?'

'No, he is not.' I rip out a handful of feathers and throw them at Luke's face.

He picks a feather off his lip and examines it for a minute. Then he says, 'He's your boyfriend.'

'He is not my boyfriend. Shane is not my boyfriend.' I spit out each word.

I glance over at Shane. He stops plucking, just for a second. Then he starts again, double-fast.

Rob clears his throat. 'We're leaving in the New Year. We've got enough.'

Sheepskin Coat comes over. 'Less chat, more work, you lot.' He lifts Rob's bird by its wing so it seems about to fly to the side. 'Don't forget these bits underneath. No one wants a mouthful of turkey fluff with their sprouts.'

He nudges Shane between the shoulder blades with his clipboard. 'You're my best worker, Shane Pearce,' he says. He holds the clipboard above his head and raises his voice. 'Everyone. Look at Shane's birds. Bald as your sister's arse. That's how all of them should be.'

Shane doesn't stop plucking.

When Sheepskin Coat's gone, I step away from my bird, wipe a hand on my skirt and fold my fingers over Rob's arm. His donkey jacket looks rough, but it feels smooth. 'I've got enough now,' I say, 'to come with you.'

Rob ups his killer lashes.

'To London,' I continue, 'we can all go together.'

'She's not coming,' says Luke. His lips are as pale as his face.

I laugh. 'Didn't Rob tell you?'

Rob's mouth hangs open, just like Shane's. He blinks at me, at Luke, then at me again.

I reach up and cup a hand round his ear, breathing in L'Oreal. The icy smoothness of Rob's gold sleeper is on my lip as I whisper to him. 'Help me.'

Rob stares at me for a minute. I stare back and mouth the word please. He runs a hand through his gel-stiffened hair.

'Rob?' asks Luke.

After a minute, Rob speaks. 'It's OK. Maybe we can – you know, work something out.' His eyebrows arch in apology and he attempts to give Luke a half-grin.

I sneak another look at Shane, who's stopped plucking and is staring at the floor. His fists are clenched, hanging in big bunches by his sides.

'We can all go together, Luke,' I say.

'And I suppose the spacky's coming too?' says Luke. He sticks his chin out of his white scarf and shoves his hands into the pockets of his bright blue Adidas jacket, pulling it down over his little hips. He faces Rob. 'I suppose she's bringing her spacky boyfriend? Why not just invite everyone, Rob?'

'He's not her boyfriend.' Rob's voice is soft. He touches Luke on the shoulder and smiles his full *Smash Hits* smile.

'It's OK. Really.'

Luke huffs over his turkey.

For the next fifteen minutes, everything seems to go quiet. There's just the ripping sound of feathers being pulled. I try not to look in Shane's direction. Luke sulks and Rob frowns.

Then I notice Shane unhooking his bird. He takes time to arrange its bald wings and bloody neck so it's all neatly packed in his basket and he carries the whole thing to the end of the shed. Sheepskin Coat pats him on the shoulder and digs in his big pocket for some coins.

On his way out, Shane stops and stands very close behind me. 'I'm going,' he says. 'You coming?'

His breath is hot on my ears.

'You coming?'

Shane's knees touch the insides of mine. Through the gash in my tights, I can feel the stiffness of his jeans. I fix my eyes on my turkey's half-plucked wing.

'You coming?'

His chest heaves at my shoulders.

I begin to wrench the stubborn feathers from round my bird's neck. Its feet groan on the hook as I go in, twist, pull, go in again.

Then Shane reaches down and tugs the hem of my skirt. He tugs so hard that the waistband digs into my hips and a blast of cold hits my midriff. I stop plucking. Shane keeps holding on to my skirt, pulling my arse towards his groin. The freezing rivets of the denim mini press into my flesh.

'I'm not coming,' I say. But my voice is barely a squeak.

We stand together, Shane's fists tight on the hem of my denim mini, his knees hard in the backs of mine. My turkey sways in front of me. For the first time this evening,

I feel warm. I become aware of my heart beating.

'She's not coming, Shane,' says Rob.

'Get back to work, you lot!' Sheepskin Coat hollers over from his table at the other end of the shed. 'I won't bloody tell you again.'

Shane's still holding on to me, and for a second I wonder what it would be like if he didn't let me go.

'Shane. She's not coming with you.'

His hands drop then. Whether he glares at Rob, or tries to answer him, I don't know. But he lets me go. I keep my eyes on my turkey's wing, and I don't move. I stand and listen to his heavy steps, feeling the cold air on my legs. I hear the creak and slam of the corrugated iron door.

It's quarter to seven and my fingers are raw from plucking. Turkey feathers look soft but they pierce your skin if you pull them the wrong way. A dribble of turkey shit has leaked into my coat cuff and dried there. Every time I lift my arm to pluck another feather I get a big raw whiff of it.

Sheepskin Coat calls time. Luke and Rob rush off, shoulders touching as they squeeze out the door. Rob looks over his shoulder and lifts one hand. Gives me a half-wave. His earring winks in the electric light.

I go to follow him but Sheepskin Coat calls me over. He leans back on his table and waits till everyone's gone and we're alone in the shed. Behind him, naked turkeys are slumped in a pile.

'What did I tell you about trousers?' he says, looking at my legs, his eyes going up, up, up.

His worn corduroys sag at the knees. Down the front of his coat there's a stain the shape of the map of Britain.

'You're distracting the others.'

'It's not my fault. They're easily distracted.'

He raises his bushy eyebrows. 'Look. I don't usually take girls on here. Not young ones, anyway. So I'm doing you a big favour. Don't bugger it up.'

'I'll try my best to be good.' I look up at him and flick my hair back.

Eventually, he smiles. 'Yeah. OK. Next time, come covered up, that's all.'

'Don't you like my legs?' I ask, pointing a suede toe at his boot.

He sighs. Shakes his head. Then he walks past me to the other side of the shed. 'Just wear the trousers, love,' he says, holding the door open.

Outside, the black sky's spotted with stars. Dad used to pretend he knew the constellations. 'That's the great elephant,' he'd say, pointing upwards but looking into my face. 'And that's Joanna. The huntress.' He'd begin to smile. 'See her bow and arrow? You wouldn't mess with her, would you?' But all I ever saw were tiny dots of glitter.

If I hurry I might catch them up.

I walk across the field, past the power station. Sometimes I think the towers must have moved in the night. From the other side of the village they can look miles away. But from the field, now, the power station looks like the closest thing to me. It looks like I could reach out and touch the fat towers. I could get my hair tangled in the wires that stretch across the fields. I could frazzle my ends on the current.

I think I see a bike light ahead. They must have been hanging about by the pools. Perhaps they've been kissing in the twitcher's look-out.

'Rob,' I call. 'Wait.'

I start running a bit. 'Rob! Wait for me.'

And as I step in an icy puddle, I get an answer. It's a very loud, sort of gargling sound. It's somewhere between a shout and a scream. And it's coming from the direction of the pools. My skin goes bumpy, like turkey flesh.

Then it happens again, louder this time.

For a few seconds, I can't move. The sound echoes around me. The stars look brighter. The steam from the towers looks whiter. One blink seems to take a long time.

'Joanna! Get out of here!' I squint into the dark. A boy is racing across the field on his bike. He pedals as far as he can, then the bike swerves on the mud and he gets off and pushes, running alongside it so fast that the back wheel keeps kicking up from the ground.

When Luke reaches me his face is grey. His eyes bulge with fear.

'What is it? What's happened?'

'For God's sake, get out of here!'

He pushes past.

'Where are you going?' I run after him. 'What's happened? Where's Rob?'

'There was an accident – he had a knife – I've got to get help – '

'What?'

He's gulping, crying. He drags his sleeve across his face, but doesn't stop running. His back wheel's bucking.

'Luke, who had a knife?'

I'm panting from trying to keep up with him.

'Shane! That bloody spacky!'

'What?'

'There was a fight – Rob fell – '

'Who was fighting?'

'Shane – he had a knife – '

I grab his arm. 'Stop a minute! Where is he? Where's Shane?'

He looks at me like I'm mad. 'I don't bloody know! He ran off.'

'Where's Rob, then?'

'He's still in there! He's in the pool!' He lets out a cry, then, like the gargling sound I heard before. 'He was cut, there was blood – he went under and –'

'Go and get someone,' I say. 'Quick.'

I run back towards the pools. I don't slip or yell this time, because my feet are light now. I have to find them, both of them. The steam is behind me as I sprint over the field.

I go faster. I go faster. I go faster. Until I get to the biggest pool, and I see his bike.

Rob's bike. Rob's racing bike is on its side in the mud. The handlebars are skewed in a smashed puddle of ice.

My breath gathers and melts in my chest.

I look around. There's a big streak in the mud by the bike, like something's been dragged through it. I step off the path and stumble through the skeleton trees, towards the pool. Brambles clutch at my tights. My foot slides on an old crisp packet and I grab hold of a knobbled branch, my feet skidding in opposite directions. I pull myself straight and peer over the silent water. Its covering of ice shines in the moonlight. It looks like cling film, sealing everything in, keeping it all down there, keeping it quiet.

I call for him. 'Rob,' I call. Then, 'Shane.' I call again. I call for both of them. I don't stop calling their names. 'Rob,' I shout. 'Shane,' I shout. Again and again I shout for them.

But there's nothing. Just dead leaves caught in the tangled twigs. The still lid of the ice on the pool. And my own breath, blooming and spreading in front of me. My own breath keeps blooming and spreading.

epilogue

Joanna
Christmas, 1985

Simon's chocolate goes soft in my mouth. It leaves a gooey layer on my teeth. I run my tongue around my gums to clean it out. But my mouth still feels clogged.

He's staring at his gloved hands. 'Your mother says you're leaving.'

Above us, the rooks scrape out another call.

He pushes his glasses up his nose and moves closer along the bench, but doesn't touch. 'I think it's a good thing. You know. You should be with your dad. I think it will be good. For all of us.'

I nod, stretching my legs out in front of me. I dig the heels of my ankle boots into the mud.

He fakes a cough. 'We'll miss you,' he says. Then, 'I'll miss you.'

I look at his face. That withered cheek. That fringe frozen into place. He tries a small smile.

'Give me some more,' I say. We look at each other, and then he hands me the chocolate.

Together, we finish off the whole bar. We sit and look out at the bare trees and the still water and we eat and eat and eat as if we're hungry. It makes my stomach feel twisted and sore, but I keep chewing and swallowing.

When we've finished, he says, very quietly, 'The police asked me about Shane.'

I screw up the wrapper and throw it in the grass.

'Joanna. They asked me about you and him.'

I don't say anything.

'They said Luke told them there was a fight. A fight with Shane.'

My mouth is dry and when I swallow it's like it's still clogged with chocolate.

'I didn't say anything,' he says. He puts his head in his hands. Rubs at his temples. 'I don't know why. I said I didn't know anything about him.'

'You don't know anything about him.'

He shakes his head. 'No,' he says. 'I suppose not. But you should have told them about him, Joanna. Even if he didn't do anything, even if it was an accident – '

'It was an accident. It said in the newspaper. Rob drowned.'

I stand up and realise my legs are shaking. But I keep my voice steady. 'Shane wouldn't have hurt him. Not like that.'

He looks at me for a long time, his eyes searching my face. My throat goes tight, but I will not cry.

'I'm sorry,' he says. Then he hangs his head again and rubs at his temples.

I turn from him but he grabs my sleeve and I let him hold it for a minute.

'Wait,' he says. He fishes in his pocket with his other hand. Then he dangles something long and shiny from one finger. 'I've got you a present. Earrings. Your reward for our tutorials. And, you know, to say goodbye.'

I look back over the pool. 'Thanks,' I say.

But I walk away without taking them, and he doesn't come after me.

Howard

January, 1986

I've taken a few weeks off work. They don't quibble over long-term illness or bereavement. If you're off with a stomach bug, there's no end of enquiry. Questions about the exact nature of the sickness, how long you had it, what you took for it and how you're feeling now. But mention death and everyone falls silent. No questions asked.

You hear about people who can't bear to enter the rooms of the dead, who can't bring themselves to touch anything that once belonged to their lost loved ones. People whose grief is so great that they seal the door of the deceased's room and leave everything just as it is, for years, as a kind of shrine.

But I haven't been able to get Kathryn to leave Robert's bedroom. Since the funeral, she sits in there every day, lost in his sea of blue. I wait downstairs in the living room, a mug of tea going cold on the table in front of me, and listen to her footsteps above. I hear the springs of the bed moan as she sits herself down on his duvet. I hear the creak of his wardrobe door, and I imagine her reaching in to touch his jumpers, shirts, socks, again. I hear the groan of his drawers as she opens each one, and I picture her flicking through his sketchbooks, looking for something she hasn't seen before.

Yesterday, I heard her close and lock Robert's door behind her. She slid the bolt home, and I sat all afternoon, listening to the sounds of my wife in our dead son's bedroom. I sat and listened, and, outside, it snowed. I didn't notice this until it was quite dark and I'd stood up to draw the curtains. A thick layer of white had fallen over my garden. Even the stumps of my roses were covered. The reflection of the street light on the snow cast a yellowy light over everything in the living room, and I stood for a moment, looking back at my own imprint in the cushions of the chair where I'd sat all afternoon, and I heard the bed springs above me moan again, and I knew that she would spend the night in his bed.

In the morning, I knock on the door of his bedroom, and there's no response.

'Kathryn,' I say. 'Can I come in?'

I hear the bed springs go. After a few moments, she slides the bolt over and cracks open the door.

'What do you want?'

'Can I come in?'

She sighs and rests her head on the doorframe. Her hair sticks out to the side. I think of our son's cockatoo touch. She closes her eyes and her dark lashes rest on her cheeks. Her cheeks seem dark, now, too. They have a hollow look.

'Why do you want to come in?' Her voice is a quiet monotone.

For a second I feel a terrible urge to shake her.

'Please,' I say.

She turns and sits on the bed, leaving the door open. She's wearing her maroon dressing gown. It has a zip all the way up the front and an embroidered tulip on the pocket. I chose it for her years ago, thinking of the book on tulips that she'd held to her chest on the day we'd had our first real conversation in the library.

I look around the blue room. Robert's old Midland Bank schoolbag is still crumpled in the corner. A pile of glossy, brightly coloured magazines is stacked by the bed. His two brushes are on the table, beneath his mirror, leaking dark hairs. The woman standing on the shell looks down blankly from the wall.

I bring the model *Somua* tank from behind my back and place it on his bedside table. I'd left it in my coat pocket for weeks, not knowing what to do with it.

'I wanted to return this,' I say.

We both stare at the khaki plastic.

'Do you remember that day?' I ask her. 'The day at the Tank Museum?'

She looks at me.

'You waited for us in a café. I took him round those awful tanks. And all the time, I wished you were there with us.'

She lifts the model tank and weighs it in her hands. She turns it slowly, examining the tyre treads, the cockpit, the gun. She peers at the tiny face of the soldier. With one finger, she flicks the turret round and round. There isn't a chip or a scratch on it. It is still perfect, despite being painted almost twelve years ago.

'I wished you were there, Kathryn.'

She puts the tank in her lap, covers it with her fist, and closes her eyes.

After a moment, I crouch down before her and place my hands on her knees. Through the soft maroon material that covers almost every inch of her, I can feel a slight warmth.

Then Kathryn lays a hand on my head. 'I know,' she says. 'I know.'

acknowledgements

I am grateful to the Arvon Foundation and the Jerwood Charity for their Young Writers' Apprenticeships Award, which enabled me to get on with this novel, and to Stephanie Norgate for putting me forward for the award. Andrew Cowan was never less than brilliant as a mentor, editor and friend during the apprenticeship, and I can't thank him enough. Thanks also to The South and the Arts Council for awarding *The Pools* a place on their Free Read Scheme. I am also indebted to David Swann, who was there and enthusiastic from the start; Lorna Thorpe, Naomi Foyle and Kai Merriott for their good advice; my agent David Riding, for not giving up; and my editor John Williams.

Nothing would have been possible, though, without the love and support of Hugh Dunkerley.

writing the pools

The process of writing *The Pools* began while I was studying for an MA in Creative Writing at the University of Chichester. When I started writing it, I didn't know it was going to be a novel. I thought these characters, this situation, might be best explored in a poem, or – what was I thinking? – a radio play in verse. (A dark secret of mine: sometimes I attempt to write poetry, and I've always had a weakness for *Under Milk Wood*). I suspect this is because I could hear the voices of the book – especially Howard's – quite clearly in my head from the start. In fact, I did write *The Pools* as a rather hysterical radio play, but it didn't quite work, and it didn't feel like the end of my relationship with the material. I wanted the thing to be quieter, gentler, more expansive. I wanted to go deeper into the characters' minds. I wasn't quite ready to let them go. So, slowly – very, very slowly – it became a novel.

I had a lot of help: first from the MA – from both my tutors and fellow students – and then from the novelist Andrew Cowan, whom I'd 'won' as a mentor for six months as part of a Jerwood award for young writers. When I was writing, I didn't think to myself: this is my first novel. I just thought about the next sentence. And the next. And the next. I didn't have a grand plot structure in mind at first. I just wrote and wrote, getting to know the characters as I went along. And then I cut most of what I wrote, and re-wrote. And, eventually, I thought about the plot, and somehow I managed to reach the end. I don't know if this is the best way to write a novel. But it seemed to work for me.

Whilst I was writing, I tried not to think about getting published. But I can't deny that I have imagined what it would be like for a very long time. I've had day-dreams about book-signings. Seen covers and blurbs in my sleep. In the day-dreams I'm entirely happy and successful and everything is very shiny. But the reality is much more everyday. Of course, when my agent called to tell me that we'd found a publisher I didn't stop smiling for weeks (except to eat, which I'm very keen on doing regularly). It's utterly thrilling – and very surreal – to see your words in print, between covers, and on the shelf of a bookshop… You even start to think: maybe I am actually a writer. Could that be true? Could it? But then you get back to your desk. And there's the blank page again. Staring at you without pity. And you take a deep breath, and dare to put down one sentence… and then the next, and then the next.

Snooping in Other People's Houses

some thoughts on writing *The Good Plain Cook*

I was just eighteen when I first visited the Peggy Guggenheim Collection, housed in the Palazzo Venier dei Leoni, Venice. Eighteen, tired from inter-railing and longing for home, a good bath and a plate of my mum's chips. I bypassed most of the big boys of twentieth-century art and found myself in a small side room, filled with puzzlingly child-like paintings by Peggy Guggenheim's daughter, Pegeen Vail, who died aged forty-two. The room displayed a photograph of her, all huge eyes and no chin, beside which was a short elegy, written for her by her mother. For the Peggy Guggenheim Collection isn't only a museum; it's also where Peggy lived.

The wonderful thing about walking around the Palazzo is the illicit thrill you get from snooping in someone else's house. There's the white plastic sofas in the drawing room, where she would have sat, backed by a Pollock, gazing out at her private gondolier (I thought); there's the Calder silver bedhead, under which she took her pleasure with her fabled string of famous lovers... In short, I found the house, and the ghosts of those who'd lived in it, much more interesting than the art.

Fourteen years later, I was still interested enough to think that Peggy's story might give me something to write about, and I embarked on what writers call 'research', which is really more snooping about in other people's houses, keeping an eye out for anything that piques your interest or chimes with your own experience enough to get a story going. I knew that I wanted to write fiction, but thought that the facts of Peggy's life might open up some avenues in my imagination. I also thought, after setting my first novel in the industrial landscape of small-town Oxfordshire, this was the perfect excuse for some much-needed glamour. I saw a prolonged period of 'research' in Venice stretching out before me. Yes! I thought. This must be why so many people dream of becoming novelists.

But then I read that Peggy and her daughter had spent a few years living fairly near me, in West Sussex, and I was intrigued. I also read that she'd employed a local girl as a cook and, dissatisfied with the girl's performance, had decided to learn to cook herself. Everything changed. There they were: the seeds of my cast of characters, just down the road from me. Writers often talk about characters 'taking over' their work, and whilst I bristle a little at such a mystical idea, once I'd found my Good Plain Cook, the novel's direction became clear. I realised that Kitty's point of view – as that of the character so often written out of the bohemian dramas of the period – was a crucial one for me. Perhaps this is because my own family's stories are full of Kittys, whose work enabled the moneyed classes to indulge their passions for art, literature, partying (and politics) without having to worry about the washing up or incinerating the fish. I was fascinated by Peggy's life, by Peggy's house – the art, the lovers, the money – but realised that the story had to include something from my own house. *The Good Plain Cook* is my attempt to put the 'below-stairs' girl centre-stage, whilst also, of course, indulging in a little bohemian glamour.

Sussex, 1936

··· One ···

WANTED – *Good plain cook to perform domestic duties for artistic household. Room and board included. Broad outlook essential. Apply Mrs E. Steinberg, Willow Cottage, Harting.*

It was the third time since breakfast that Kitty had read the notice she'd cut from the *Hants and Sussex Herald*. Folding the slip of paper back into the pocket of her raincoat, which she'd belted tightly because her waist – as her sister Lou often pointed out – was her best feature, she walked along the slippery grass verge towards her interview at Willow Cottage. Beneath her blue beret, the ends of her hair were beginning to kink in the mist of spring drizzle.

Lou had told her that the cottage was now in the ownership of an American woman, and that she lived with a man who was, apparently, a poet – not that you'd think it to look at him; he was quite young, and didn't have a beard. No one was sure if the poet was the American woman's husband or not. 'No one else will answer that advert, knowing who *she* is,' Lou had said. 'And I'll bet they want one person to do it all: cooking and skivvying both.' But Kitty had had enough of living with her sister, despite all the modern comforts laid on at 60 Woodbury Avenue, and so she'd written, not mentioning that she'd no experience as a cook. At the last minute, she'd added the words, *I have a broad outlook*.

She turned into the lane which led to the gravel driveway. The cottage was just off the main road out of Harting and was the largest in the village. Through the dripping beech hedge, she caught glimpses of the place. It was red brick, and had exposed beams, like many in the village, but the front door was crimson, with a long stained-glass panel of all colours, much brighter and swirlier than anything Kitty had seen in church, and obviously new. There was a large garage at the end of the drive, from which a loud *chuck-chuck* noise was coming. Kitty recognised the sound: there'd been an electricity generator at the Macklows' too, where she'd worked as a kitchen maid after leaving school.

As she approached the house, Kitty noticed a woman's round-toed shoe on the front lawn, its high heel skewed in the mud. Bending down, she tugged it free. It was quite large for a woman's shoe, and the sole was shiny with wear. The inside was soft cream leather, the outside brilliant green and scuffed. She tapped it on the stones to remove some of the mud, then walked around to the back of the house.

Squinting through the rain, Kitty could see a stream and a line of willow trees at the end of the garden, before which was some kind of building that looked like a tiny house. Plants seemed to be everywhere, spilling over the paths without any apparent order; the large lawn needed a cut. Amongst the daffodils, Kitty caught a glimpse of a woman's rain-streaked backside, sculpted in stone.

She adjusted her beret, tried to comb out the ends of her hair with her fingers, and knocked at the back door.

Immediately there was a series of high yaps, and when the door opened, a little grey dog with large ears, a straggly beard and black eyes jumped at Kitty's legs. Kitty stooped to scratch its head. When she was very young, her father had owned a docile Jack Russell, who'd never minded the sisters dressing him up in bonnet and bootees. The grey dog caught hold of Kitty's cuff and gently licked the rain from its edge.

'Don't mind Blotto, he gets excited with strangers.' A tall girl of about twelve stood in the doorway, chewing a piece of her long blonde hair. 'Who are you and why didn't you knock on the front door?'

Kitty straightened up and held the shoe behind her back, suddenly worried that the girl would think she was stealing. The rain was coming down harder and she hadn't brought her umbrella. Her beret must look flat and ridiculous by now, like a wet lily pad on her head.

'I've come about the position, Miss.'

'Position?'

'Is your mother – is Madam in?'

'Who?'

'Madam – Mrs Steinberg, Miss.'

The girl frowned and chewed. 'I don't know,' she said, not letting the strand of hair drop from her mouth. 'What have you got behind your back?'

Kitty glanced down at the girl's dirty knees. She was wearing a very short and ill-fitting tulle skirt with an orange cardigan.

'I found it on the front lawn, Miss.' Kitty held the shoe out to the girl, who shrugged.

'That's been there for ages,' she said.

Kitty let her arm drop. 'Have I come to the right place?'

'*I* don't know.' The girl bent down and scooped up the dog, which buried itself in her hair and began licking her ear.

'There was a notice, in the *Herald*. For a plain cook, Miss.'

Rain was dripping into Kitty's collar now. She tried to see into the kitchen, but the girl shifted and blocked Kitty's view.

'Ellen never said anything to me.'

'Perhaps I'd better be going.'

The girl stared at Kitty for a moment. Her eyes were startlingly blue.

'But then, she never tells us anything, does she, Blotto?' She kissed the dog on his nose and was licked right up her forehead. 'My name's Regina, but that's horrible so everyone calls me Geenie, and this is Blotto, he's a miniature schnauzer, which is a very good breed of dog.'

'I think I've made a mistake.'

She'd be dripping all the way back on the bus by the time it came.

'Geenie! Who's there?'

So she *was* American.

'She won't tell me her name and she's got your shoe.'

A tall woman came to the door. She was wearing an embroidered red jacket and wide-legged mauve slacks. Her hair waved above her high forehead and was the colour of brown bread. She wore no jewellery. Her nose was huge; the end of it looked like a large radish. She blinked at Kitty.

'What's your name, please?'

'Allen, Madam, Kate – Kitty – Allen. I've come about…'

The woman stuck out a hand and Kitty met it with the shoe.

'What's that?'

'It's been on the lawn for ages,' said Geenie. 'I wear it

when I'm being Dietrich.'

The woman ignored this. 'Is it Kate or Kitty?'

At the Macklows' she'd been plain 'Allen'.

'Kitty, Madam, please.'

'I'm Ellen Steinberg. Do come in. You could have used the front door, you know, this isn't London, and it's only a cottage.'

'Yes, Madam.'

'Get out of the way, Geenie, and let the girl through.'

Geenie ducked under Mrs Steinberg's arm and fled, taking the dog with her.

'You'll have to excuse my daughter. I'm afraid she's always been highly strung.'

Kitty followed the woman into the cottage, still gripping the sodden shoe in one hand.

. . . . .

There was no fire in the sitting-room grate. Ashes floated in the air as Mrs Steinberg walked past the enormous fireplace, dropped into a velvet armchair, and drew a fur rug across her knees. 'Take a seat, please, Kitty.'

Kitty sat on the sofa, which was covered in a tapestry-like fabric, threaded with gold. She thought about putting the shoe on the floor, but changed her mind and folded her hands around it in her lap. Then she looked up and noticed, above the armchair where Mrs Steinberg was sitting, a hole in the wall. It was as big as the woman's head, and its edges were ragged.

Mrs Steinberg twisted around and looked at the hole too, but said nothing.

Kitty let her eyes wander over the rest of the room. The walls were all white, except for one which was covered in wooden racks filled with records. The floorboards were bare, apart from a red rug in front of the hearth. The curtains were pink and green chintz, lined with purple satin. On the mantelpiece was a large bunch of irises and daffodils, stuffed into a blue ceramic jug. The flowers were interspersed with long blades of grass.

'Mr Crane loves grass,' said Mrs Steinberg.

Kitty dropped her eyes.

'He says the grass of Sussex is the best in the world. He's worked wonders with this place; it's really all his doing. He's an absolute whiz with interiors. We're both very keen on modernisation. But it's still damned icy, don't you think? And the rooms are ridiculously small.'

The woman's voice was strange – not as American as Kitty had imagined, and high-pitched, like a girl's. Kitty shifted her feet. Mrs Steinberg had hung her raincoat and hat to dry in the kitchen, but her shoes were soaked.

'However. We *have* got gas *and* electricity, Kitty! A very recent addition out here in the wilderness. So it will be easy for you – in the kitchen. And music. We've got plenty of music. I hope you like music?'

'Yes, Madam,' said Kitty, wondering what music had to do with anything.

'Excellent. Geenie's never been musical and Mr Crane is hopeless. He thinks brass bands are a good thing! So, you see, I need an ally.' She adjusted the fur rug and stretched out her feet. Her shoes were made of a soft material, gathered in a visible seam around the sole; to Kitty, they looked like a pair of man's slippers.

'Every woman needs an ally in the house, don't you think? It's no good just having men and children. You must have dogs, too, and other women.'

Kitty plucked at her skirt. She'd worn her best – blue boiled wool with a pleat at the side – and now it had a damp patch on the front from the wet shoe.

'How old are you, Kitty?'

'Nineteen, Madam.'

Mrs Steinberg frowned. Kitty wasn't sure if she was too young, or too old, for the job. At the Macklows', all the girls had complained about this problem: when you were young they didn't want you because you'd no experience, but as you got older they were reluctant to promote you for fear you'd go off and get married.

'And what was it you did before?'

'I'm a cleaner in the school, Madam, at the moment. But before that I did a bit of cooking for a lady in Petersfield.' In reality, she'd scrubbed the zinc, laid out the cook's knives, and fetched, cleaned or carried anything she was told.

'Are the schools here awful? The ones in London were really dreadful. Geenie was very unhappy in all of them. The English seem to believe children can learn only through punishment.'

Kitty thought of her school, of the hours spent copying words and numbers from a blackboard, the dust that gathered in the grooves of her desk, the teacher who used to pick the boys up by their collars and shake them. 'I – wouldn't like to say, Madam.'

'Can you brush hair?'

'Yes, Madam.'

'Because Geenie's hair needs a lot of brushing and although I don't expect you to be her nanny there will be times when I may need help—'

'Oh.' Kitty grasped her knees. 'I hadn't realised...'

'Our old nanny, Dora, left us recently. Geenie was far too attached to her, so in the end it was all to the good.'

Mrs Steinberg fixed Kitty with her grey eyes, which seemed to be smiling, even though her mouth was not. 'So. Tell me. What can you do?'

Kitty wanted to ask about the times when Mrs Steinberg would need help with the girl, but she'd been rehearsing her answer to this question, so she replied, 'I'm schooled in domestic science.'

It was what Lou had told her to say, insisting it had enough meaning without having too much. She'd read about it in one of her magazines.

'Whatever does that mean?'

A sharp heat rose up Kitty's neck. Her mouth jumped into a smile, as it always did when she was nervous.

Mrs Steinberg laughed. 'Do you mean you can cook and clean?'

Kitty nodded, but couldn't seem to find enough breath for words. Her feet were numb with cold now, and she was beginning to feel awfully hungry.

Mrs Steinberg waved a hand in the air. 'So what can you cook?'

Kitty had prepared an answer to this as well. She'd always cooked for Mother, and had seen enough, she felt, in the year she'd spent in the Macklow house to know what the job was. The most important thing seemed to be always to have a stockpot on the go.

'Meat and vegetables both, Madam. Savouries and sweets.'

Mrs Steinberg seemed to be waiting for more.

'I can do meat cakes, beef olives, faggots... And castle pudding, bread and butter pudding, and all of that, puddings are what I do best, Madam.' She could eat some bread and butter pudding now, with cold custard on it.

Mrs Steinberg's face was blank. 'Anything else?'

Perhaps they were vegetarians. Lou's husband Bob said that some of these bohemians were. 'Fruit fritters... and, um...'

'Nothing more... continental, Kitty?'

'I can do cheese puffs, Madam.'

Mrs Steinberg laughed. 'Well. Never mind. I hope you won't mind doing some housework, too. I'm not very fussy about it, but there'll be a bit of sweeping and dusting now and then, keeping the place looking generally presentable.' She twisted round in her seat and looked again at the hole above her head. 'It will be easier for you when Mr Crane and Arthur have finished knocking these two rooms together, of course. One large, light, all-purpose room, that's what we want. I don't believe in all this *compartmentalisation*, do you?'

'Yes, Madam. I mean, no, Madam.'

'Stop calling me that. It makes me sound like a brothel-keeper. You can call me Mrs Steinberg.' The woman's long fingers rummaged at her scalp as she spoke. 'Now. Would you like to ask me anything?' She perched on the edge of the armchair and held the wave of her hair back from her forehead with both hands. 'Anything at all.'

Kitty looked at the woman's clear forehead for a moment.

'Anything at all, Kitty.'

'Are there any other staff here, Mrs Steinberg?'

'Just Arthur, the gardener and... handyman, I suppose you'd call him. He doesn't live with us, but he's here most days.'

Kitty shifted in her seat. 'There's no housemaid or parlour-maid?'

'You won't be expected to wait on us, Kitty, if that's what you're worrying about. We don't go in for all that.'

'No, Madam.'

There was a pause. Kitty squeezed the green shoe in her hands.

'Are we settled, then? Could you start next week?'

She must ask it. 'Will I be expected to – what you said

about when you're not here... your daughter...' She mustn't be the nanny. That was not what the notice said. 'What I mean is, what will I be doing, exactly?'

'Kitty, I'm probably the only bohemian in the country who likes order.' Mrs Steinberg smiled and widened her eyes. 'Let's see. Start with the bedrooms. There are four rooms, one for myself, one for Geenie... And one for Mr Crane, of course.' She paused. 'Then a guest room. And, downstairs, sitting and dining room – soon to be one – bathroom, a cubby-hole that's supposed to be a library, but you don't have to bother with that: only I go in there. So it's not very much. A little cleaning and polishing, fires swept and laid when it's cold, which it is all the damn time, isn't it? And the cooking, of course, but we quite often have a cold plate for lunch, and only two courses for dinner, unless we've got company. Geenie eats with us; we don't believe in that nonsense of hiding children away for meals. And we don't go in for any fuss at breakfast time, either. Toast will do for me, but Mr Crane does like his porridge.'

Kitty blinked.

'He has a little writing studio in the garden, you probably noticed – it's where he works. But, if you'll take my advice, you won't go in there. The place is always a mess, anyway, and he hates to be disturbed. He's a poet, but at the moment he's working on a novel.' Here she paused and smiled so brilliantly that Kitty had to smile back. 'I'm encouraging him all I can. That's why he's living here, you see; it's a vocational thing, really; if one has artistic friends, one must help them out.'

Kitty looked about the room for a clock but couldn't find one. How long had she been here? Her stomach felt hollow. She thought of sausage rolls, of biting into the greasy pastry, the deep salty taste of the meat.

'And then there's Geenie. Well, of course, I would really

appreciate it if you could keep an eye on her occasionally but she's my responsibility now.'

If Kitty didn't move, her stomach might not growl.

'Children need their mothers first and foremost, don't they?'

Kitty nodded, relieved. 'Oh yes, Mrs Steinberg.'

There was a pause. The growl was building in Kitty's stomach, pressing against her insides as if some creature were crawling around the pit of her.

'So. Can you start next week?'

As she nodded, Kitty's stomach gave a long, loud rumble. Mrs Steinberg raised an eyebrow and smiled. 'It's lunchtime, isn't it? Yes. I must let you go.' She clapped her hands together. 'Kitty, I think you'll do nicely. Forty pounds a year, and two afternoons off a week, all right?'

'Thank you, Mrs Steinberg.'

The woman stood, and Kitty followed.

'Are you still holding that shoe?' Mrs Steinberg laughed. 'Why don't you keep it? As a welcome gift. We might even be able to find the other.'

Kitty looked at the sodden shoe. It was at least two sizes too big for her. 'Thank you, Mrs Steinberg,' she repeated.